The School for Monsters and Misfits

Rob Preece

BooksForABuck.com

2015

BooksForABuck.com
January 2015

Chapter One

"**M**athew Carnecero, do you accept your responsibilities as a member of the Fae community, to preserve our secret, to use your powers responsibly, to honor the elders in both your family and those of your totem beast, your true form, whatever that form may be?"

Matt looked around. Friends, family, and especially friends of his father's had gathered at Frisco's historic Wildebeest Hall to celebrate his first change. Smoke-darkened paintings of wolves, bears, tigers, and a solitary Tasmanian Devil hung from draped walls. Although Frisco was mostly a new suburb, Wildebeest Hall dated to the time when it had been a tiny farming community—founded by Matt's ancestors.

On his magical thirteenth birthday, he was finally old enough to drink the mix of hormones and pain drugs that would enable him to transform to his true form. Today, he'd find his shape, his personality. Today he'd become a man— and a beast. He'd join the community of shapeshifters, become part of the great hunt.

He swallowed hard and his brother, Scott, slapped him on the back. "Don't worry, Matt. Younger children are more magical than the older. You'll probably be a tiger. Maybe even a dragon—wouldn't that be cool?"

Matt nodded—his throat clamped so tight he couldn't talk. The hall should probably have been named which-a-beast instead of wildebeest.

He looked around, halfway fearful, halfway hopeful someone might stand and argue against his readiness. The hormone mix was supposed to ease the transition but everyone said it was still the most painful experience they'd ever been through.

Nobody objected though. Which meant he was in. In moments, he'd join the ritual feast celebrating his first transformation.

His father, Arn Carnecero, surveyed the crowd, then looked down on Matt. "Are you ready, my son? Have you fasted for twenty-four hours, consuming nothing but water? Have you purified your mind with contemplation? Have you completed your reading of the lives of the great changers?"

Matt started to nod, but the experience of dozens of rehearsals conducted by his parents, Scott, and even his younger sister, Ophelia, kicked in.

"I have purified and prepared myself according to our traditions." For once, his voice didn't break—that would have been just too humiliating.

"The feast has been prepared," his father said. "We will dine together in our true forms, once you have joined us as an adult."

Again, months of practice made the response automatic. "I will savor the feast—and long for the day when I can contribute to the great hunt."

"That," his father chanted, "is the way of the world, as child becomes adult. Take and drink, my son, then look into the mirror as you assume your true form. From your animal form will flow your nature. A bear is strong and enduring. A wolf lends support to the pack. A hawk sees danger from far away and calls out warning. None is superior for every animal brings its special advantage to the hunt."

Arn placed a mirror in front of Matt, who resisted the urge to make a face at it. So far, he looked the same as always. Then again, so far, he hadn't swallowed the drink.

Satisfied with the mirror's placement, Arn reached into a small red cooler and removed not a golden chalice but a chemistry beaker containing a steamingly cold jell-like liquid of an intensely green color.

Matt accepted the beaker. Rumor had it that the hormone mix was the nastiest thing anyone could taste. According to whispered confidences by older teens, more than a few prospective shifters had gagged in drinking it, embarrassing themselves and their families. Matt had promised himself he wouldn't bring shame to himself or his family, but he took the moment to compose himself

It could be that his hands shook a bit but it certainly seemed as if the viscous liquid writhed under its own power as he grasped the beaker. He sniffed at the open top to the flask but could only smell the sizzling brisket and sausage prepared for the barbeque afterwards. In animal form, carnivores need meat—his mother, for example, was a panther and, like all cats, an obligate carnivore. He rather hoped he'd be a bear like his father—but a grizzly rather than a polar bear.

Still, his father's words warmed him—whatever animal he became, from the lowest ferret to the Siberian tiger, he'd have special abilities he'd contribute to the pack. All were welcomed.

Matt blinked and realized he'd stared at the beaker for too long, that his audience was impatient. Although the ritual didn't require it, his family had fasted along with him. Unlike him, their nerves wouldn't tie their stomach into knots. They had to be hungry—anxious to get to the feast.

He tipped the beaker over his mouth and swallowed its contents in three practiced gulps—three being a number of power.

The jell stuck and burned when it hit his tongue. He nearly hurled but he'd been prepared for his reaction and swallowed a fourth time to keep it down. He managed to hand the now-empty beaker back to his father.

Arn examined the container, nodded, smiled, and set the beaker aside. "We have a new brother joining us," he chanted. "Our true natures will be no secret to him just as his will be open to us. All may take their true forms now."

He raised his arms and began his transformation to polar bear.

The hormone mix hit Matt's stomach like a sledgehammer. Supposedly, it served as a catalyst, making it easier for a body to find its true form the first time. Certainly it wasn't necessary for the adults, who could flow between animal and human at will.

Arn was leader of the pack partly because he was an intelligent and charismatic man, but also because his animal form, the polar bear, was that of perhaps the fiercest and most intelligent land predator in the world.

Beside Arn, Matt's mother dropped to all fours. Her skin seeming to liquefy, her face elongating as fur sprouted from her face.

Scott growled, becoming a dire wolf. His older sister, Camilla, gave a harsh shriek. Her arms extended, transformed, became wings, and she flapped over to the table and snared a hunk of brisket, then found a perch on one of the hall's exposed rafters. Ophelia wasn't there, of course—the ceremony was limited to those who already shifted both to preserve the mystery and to protect soft humans from dangerous predators whose human minds were partially submerged while in animal form.

Braced as he was for the pain, at first, Matt felt nothing although the gel's aftertaste had a bitter feel. The mirror simply showed a teenage boy with dark hair, brown eyes, and a worried look on his face.

Then, with an abruptness that shocked him no matter how often he'd seen his parents and older siblings transform, his bones seemed to shatter inside him.

Despite the pain medicines in the hormone drink, his body contorted with agony and he swallowed one more time to keep the mix from coming back up.

He'd been warned of the pain, of course. Even bending a stiff muscle can hurt. Transforming both muscle and bone into radically different forms hurt even more—at least the first time. Supposedly, once he completed his first transformation, his muscles and bones would remember their animal shape and he'd be able to transition without artificial aid. At the moment, he could only think about how much everything hurt and wonder if the pain would go on forever.

His eyes blurred with tears, which he did his best to blink back.

Obviously, though, blinking didn't do the job—his eyesight transformed. Around him, the hall expanded in his vision, becoming impossibly large. *It's an optical illusion*, he reminded himself. He and his vision were one changing, not the building. Still, it seemed horribly real.

The sounds of humans assuming their predator shapes, went from a soft whisper to a harsh and frightening roar. Their raspy breathing, and what had been soft whispers, increased in intensity. If it weren't for the pain, Matt thought he could make out every word spoken from the far end of the hall. That would, his frazzled brain managed, be kind of fun.

His sense of smell grew more dominant.

The muscles in his legs quivered and he felt as if he could jump a thousand yards. Could he have become one of the extinct carnivorous kangaroos that had once dominated Australia? Now *that* would be cool and different. Maybe it would be cooler even than a grizzly.

He blinked again and studied himself in the mirror. From the look of it, he'd halfway changed. His human nature remained dominant, but his ears had migrated upward on his head and grown larger. His black nose wiggled as it sniffed the air. Pale brown fur sprouted from his hands and face.

As he watched, whispers sprouted beside his nose and he hunched forward.

His eyes still watered, but he wanted, needed to see what form he would take. He didn't look exactly like a kangaroo, but an extinct carnivorous kangaroo would look different from the modern vegetarian ones that roamed the Australian outback.

His father reached a huge white paw toward him and panic swept over Matt. This wasn't a part of the ritual.

"No." His mother halfway transformed back to human shape and knocked away his father's paw. She stood over Matt, her snarls warning away the dozens of predators that circled her—and Matt.

Nothing in any of his rehearsals had prepared him for this. His body shook—possibly from the aftereffects of his shift—and he seemed frozen in place. The sensation of being impossibly small, weak, and helpless wouldn't go away.

What was going on?

He looked *up* at his mother, which he hadn't done in more than a year. She wasn't especially tall as a human. In her jaguar form, she stood only three feet tall at the shoulder. A carnivorous kangaroo would be taller than she, right? So why did he cower under her four-legged stance like a man hiding under an elephant.

"He's my baby," his mother howled. "He shall not be prey to you."

Prey?

Shapeshifters were predators, participants in the great hunt. Perhaps, he reasoned, they'd mistaken a carnivorous kangaroo for the vegetarian kind?

Matt blinked one more time and the blur covering his eyesight finally cleared.

He took half a hop toward the mirror and stared.

Hop? Okay, that made some sense for a kangaroo.

The vision that stared back at him, didn't make any sense at all.

Tall ears reached for the ceiling. Huge rear legs would propel him to ultra-fast flight. His wiggling nose could smell danger from hundreds of yards away. Matt had transformed not into a bear, not into a tiger, not even into a carnivorous kangaroo.

Could he really be a rabbit?

With what looked like enormous effort, his father shook his bear-body and became human once more. He stretched his huge hands down and scooped Matt up. "My friends," he shouted. "Enjoy the feast. This one prey animal would not do more than whet your appetite and his loss would sadden my family."

"Not to mention, if any of you tries to stick a tooth into him, I'll claw your face off," his mother, her voice a hoarse snarl. Then she licked her chops—staring at Matt with an expression that sent panic through his body.

If he hadn't been sick with worry, Matt would have cried. He wasn't being welcomed as an equal member of the shifter community. He certainly wasn't the guest of honor. Only fear of his parents kept him from becoming the feast's featured entree.

He wondered if how long he could survive in a house full of meat-eaters.

* * * *

The buzz of overhead florescent lights at the Dallas Greyhound station created a jarring dissonance with the beat from Barley Harris's iPod. The station walls had been painted gray once—perhaps to match the bus line's name, but the color had long-since faded and blotched. The terminal stunk of vomit, old sweat, stale cigarette smoke, and fear.

Part of that fear, Barley knew, was his own. Other than a few scout trips, he'd never been away from his family. Now, he'd probably never see them again.

He stepped over to the counter, trying to walk as if his legs ended in feet like everyone else, as if he wasn't on the verge of breaking into dance despite, or perhaps because of his sense of danger.

The cashier ignored him, finishing a solitaire game with a deck of cards so battered Barney suspected they'd been original equipment in the days when Greyhound used dog wagons. Barley waited at least three minutes before the man gave Barney a snarl. "Yeah?"

"A one-way ticket to San Antonio, please."

The man gave the battered cards a couple of shuffles. Finally, reluctantly, he punched a couple of keys on his computer. "Thirty-eight bucks."

Barney handed over two twenties and the cashier sniffed them. "You some sort of religious group. I saw a couple of other kids with those red tags you got around your neck."

"Sort of like that," Barley admitted.

"Hey. Good luck converting the heathen down there."

Yeah, right. Still, Barley forced a smile. "Thanks. Where did you say those other students were?"

The clerk didn't look up from his playing cards.

"There's a kid, maybe your age, in the waiting room. A couple of chicks around, too." He licked his lips. "Not bad looking if you know what I mean."

Barley nodded glumly. It wasn't that he didn't find girls interesting—he did. When he tried talking to them, though, he tensed up and blurted nonsense—when he managed to say anything at all. Not that it mattered. He could be as suave as James Bond but when girls learned his secret, they ran away faster than Barley could stump in his cowboy boots.

As the attendant had suggested, the boy was easy to spot. With his red tag and a furtive look that said he was expecting an attack, the kid stood out from the panhandlers, homeless people, and bored passengers that made up most of the Greyhound terminal's population.

Barney snuck a look at kid's tag. Hand-lettered in what had to be female writing was the name 'Matt.' Barney had printed out his own label—his parents couldn't be bothered.

Matt's brown eyes looked intelligent and Barney noted the large ice chest beside him.

Barney's stomach rumbled. He might as well try to make friends After all, if he was being sent to the School for Monsters and Misfits, Matt couldn't be too fussy about who he hung out with. And maybe he'd share some of whatever he had in that cooler. Barley had long-since consumed the sack lunch he'd packed for the bus. He was really—

"I'm hungry."

The words echoed his thoughts so closely that Barley suffered a moment of vertigo. Despite his unfortunate recent changes, though, his stomach didn't talk. If it ever did start talking, he hoped it wouldn't sound like a tired old lady.

That tired lady had bent over Matt, sticking her face in his and, not coincidentally, reaching a hand into his pocket while she distracted him.

"Hey, you," Barley shouted. "What do you think you're doing?"

"Mind your own business, punk." Still, she pulled her hand back.

Matt looked up, his nose wrinkling like he smelled something suspicious. No surprise there—the panhandler stunk.

"I'm making it my business." Barley did his best to puff up.

"You and what army."

"It's all right."

Typical. Matt thought Barney was butting in rather than saving him from a pickpocket.

"I'm a hungry woman," the panhandler whined, holding out her hand.

She might be hungry but Barley doubted she was that interested in food. He'd grown up in Richardson where panhandlers were rare but not invisible. A couple of times, he'd followed after they'd collected their money. Every time, they'd headed for a convenience store for cheap wine, cigarettes, or, in one case drugs.

This lady might be different. Barley wouldn't bet on it.

Matt fished a couple of carrots from his cooler. "These are really go—"

Barley wasn't surprised when the panhandler slapped Matt's hand, dumping the carrots on the floor. "I don't want lousy carrots," the woman screeched. "I want money."

Matt scrunched back in his chair, his expression a mix of surprise and pain. "You said you were hungry."

"Hungry for something that will nourish my kids—not rabbit food."

She looked closer to eighty than thirty, but Barley had seen what life on the streets did. He tried to evoke his talent but couldn't tell whether those children were real or figments of her imagination. His failure wasn't unexpected. He always failed when it came to magic.

Matt reached into the pocket the woman had pawed at earlier and pulled out a five. "How old are your children."

She snatched the bill. "None of your business, pervert." She jammed a thumb into Barley's chest, rocking him back. "None of yours, either, creep."

The woman smelled like she hadn't bathed in years. That didn't bother Barley too much. Until his horrible thirteenth, he'd played football. He was used to sweat.

Apparently Matt was more sensitive to stink. His nose wiggled like it wanted to be a long ways away. "I'm not trying to get their address or anything," he said. "I was just concerned about them, that's all."

"Worry about your own kids." The panhandler rolled her eyes rolled backed away, clutching the five like it was a religious symbol.

It looked to Barley like she was getting ready to attack, but then she scurried toward a pretty teenage girl in a cut-off public school uniform—way too skimpy for the chill wind blowing from the north.

When Barley put a hand on the kid's shoulder, Matt jerked in the seat like he'd been hit with an electric prod.

"You'd think," Barley said, "they'd lock up crazy people like that—sort of the same as locking us up."

"You think she's crazy?" Matt scratched his head. "I thought she was hungry."

"Could be both. For sure she's crazy. They shut down all the institutions years ago. The nice suburbs hire cops to keep them out so they end up in the cities wandering the streets—when they're not in jail."

Matt looked sad. "At least they don't lock *everyone* up."

"Tell me about it." Barley grabbed the empty seat near the cooler. "You don't look like a monster. What are you in for? You give your instructor a bar of Ex-Lax or something?"

"Huh?"

Barley tapped the red card on his chest. "You know, School for Monsters and Misfits. If you're not a monster, you're a misfit. Come on—what do you do? Start fires by staring? Turn girls' clothes invisible." Barley was nervous about talking *to* girls but he didn't mind talking *about* them. "Just so you know, I'll happily pay to see the invisible clothes trick."

"Of course I didn't do anything like that."

"Hey, no need to be ashamed. You're going to do the time, you might as well be proud of the crime. I'm Barley, by the way. Barley Harris."

"Matt Carnecero."

They shook hands. "So, Barley," Matt asked. "Why are *you* being sent to the, ah, School for Advanced Fae Studies?"

Barley had known that question would be coming ever since his parents had informed him of the council's decision. Fortunately, he'd come up with an answer. Now he'd get to try it out—anything was better than the truth.

He ticked them off on his fingers. "Let's see—I torture and kill cats and dogs, wet my bed, and start fires. My parents—"

"Really?" Matt's mouth formed an astonished 'O' that gratified Barley considerably. Since his terrible thirteenth, he'd come to love telling stories—whether on himself or on others. That might have been a part of the reason he was being sent down, of course. That didn't mean he could stop.

He laughed. "Not really. I was messing with <u>Wikipedia</u> this morning before my folks dragged me to the bus station. Supposedly, that's the FBI profile for serial killers. Do you think, if I told the school administration those were my issues, they'd treat me with a little respect?"

"I'm sure they'll treat everyone with respect. I mean, we pay their bills, right?"

Barley laughed. "*We* don't pay anything, we're just kids."

"You know what I mean."

He leaned closer. "As far as I can tell, people who go there just vanish. Sort of reminds me of this story I once read about a guy who drives around the country picking up hitchhikers and turning them into dogfood. It's—"

"You can quit trying to scare me because I'm not buying it. My family wouldn't send me anyplace where they'd turn me to food." Matt looked very certain of that.

"Right—your loving family. If they loved you so much, why are you going to the school?"

From the frustration that raced across Matt's expressive face, he didn't have an answer to that question.

The Greyhound P.A. system grumbled something, which Barley ignored because it had been making screeching noises ever since he'd gotten there and he hadn't understood any of them. The speakers probably hadn't been state of the art in the 1950s when they'd been installed. They'd suffered a lot since then.

Matt, apparently, had other ideas. His ears wiggled and he grabbed his cooler. "That's our bus."

"Says who?"

"They just announced it. Weren't you listening?"

"I was listening but I didn't understand a word."

"If you say so. Anyway, they just announced our bus."

Maybe Matt's problems should have been his own business but Barley couldn't help being interested. Super-sharp ears and a super-sharp sense of smell added up to a clue. Unless he missed his guess, Matt was some kind of shapeshifter. Considering the reputation of the school, and the types of shapeshifters who *didn't* get sent there, the kid was probably a lot more dangerous than he looked.

"You see anyone else going to the school?" Matt asked as he held out a carrot to Barley.

Barley really would have preferred a cupcake, but he took the carrot and waggled his eyebrows. "The ticket seller said there were a couple of girls. I saw one with a badge at the snack counter."

Chapter Two

Annie Fish had noticed the two boys with red tags when they were sitting together talking about whatever boys discuss.

A couple of times, when they'd appeared to reach a lull in their conversation, she'd strolled by, close enough that she almost brushed against them as they sprawled, like boys do, in the Greyhound waiting room. They ignored her, of course. Boys pretty much always ignored her.

Which was part of what made her an outcast. Among her people, the females got noticed—except for her.

That didn't mean she couldn't watch them, though.

Apparently the boys interpreted the squawk of the loudspeaker as instructions to get on the bus. They collected their sprawled legs and arms and shambled to their feet.

It seemed like a good time to meet them.

She pasted on a smile—and instantly dropped it when she remembered. "Hi, guys." She tapped the red badge hanging in the clear plastic container on her chest. "Looks like we're all heading the same direction."

The two had been involved in an intense discussion. They replaced that with slack-jawed stares.

"Huh?" the bigger one managed.

"Oh." The smaller boy popped what remained of the fourth carrot he'd eaten since she'd first noticed him into a pocket. "You're going to the School for Advanced Fae Studies, too?"

She nodded glumly. "Yep. My parents finally gave up on trying to take care of their local monster."

The bigger of the boys swallowed audibly, his Adam's apple chunking up and down his throat. "I'm Barley. This is Matt. Don't bother asking what we were sent up for—neither of us is talking."

"That makes three of us."

Barley might think he was keeping secrets, but *he* wasn't hard to guess. He looked like a guy searching for a party, his

cowboy boots tapped in time to music only he could hear—
and while he had an iPod attached to his belt, the earbud
drooped from his T-shirt pocket. When she'd seen him
walking earlier, he'd moved with just a hint of
awkwardness—as if his boots didn't quite fit. Putting it all
together, she suspected he was another throwback, something
that shouldn't exist in the modern world.

The smaller kid, Matt, was harder to figure—but she'd
been watching him. His face had more expressions than a
normal human's. She guessed he was a shifter of some sort.
Not that the Fae had anything against shapeshifters in general.
But she could imagine forms that would cause big trouble.
Maybe he turned into an elephant or something and rampaged.

While the two boys were obvious, Annie hoped the same
wasn't true of her. As long as she kept her mouth shut, neither
of them should be able guess her condition. She hoped.

"You have any idea how long they'll keep us there?" Matt
asked.

"Keeping us *is* sort of the point." Annie was surprised they
didn't know that.

"Really?" Matt wiggled his nose. "I thought we were
supposed to learn—"

"Learn how to deal with what makes us different from
other members of the Fae community so we can assimilate?"
She fed back the School's official line as they stood outside
the bus, waiting for the door to open. With the noise from
busses coming and going, they could speak freely without
worrying about violating the prime secret.

"Yeah. Assimilate and all that stuff. It wasn't safe for me
to stay with my pack, so I have to learn to…"

"Oh, brother. You are so pathetic."

Annie whirled around to see the speaker, an exceptionally
pretty girl in a too-short plaid school uniform skirt and white
blouse unbuttoned two buttons deeper than Annie would have
dared. The barest hint of a red tag poked from under that top.

Although Annie had just met the boys, she felt protective
of them. "It isn't Matt's fault his people didn't tell him what
was going on."

"You and I figured it out, didn't we?"

The girl had a point—but boys tended to trust more than girls did. She held out her hand. "I'm Annie"

The other girl ignored both the hand and the introduction. Instead, she stared at the guys for a couple of seconds. Finally, she shook her head. "I'd hoped for better. They'll chew you up and swallow you."

Barley swelled his chest. "Like you know any more of what we're getting into than we do."

"Like I don't."

Annie suspected the other girl was right. A badly concealed satyr and a shifter whose pack had rejected him would have a hard time if the stories she'd heard were true. So would a *murdhuacha*, if she had nobody to watch her back.

"Maybe if we stick together, uh…," she snatched the red tag from the other girl's top, "Taylor Bang, we'll have a better chance."

"Sticking with losers is like gluing your feet to the Titanic." Taylor turned and walked onto the bus.

Annie wondered if it was coincidence that the bus doors opened just when Taylor got there. She hadn't seen the other girl make any gestures or mouth any words, but then, if a witch with any kind of power doesn't want you to see, you just don't.

The guys both stared at Taylor's rear as she stepped into the bus—which wouldn't have hurt as much if they'd even acknowledged that there was another girl right there with them.

If Annie had just been normal, they would have noticed her, would stare at her like they did Taylor. Instead, she might as well have been invisible to them. Unfortunately, she was stuck with them—her kind didn't do well as loners.

"We'd better go, too," she said.

* * * *

How much would it have cost to buy a ticket on Southwest Airlines and let her avoid this miserable trip? Sure Taylor's mother and stepfather had wanted to get rid of her, but she'd had never known them to be cheap. So, now she was stuck on a bus with two dweeby guys and a nerdy girl who… well, she hadn't figured out the girl—but she would.

By air, San Antonio was an hour from Dallas. By car, might be four hours. The bus was scheduled to take eight— assuming it didn't break down along the way.

Taylor headed for the back of the bus, then rolled her eyes as the three losers clomped after her.

Was it completely impossible for destiny to give her someone cool to arrive with? Kids like them, nice kids from rich families, might as well wear kick-me signs on their backs.

Because they were rich kids, Matt lugged on a cooler stuffed with a mix of super-healthy things like celery sticks, and treats. As she watched, he handed a baggie of what looked like homemade cupcakes to Barley and nibbled on a celery stick. Taylor was more interested in Annie.

Finally, when she thought nobody was looking, Annie gave her a clue. She snatched a couple of ice cubes out of Matt's cooler and just held onto them.

Not a single drip hit the ground and when Annie opened her hands again, they were dry, with no sign there'd ever been any ice at all. What was that about?

For a weak second, Taylor considered asking for a cupcake but she fought the temptation. She wouldn't be a hypocrite even for cupcakes. She wouldn't pretend to be their friend just to get them to share their stuff.

Instead she sat, alone, and tried not to listen to her stomach growl while the other three chattered like cockatiels.

The second the bus rolled out of the station, already half an hour behind schedule, Barney reached into his backpack and pulled out a stack of comic books at least six inches thick. He handed a bunch to Matt and a few more to Annie. When he glanced in Taylor's direction, she purposely stared out the window as if she cared about the abandoned warehouses and boarded up gas stations that seemed to make up most of the buildings on their route out of Dallas.

She had a feeling something bad was coming. Like Cassandra in the old-time stories, her feelings were always bad and they always came true. This time, though, knowing trouble was coming didn't take magic—it came from knowing where they were going. The School for Monsters and Misfits was dangerous—deadly.

Trouble hit them before they even got close.

The Austin Greyhound Station was close to downtown and they were scheduled for a forty-minute wait.

"Come on, kids. Off the bus." The driver, a fat, sweaty man with no eyebrows, gestured them forward.

Her apprehension reared up. The bus wasn't much protection but the seats would slow any attacker. "You're not making *them* get off." Taylor pointed to an old couple who looked superglued to their seats.

The driver ran his fat fingers through greasy hair. "That's because they're not going to tear things apart if I leave them alone. Now, off."

Taylor was tempted to refuse, to grab onto one of the seats and demand that she be allowed to stay. Except, the only thing that would accomplish was that he'd call the cops. Arriving at the School with a couple of losers would be bad. Arriving in the back seat of a cop car would be far worse. Or at least that's what she thought.

"I'll let you on in half an hour," the driver promised. "Stay out of trouble."

Like that was going to happen.

Texas's state capitol gleamed from just a couple of blocks away, but the bus depot might as well have been in another world. Diesel fumes danced across the parking lot like living things and the waiting room, with its depressed coffee shop, seemed a million miles away.

"Anyone want ice cream?" Matt gestured at a machine in the coffee shop, oblivious to the air of dread hanging over the station like a dung-covered horse-blanket. Then again, why shouldn't he be? Being sent to the School for Monsters and Misfits was probably the first bad thing that ever happened to him.

Barley and Annie trotted after Matt, anticipating their sugar rush, leaving Taylor to watch for the danger she knew was coming. Sometimes it helped to see trouble before it got there.

Usually, of course, it didn't.

* * * *

Taylor was being weird, and hadn't even responded when he'd offered to buy ice cream, but Annie and Barley joined Matt at the freezer, selecting from all two flavors available.

Although it was barely noon, a couple of big guys who looked like they had either snuck out of school or had just graduated were smoking cigarettes and drinking beer at a table near the ice cream machine. They didn't look friendly, so Matt led the others back out to the bus lot where a couple of benches had been set up under an overhang.

The bus depot wasn't the most beautiful environment and the summer sun beat down like an overly-energetic microwave, but the benches were better than inhaling someone else's smoke.

He opened the door for Annie and Barley and, once they'd passed him, started out himself.

He didn't make it.

One of the big guys grabbed his arm and jerked Matt toward him, pressing his face down until it was only a couple of inches away. "Funny, you don't look like monsters to me. What makes you so dangerous, kid?"

Matt dropped his ice cream as he struggled to get away.

"Watch out," Annie shouted. "He's a troll."

Sure enough, the guy who'd grabbed him swelled up, growing to almost seven feet in height with shoulders so broad he had to turn sideways to make it out the door.

"We're not looking for trouble," Matt tried.

The troll jabbed his red tag. "Too bad, loser. You found it anyway. Right, Ryan."

The other guy dropped his cigarette and transformed to troll himself. He shoved past Matt and poked Barney in the gut. "We're only trouble for scum, Eric."

"That's what I thought. That's why cleaning up this mess from Dallas is our job."

"Let him go." Annie grabbed Eric's hand and tried to pull it from Matt's arm—but the troll stuck an elbow in her face and she reeled away.

Barley tried to help as well, but Ryan caught him as he charged past and twisted both arms behind him in a full-nelson. "What do you say we clean up this filth and save our parents the money it costs to send them to the School for Morons."

"Good plan," Eric said. "My mother always tells me to flush when I find a mess." The troll shoved Matt into the wall hard enough he bounced off it, then whirled around and punched Barley, still being held by Ryan, in the stomach.

Barley turned green and gagged.

Matt looked around, desperate for any type of assistance. In the early afternoon, the bus station should be full of people. He'd seen a couple of cops when they'd first climbed off the bus but that was then. Whether it was just bad luck or if the trolls had planned ahead, the lot was deserted now—except for his two friends, the two trolls, and the mysterious Taylor.

Annie wasn't going to be any help—she'd sagged to the ground after taking Eric's elbow. Taylor, of course, pretended she didn't know any of them.

But they'd let go of him when the two trolls had ganged up on Barley. That left him free.

Few bunnies turn on larger predators and hunt them down. But his father had always explained that bullies are fundamentally cowards. If he just confronted them, maybe…

He put down his head and charged. If he could catch Eric from behind, possibly Barley could get free, and then, perhaps, the two of them could figure a way to help Annie up and get away from the trolls. Maybe…

Instead of Eric's back, he ran into the older boy's fist.

Something went crunch and his nose twisted sideways.

He told himself to keep going but his knees wobbled under him and abruptly he was sitting on the concrete parking lot.

"Guess *these* monsters aren't so fierce after all," Eric announced. He had blood on his fist and, for an instant, Matt wondered if he'd at least injured the troll. Then he realized the blood was his.

"I've been thinking about this," Ryan observed. "I'm thinking, if they're not people, killing 'em isn't murder. More like vermin elimination. My pop always says there's no off-season on vermin."

"Excellent thinking, Ryan. An apt comparison."

If he transformed, Matt might get away. But rabbits <u>are</u> vermin and he'd simply confirm what these guys already thought. Then they'd take out his escape on Barley and Annie.

Matt had never been the kind to crybaby home to his parents. Now, though, he didn't see any alternative.

Pain and the damage to his nose made Matt's eyes water so hard he couldn't make out the buttons on his phone, but he didn't need to see the numbers to dial home.

He knew he was just confirming his father's judgment that he was a coward and a disappointment. He knew a real man would stand and take whatever these guys chose to dish out. But Matt thought they were deadly serious about killing him and the others. Maybe he was less than a real man—the part of him that was a rabbit had no bravery in it at all. But he'd swallow his pride if doing so kept him and his friends alive.

He pushed the speed dial number. "Dad, it's Matt. Some Fae kids are beating us up in Austin. Their names are Eric and Ry—"

A heavy boot smacked into his hand, sending his phone flying.

It landed with a thunk—followed by the tinkle of electronic parts scattering across the parking lot asphalt.

"Now that was stupid," Eric told him. "Do you really think your mommy is going to—"

"You'd better hope there are a lot of trolls named Ryan and Eric."

Taylor might as well have been on another planet until then. For some reason, she'd decided to pick that moment intervene. Maybe she'd realized that the trolls would have to kill her too if they didn't want witnesses.

"Otherwise," she continued, "you might as well buy your own bus tickets for San Antonio."

"What are you talking about?"

"You don't even know who you're beating up on?" Taylor laughed. "That's Matt Carnecero. As in *the* Carneceros of

Frisco. His daddy, the one you just broke up is call to, is head of the Dallas shifter community."

"Good thing you're in *our* neighborhood, then," Eric said. "We'll just—"

Whatever they would "just do" was interrupted by Eric's phone.

"Yeah? ... Yes, dad." Eric looked like his winning lottery ticket turned up counterfeit. "But dad, I'm just cleaning up some ... Okay. If you say so." He snapped his phone shut.

"Guess you've got a pretty important father." Eric hauled Matt off the ground where he'd fallen after running into Eric's fist. "Guess you think that makes you important too."

"I don't..."

"I didn't hear anything about your friends being important, though." Eric hit Barley twice more in the stomach, then stomped over to Annie and drove a knee into her belly.

He strolled back to Matt, pretended to brush him off, then picked him up like a football, and drop-kicked him. "Oops. Sorry."

Matt wasn't a football and he didn't fly far, but the kick hurt more than the punch in the nose had, more than anything he'd ever experienced—except his first and only transformation to animal form.

"I'd say we'll see you losers later," Ryan taunted. "Except we won't—because where you're going, they don't come out." Let's get out of here, Eric."

As they headed out, the trolls exchanged high fives and bragged on facing monsters and prevailing.

Matt wondered if he'd just got his first taste of the rest of his life.

The thought was not reassuring.

* * * *

"Good thing you're all looking out for each other's backs." Taylor had hoped it wouldn't work out like this, but she probably had more experience with the whole monster thing than the others—except, maybe, Annie. She'd seen a flash of green when Eric had rammed his knee into Annie's stomach and had a guess why Annie never smiled.

Barley glared at her. "What's that mean?"

"You might have gotten into trouble if you weren't."

"We got out of it."

"You wouldn't have if I hadn't given Matt the chance to call his dad."

It should have been easy for her to watch. They were three spoiled kids from the rich side of town, children of the powerful elite in Dallas's Fae community. She probably shouldn't have interfered as much as she had, but mentioning Matt's parents had seemed harmless.

She'd waited a good three minutes after the fight to make sure the trolls were really gone before coming over and helping Matt to his feet.

"Thanks for your help." This time Annie didn't bother hiding her smile—which was more of a grimace. Yep, Taylor had seen right. The girl had green teeth that came to sharp points. The punks had attacked Matt and Barley. They'd barely bothered with the real monster.

She'd read about murdhuacha, the Irish version of mermaids, who never sat combing their hair and being beautiful, but instead dragged sailors into the water and drowned them. Annie was one of those.

Unfortunately, just because she was a monster didn't mean she could fight like one. Annie might as well have been a fully human girl like Taylor for all the help she'd been.

"Did you expect me to do more?" Taylor laughed, pretending she didn't mind they hadn't thanked her for interrupting. Without her, Eric's father's call would have been too late. "I don't remember being part of the 'stick together' gang. Like I said, though, sure worked well for you."

"At least we tried."

"Did I say stick together?" she continued. "Sink together is more like it." She wished she could believe that "trying" and good intentions resulted in good outcomes, but she'd never seen that. Maybe the meek *would* inherit the earth—but the tough guys would ruin it and move on to something better first.

Annie jerked Matt away from Taylor as if staking a claim—as if *she* might be interested in a kid doomed to be stepped on by everyone.

She hadn't figured him out yet. Coming from the Carnecero family, he had to be a shifter. She wondered if he was a kitten—he certainly seemed skittish enough. And they might not like the image of a humble house-cat being part of their pride.

The beating had taken its toll—he looked about as steady on his feet as her stepfather did when he stumbled home from a twenty-four hour drunk.

Her guts tightened when she remembered what that man had tried to do the last time he'd come home drunk and found her alone.

"Come on, Matt." Taylor would have shaken him, but Annie held both of his hands and looked intently into his eyes. "You're a shifter," Annie said. "Transform into animal form. When you shift back, a lot of your injuries will be healed."

"How do you know that?" Barley demanded. "You a shifter."

Annie sighed. "Didn't you pay attention to anything they told you when you were getting ready for your thirteens?"

"Uh, sure. Anyway, I'd love to be able to become a T-Rex myself."

"I'm getting back on the bus." Taylor shook her head in disgust. "It really doesn't matter to me, but if you have any sense, you'll get back on, too. And think about this, Annie. If Matt wouldn't transform when he was in a fight, why would he do it now, just because you ask? Maybe he can't transform, or maybe he transforms to something out of place—like a miniature shark."

That was a clever slam—and hinted to Annie that Taylor had seen through her secret. "Maybe that's why he's a magical misfit."

Annie gnashed her sharp green teeth and growled at Taylor. "Considering how much help you've been to us, I don't know why we're even listening to you. Come on, guys. Let's get on the bus. You've got a broken nose, Matt. And

Barley, you look like something you ate didn't agree with you."

Barley rubbed his stomach. "Right now, nothing I've ever eaten agrees with me."

The three clomped over to the bus just as the driver headed out of the station coffee shop.

Once, Taylor would have been hurt by their attitude. But that had been a long time before—back when she'd let other people's opinions matter. She'd learned her lesson the hard way. Never depend on anyone, never count on anyone. And watch your own back.

She pretended she didn't mind the way the kids shut her out, found her seat at the back, and stared out the window as they headed down Koenig Lane toward the onramp to I-35.

Her stomach growled as she sat, but she glared at Barley as if accusing him of making the noise. She'd recognized Matt's offer to buy everyone ice cream for the trap it had been. Accepting it would have committed her to, if not friendship, at least a vague alliance with the others. She couldn't afford to hang her future off their sinking ship. That didn't mean she wasn't hungry.

She opened the celebrity magazine she'd lifted at the station from a lady who'd probably finished it. She planned to spend the rest of the journey pretending she was fascinated by the supposed lives of the supposedly glamorous.

She wondered how ordinary people would react if they learned how many of their idols were Fae. Maybe they wouldn't care—maybe the whole idea of keeping the Fae secret was about control rather than to protect the people.

One thing was certain—there was nothing glamorous about being sent to the School for Misfits and Monsters—a place where people went and never returned.

Chapter Three

In a million years Barley wouldn't have admitted it to anyone in the Fae community, but he was a Harry Potter fan. Sure, Potter's world could never happen to him—Texas was about as far from England as you can get both geographically and socially. Still, in his gut he hoped the School for Monsters and Misfits to be a combination of Hogwarts and Azkaban. He wanted, almost needed, the fancy carriages, the magically propelled boats, the flying-on-broomsticks ambiance of Rowling's magical stories.

If only he'd been English rather than Texan, he might have gone to the real Hogwarts, learned real mage secrets, maybe even played Quidditch—he wasn't sure if that was completely fictional.

Texas wasn't like that, of course.

It started at the San Antonio Greyhound station. No secret gates, no magically drawn coaches, no beautiful floating gondolas. Instead, a fat guy with a rent-a-cop uniform, a shiny bald head, and a third-eye tattoo on his forehead grabbed them as they exited the bus, patted them down, dug through their baggage, then escorted them to a green van with bars between the driver's seat and the back. A second guard, also with the blue tattoo on his forehead, stayed about ten feet away, his hand resting on his unsnapped holster.

"I'm Barley." He stuck out his hand figuring it couldn't hurt to make friends with the staff.

The driver ignored Barley's hand just as he ignored the blood all over Matt's shirt.

When the second guard opened the van door, the driver jerked a shoulder for them to get in.

Annie made a hushing noise when Barley started to object.

Two minutes after they'd pulled out of the station, Annie stuck an elbow into Barley's still-sore stomach. "Check it out."

He wasn't up to checking out anything. Since he even more wasn't up to arguing—especially not with a girl, he followed her pointing finger.

"An old building. Boring."

"Don't you know what that is? It's the Alamo. You know, where Davy Crockett and…"

He noticed Taylor was checking it out—while pretending complete indifference. Something about that girl didn't quite line up—and he didn't mean because she wasn't in a hurry to be his friend. Which was too bad—Barley needed friends. At the ceremony celebrating his thirteenth birthday, his belly had expanded, horn nubs grew just above his hairline, and his feet had shrunk into little hooves—hooves he kept hidden inside cowboy boots. He'd become a useless party animal.

The Dallas/Richardson Fae community had no use for Satyrs. Then again, nobody had any use for Satyrs—unless, maybe, they were looking for a D.J. Barley had wanted magic—instead, he had a talent for music. Before the change, that hadn't been a bad thing—people sought out his advice on their play lists, asked him to check out their demo CDs. Once they learned he was musical only because he was a Satyr, even his former friends had simply shaken their heads and avoided him.

And now he was supposed to look at some old building—which would have been considered pretty much modern in England—as if it mattered?

"Big deal—the Alamo," he said. "Couple dozen guys got killed because wouldn't follow orders and had some sort of martyr complex. What's that supposed to be—an inspiration?"

The driver peered at him through the rear view mirror and Barley got the uncomfortable feeling he'd just failed a test. No big surprise there—he'd failed at just about everything since his birthday.

"It's so cool," Annie clutched his arm. "Imagine, a few dozen brave men and women, with the hordes of Santa Anna raised against them, bravely fighting for liberty—"

Barley snickered. "That's if you define liberty as the right to hold slaves. You know that's what the Texas Revolution was about, right? The anglo settlers really didn't like those new Mexican laws against holding slaves."

Annie gave him a look and Taylor raised one eyebrow at him—he wasn't sure if it was condemning or if he'd actually impressed her. Just because he wasn't the most brilliant student in the world didn't mean he couldn't read.

"That," Annie said, "isn't very romantic. I also happen to think there was probably a lot more to the Texas independence story than fighting against abolitionists."

"Always good to believe fairy tales rather than evidence."

Whatever the story might have been, the Alamo was not the School. Their driver headed past a long strip of dirty paint-and-body shops before finally pulling to a stop in front of what looked like an abandoned army base a few miles from downtown.

The buildings behind the fence looked dilapidated—decades of Texas's hot sun had faded their paint, crumbled the asphalt, and dehydrated nature's optimistic attempts to let things grow.

If the buildings were in sorry shape, the fence wasn't. Tangles of razor-wire glistened where they wrapped through the rusty chain link that had probably served the army base. Guard stations towered over the fence and Barley was pretty sure he saw machine guns poking out. An ugly water tower, also rusting, rose over everything.

The driver honked his horn at a reinforced gate—also studded with razor wire and another guard peered out. Barley wasn't sure whether it was his imagination or magic, but this guard's third eye appeared to move independently of his head.

"Abandon hope, all you who enter here," the driver muttered.

"We're definitely not at Hogwarts." He spoke to himself, but he noticed Taylor's disgusted look. So much for impressing the girl.

The driver pulled past a series of dusty rust-brown Quonset huts mingled with a few clapboard buildings before braking in front of a building that didn't look any newer than any other but at least had a fresh coat of white paint.

When the van stopped, Barley fumbled for the van door—
but the latch didn't catch and the door stayed locked.

The second guard turned and glared at him. "Wait for the
headmaster."

Finally, a door at the front of the white building opened
and a tall fat man emerged, a huge smile lighting his face.

"He looks like Santa Claus," Annie said.

"Uh-oh," Taylor whispered. "When they're happy to see
you, you know you're in trouble."

Barley didn't feel that way. Sure, there were scary rumors
about the School for Monsters and Misfits. But could it be that
much worse than staying in Richardson and suffering
contempt from everyone he knew? Yeah, the decor fell short
of fancy England, but the headmaster's smile went a long way
to reassuring him.

"Oh, let them out, Gus," the headmaster shouted through
the van windshield. "What are they going to do-set fire to the
school?"

"Safety first," the driver, apparently named Gus,
responded. He and the second guard opened their own doors
and got out.

Again, the second guard stayed back. This time he actually
drew his gun before signaling to Gus to open the door and let
the four emerge.

Then Gus produced a form and handed it to the
headmaster. "Please acknowledge delivery of four prisoners."

"Students, not prisoners."

"Prisoners until you sign the form. We can dispose of them
if you won't take them."

The headmaster quickly signed and the guards got back in
their van and drove away.

Unlike Gus, the headmaster tutted over Matt's injuries and
inquired as to the others' health.

He put his hand over Matt's nose and closed his eyes.
Barley didn't close *his* eyes, though. He saw the flash of
power.

"Good as new," the headmaster proclaimed. "You'll have
a pair of shiners tomorrow, but that's normal healing. And as
for you, my friend." He turned to Barley. "The best thing for

your sore stomach is to put something into it. I assume you're hungry—teens are always hungry, I've discovered."

"We're hungry," Annie admitted.

Barley noticed Taylor didn't actually admit to anything as mundane as hunger—that would make her seem fallible or something. Still, she didn't complain when the headmaster led them into what turned out to be his home and office.

"I am Julian Hoffbrewer," he admitted when they were arranged in his living room. "Headmaster at the School for Advanced Fae Studies."

He patted the stack of papers he'd picked up as they'd entered the room. "We've never had anyone try to sneak in here, but let's take a look. Matt Carnesario?"

Matt raised his hand.

"And which of you lovely young ladies is Annie Fish?"

Annie admitted it.

"So, you must be Taylor Bang and this is Barley Harris. Have I got it right?"

"That's right," Barley said. "And thank you for—"

"I've got your dorm assignments and class schedules ready. I got your transcripts and test results from your prior schools, so you should be able to cope, but there are tutorial sessions for any class you need to catch up on." He handed each of them a sheet of paper.

"I've put you boys together," Headmaster Hoffbrewer said. "And you girls, of course. It's so much nicer, don't you think, when you've already got a friend to help you deal with all the changes?"

"Oh, joy," Taylor said.

Barley shook his head. Taylor was mad and mean—but that wasn't his problem. His stomach was his problem. "You did say something about food."

"So I did." The headmaster opened a door that led to a dining room with a table practically groaning with food. "Our dining halls are closed, but since I knew you'd be late, I prepared a small snack."

Barley studied the table and thought about the words, *small snack*. For the first time in months, he let his own smile out.

He was home in a way he'd never been even before his change. Headmaster Hoffbrewer knew what he was and didn't hold it against him.

This was going to be wonderful.

* * * *

A rabbit is always afraid.

That was the sum of Matt's experience since his change. His family and friends barely restrained themselves from chowing down on him, he'd been relegated to a school nobody wanted to attend, the cutest girl he'd ever met looked at him like he was so much bat guano, and he'd been beaten up by trolls because they thought *he* was the monster.

He wanted to believe things would be different now. Certainly Headmaster Hoffbrewer <u>seemed</u> friendly. But bunny instincts urged caution.

Until, that is, he saw what Hoffbrewer called a *snack*.

While Barley stuffed himself with cake, Matt filled a plate with lettuce, legumes, and carrots.

He looked around until he found a chair overhung by a bookshelf that looked vaguely den-like, then sat there, his senses alert to possible attack as he dug in to the treats.

He didn't feel safe, of course. Still, with Hoffbrewer smiling at his four new students, with the knowledge that he'd be sharing a dorm room with a kid who liked him and who seemed more interested in sweets than in a high-protein rabbit snack, and with food treats in front of him, he felt as close to comfortable as he'd gotten since his change.

Hoffbrewer waited until they'd all gotten something to eat, insisting that Annie take a huge portion of what looked like raw tuna, then crunched down on a carrot of his own.

After clearing his throat, he smiled at all of them again. "Again, welcome to the School for Advanced Fae Studies. I look forward to working with each of you to develop your Fae abilities."

"Why?" Matt's rabbit side demanded that he keep silent, unobserved, but he was more than simply rabbit no matter what his family thought. Or maybe he just had an overdose of rabbit curiosity. He seemed to remember children's stories about curious rabbits. "We're here because the world doesn't *want* our magic. Why shouldn't we let it atrophy? Maybe we'd get safe enough that they could let us out."

Hoffbrewer peered at Matt through his gold-rimmed glasses. "An excellent question, young Carnecero. You're all feeling down, a natural result of what's happened to you since you came into your powers. I know there are those out there who even call our school the *School for Monsters and Misfits*." He laughed easily, as if that was ridiculous and they were there because they *wanted* to advance in Fae Studies. "But think about this," Hoffbrewer continued. "Leonardo da Vinci was a misfit. Picasso, Einstein and Winston Churchill were misfits. Not fitting in may mean that you're ready to fly higher than the others."

Matt hadn't thought Barley would ever look up from the chocolate cake he hovered over like an overprotective parent, but he did now, nodding firmly as Hoffbrewer finished his lecture.

"Like those misfits—" the headmaster began.

"Oh, give it a rest," Taylor interrupted. "So what if a few losers made history? They weren't stuck in what's essentially a prison with no exit door. The Fae community doesn't send people here to learn magic, they send us here so we're kept out of the way."

If Hoffbrewer was angry that Taylor had cut off his little speech, he didn't show it. He shook his head sadly. "You're quite right. The Fae community of Texas has rejected you, tossed you to a place where, as far as it is concerned, you essentially vanish."

"Going back to my question, then," Matt said, "what's the point of us developing our Fae skills? If the world thinks we're monsters, wouldn't further honing those skills be seen as dangerous?"

"It would indeed," Hoffbrewer boomed. "But you see, the Fae outside happen to be wrong. Every one of your talents is precious and wonderful."

"So wonderful we're locked up for life," Taylor grumped.

"That," Hoffbrewer said, "is what the community believes. I, however, have a different opinion. I've decided not to *let* them lock you up—not, at least, on a permanent basis."

Matt's head whipped from Taylor back to Hoffbrewer so quickly he was surprised it stayed attached. "*You've* decided?"

"Why do you think I volunteered to be headmaster? Do I look like a prison warden?" Hoffbrewer slapped his oversized belly. "I intend to prove your value—first to those of you here, and then to the rest of the Fae. So what if I'm supposed to keep you locked up? My goal is to let you free."

Matt shook his head. He couldn't be happy about serving a life sentence in a defunct army base, but at least he was alive. How long he'd survive outside was anyone's guess but the shorter the guess, the more likely it would be right.

Annie, apparently, didn't agree. Blood ran down her chin as she looked up from her plate of raw tuna. "You're going to let us out?"

"I'm going to help you develop the skills you need so we can *all* get out."

She licked her lips. "Cool."

Matt glanced from Annie, who looked dangerous but happy, to Taylor, who looked suspicious, to Barley who looked like he wanted another piece of chocolate cake. Taylor's reaction was what he would have expected—she seemed suspicious of everything. And Hoffbrewer sounded too good to be true. Barley's reaction was even more predictable.

Taylor asked the question Matt wished he could. "Exactly how many of your students have returned to the Fae community, Headmaster Hoffbrewer? When my stepfather decided to send me here, I did some research. You know what I found? Zero."

Hoffbrewer shook his head, the twinkle fading from his eyes. "You're quite right, Miss Bang. Previous headmasters, and even much of our current faculty, haven't had my commitment to re-engaging the community. We'll hone your skills, develop self-control, and show the Fae community that you're not the danger they think you are. I wouldn't be surprised if you're able to go home at the end of the year.

"Maybe *you* wouldn't," Taylor muttered. "I sure would be."

Hoffbrewer glanced at his watch. "Your dorm monitors should be arriving in a few minutes. Matt and Barley, you'll be staying in Forester Hall. Taylor and Annie, it's Geneva for you."

Annie set down the remains of her third slab of raw tuna. "When we drove up and I saw the barbed wire and the run-down facilities, I expected you to be more like a prison guard."

"You'll see guards," Hoffbrewer admitted. "They're quite evident and not under my chain of command. Please be careful and don't go anywhere near the fences."

Matt forced his quivering nose muscles still. Hoffbrewer was a rebel with a dream. Maybe Matt could be a part of that dream in a way he could never be a part of his family again. "I'll do what I can to help you."

"Good spirit." Hoffbrewer slapped him on the shoulder. "We'll work together to change the situation."

* * * *

Annie desperately wanted to talk to someone, to see if their impression was the same as hers. Unfortunately, Phaedra, the dorm monitor who'd collected them from headmaster Hoffbrewer's home, had been more interested in flirting with her male counterpart than in answering Annie's questions.

Phaedra led Annie and Taylor to a dorm room in the back of a rusting Quonset hut. The bare lightbulb hanging from the ceiling generated about as much light as a firefly, which Annie considered just as well considering the filthy walls and floors.

Pushed against one wall, a steel bunk bed held a single mattress. Against the tin side stood a three-legged desk with no drawers and two wooden chairs, one missing its back.

"You got a window and everything," Phaedra said. "Not all the rooms do."

Outside the tiny barred window, spotlights danced across the open ground between the dorms and the razor-wire fences and the water tower loomed darkly, like an Imperial Walker from *Star Wars*.

"What about the second mattress?" she said.

Taylor dumped her bag on the top bunk. "Good question. Where's Annie's mattress? Although if you happen to find a clean one, Phaedra, I wouldn't mind switching this out."

"New kids get what's left. Unless you want to fight for more than your share." Her voice dropped three octaves as she put out the challenge and she swelled up just enough that Annie realized she could grow a lot more. No way was Annie going to challenge her. Not, at least, without knowing a lot more about how things worked here.

The iron bunk bed squeaked when she put her hand on the rusty springs. "I'm just saying, this doesn't look very comfortable."

"Anyone who told you the School for Monsters and Misfits was a luxury cruise was lying, girlfriend." Phaedra's voice was a snarl. "Now, get some sleep. Breakfast is at six. Classes start at seven. And trust me, you don't want to miss a roll-call."

The building's concrete slab shuddered as she closed the door behind her and walked down the hall.

"Nice going." Taylor grabbed the rails and climbed on Annie's bed frame on her way to inspect the top bunk. "That's one giant, three trolls and me you've pissed off so far today. Next time, warn me in advance so I can get out of the firing line."

"It isn't fair that you get the mattress and I've got to sleep on the springs."

Taylor laughed. "You're right. It isn't fair at all."

Annie joined Taylor on the side of the bed and inspected the sweat-stained mattress. "Then again, at least there probably aren't any fleas in the metal springs. Try not to drop any down on me, would you?" She inhaled a definite canine scent from above—and she didn't think it came from Taylor.

Taylor froze, one leg suspended in air over the mattress. "You think you zinged me, don't you?"

"I know I zinged you. Enjoy your bugs."

"Well, all you did was help me out." Taylor climbed back down and reached into her bag.

They'd all gone through tough times before they got sent to the School. In Annie's case, at least, her parents had gone to bat for her, argued she should be allowed to stay with the others. They'd lost that argument and the merfolk monitors had literally torn her from her parents' arms. Still, Annie knew that somewhere, were people who loved her—even if they couldn't help her. She suspected Taylor didn't have anyone like that. She knew Taylor wouldn't appreciate it if she pointed that out.

"Bug investation happens to be a problem I can deal with," Taylor said.

Annie bit her tongue to force herself to stay silent but it didn't work. "I imagine you've had plenty of practice."

Taylor whipped around so quickly her body blurred.

Annie didn't mean to move but her body responded. She reached up—and caught Taylor's arm as it descended. Only when she held Taylor's hand a few inches from her face did she see that her new roommate held a bar of soap with a razor blade embedded in it.

"You're fast, green-tooth. I'll give you that. Now let go of my arm."

Annie realized she'd been dragging Taylor's hand toward her mouth. She shuddered and shoved Taylor away, suddenly sick to her stomach.

Taylor took a couple of steps back and looked at her with something approaching respect—which was so not the reaction Annie wanted. It was moments like this, instinctual reactions to possible danger, that had finally swayed her pod to cast her out. The worst part was, her responses weren't even dependable. She could have used them when the trolls had grabbed her instead of being a helpless girl. And this time, she'd been ready to take a bite out of Taylor. She'd probably reinforced Taylor's sense that violence was the only answer to any problem while destroying any chance she had to make the other girl a friend—and Annie needed friends—soon. Merfolk kept together because they needed social groups for survival— unless Annie replicated that environment quickly, she'd die.

"At least you're here for a reason," Taylor muttered. "Let you loose on society and you'd tear them up."

"Like there aren't a lot of worse monsters who never got sent here."

"That's a point." Taylor grabbed her bag from the filthy floor where she'd dropped it, then started yanking things from it. The celebrity magazine Taylor had stolen while Annie had watched amazed came first followed by two bananas, four of Hoffbrewer's mini-sandwiches, and finally three candle stubs.

By the time she'd fished out the candles, her bag flopped around empty. It reminded Annie that Taylor hadn't had any other bags. So, where were her clothes, her books, her electronics?

"Don't you have—"

"No, I don't." Taylor placed the three candle stubs around the bed, using strings and chalk to mark out the boundaries of a perfect isosceles triangle.

Then she slapped her skirt, apparently searching for pockets that weren't there. From the glare she sent Annie's way, asking for help was somewhere on her list down around eating dog poop. Finally, though, she brought herself to do it. "You have any matches."

"Of course not."

Taylor seemed gratified. "Figures. You were little Miss Perfect one day and a monster the next. Now you can't decide which you are."

"If you say so."

Taylor shook her head, then snapped her fingers three times, pointing to each candle in turn.

On the third snap, all of them glowed, smoked, then flamed up.

"Good trick."

"That? It's nothing."

Annie thought, though, that she saw a hint of a smile on Taylor's face.

"You know, if you ever want to borrow any of my—"

"If you're thinking how pathetic I am, remind yourself of this—I'm the one who's sleeping on a comfortable mattress tonight. While you're getting poked by hundreds of metal hooks, I'm luxuriating."

"Luxuriating along with your bug friends and the rich scent of werewolf pee."

"I'm taking care of those."

"I was just wondering—what are you going to do about clothes?"

Taylor glared at her, then hitched her too-short skirt a bit higher up her thighs. "You saying there's something wrong with this?" It's a lot sexier than anything *you've* got."

"As if you know what I have. Besides, even if a uniform for a school you don't go to any more was cool, it's only one outfit."

"I'll keep it clean the same way I'll clean this mattress." Taylor shook her head as if disgusted, then flicked off the overhead light.

The room plunged into the golden glow of candlelight.

"What are you planning on—"

Taylor put a finger to her lips. "Watch and learn, mergirl."

"You knew?"

She laughed. "If I hadn't guessed from your green teeth, the raw tuna would have given it away. Now that was a disgusting display."

Annie knew she'd regret any confidences but she couldn't help herself. Even an enemy was better than being ignored. "Ever since I had my birthday, I've craved raw fish. Makes me weird, right?"

Taylor laughed. "Makes me wonder about your friend Matt. You think maybe he's a werehorse? He sure seems interested in vegetables. Maybe you should take him for a ride some time."

"That is so disgus—"

"Shush."

Taylor sang the song about the Eensy-weensy spider while she ran her fingers over the mattress.

For what felt like a long time, nothing happened. Annie wondered if lighting candles was the extent of Taylor's talent and if she was faking it.

Then her roommate plunged her entire hand straight through the fabric and deep into the mattress's foam padding.

"Jeez. If you were just going to ruin..." Annie let her voice trail off when Taylor pulled her hand back out—leaving the mattress unharmed.

"That's another good trick."

Taylor's gray eyes rolled back in her head. "Where one goes, all go. Never to return."

She turned to Annie as if they'd been engaged in an ordinary conversation—except that only the whites of her eyes showed. "Open the window."

"It's painted shut."

"You're stronger than you know." Taylor's voice was soft and weirdly musical. She put a beat on the word *stronger* and abruptly, Annie noticed that gravity pulled on her a bit less. She grasped the window frame and yanked it upward.

To her surprise, it opened.

Taylor kept chanting about the spider as she walked to the window and flicked her fingers.

A tiny spot—a flea, Annie guessed, vanished into the darkness.

Seconds later, a line of insects, there had to be hundreds of them, formed on the bed rail closest the window, climbed down, hopped across the floor, then headed out the window.

A green fog, a fog that smelled distinctly of dog, accompanied them.

"That's amazing." Annie knew there were mages in the world, but she'd always heard about the price they paid, the blood and effort required as sacrifice. Then again, merfolk generally kept to themselves—they might have made up those stories to terrify the little ones.

"'Amazing' would be for me to let a bunch of disgusting bugs keep me awake all night. So, are you going to close that window or not?"

"Yeah." Annie jerked it down. "If I had to get rid of a bunch of bugs, know what I'd do?"

"Huh?"

Annie let her murdhuacha aspect dominate. She knew she dripped seaweed, that her teeth gleamed green and bloody, and that her hair—so unlike the traditional mermaids, became a tangled net. Still, it was worth it to see Taylor's reaction. "I'd scare them."

Chapter Four

Something clunked.

Matt froze in his bed, his rabbit true-form quivering inside, urging him to transform, flee, burrow and hide.

Above him, Barley's gentle snores continued, apparently unaffected by the noise.

The scraping sound confirmed Matt's deepest fears. Someone outside had decided to come in—and his improvised barrier of a chair stuck beneath the doorknob wasn't holding.

He stood quietly and pulled on a pair of jeans and t-shirt so he wouldn't confront the invasion naked.

"Matt Carnecero." The voice echoed from the hall outside his dorm room. "Let me in."

It took Matt a moment to place that voice. For one thing, it had changed since the last time he'd heard it, deepening and becoming rougher. For another, it belonged in Frisco, in Wildebeest Hall, not in the prison-school.

"Larry Trent? Is that you?"

The Trents were cousins of his. Larry had never been a particular friend—he was a couple of years older and scorned playing with younger relatives—but he was family, someone Matt knew, a familiar face in a strange world. Part of the pack.

Matt jerked the chair away from the door and opened it.

Larry, along with a handful of other guys, slouched outside his door. A few of them remained in fully human form but most had halfway transformed to their true shapes, just keeping enough of their humanity so they could stay dressed. Larry was at least as much wolf as man, although he walked on his hind legs.

He'd grown a lot since Matt had last seen him. At well over six feet in height, he towered over Matt. Tattoos sprawled up his arms although Matt couldn't make out what they represented because of the wolf fur in the way, and he needed a shave.

"Come on, kid." Larry's voice seemed friendly enough. "We're going to initiate you into the Hans."

Matt glanced at his watch, then looked again. Three o'clock? Unless the School had ridiculous hours, this was not a normal wakeup call. "You've got to tell me what's going on, Larry. I'd heard you went away to school, but I had no idea they'd sent you to *The School*, if you know what I mean."

His cousin nodded. "We can talk about that later. Because you're family, I spoke up for you with the guys, told them you were a Carnecero, which means you can be trusted, that you're a stand-up guy. But you've got to stop asking questions and come with me."

"I can do that."

"You should thank your stars I spotted you. If you're going to survive, you need a pack to watch your back and the Hans is the best pack in the school." Larry snickered. "It didn't hurt that you brought a couple of chicks with you."

"What's that got to do with anything?"

"You haven't had time to look around much. Tomorrow, when you do, check it out. There's an easy five guys for every girl here. The guys think you're a lucky omen when you bring in two chicks and only one guy—especially since Barley is an obvious short-termer."

Matt wanted to defend his friend, but he didn't know what he could say. Besides, he could help Barley more by learning about the school than he could by getting into an argument with his cousin.

"We're wasting time." The speaker was a strange half-beast with a long snout, hairy legs and front claws that looked like they could tear holes in a battleship. Matt had wondered about the long scrapes in the concrete hallway. He didn't have to wonder any longer.

"Shut up, Marcus," Larry said. "He's my cousin. I say he'll be a Hans."

Matt's rabbit fears reared up when someone pulled a stocking cap over his head, dragging it past his eyes so he couldn't see. But Larry held his arm and guided him down the hall, around a corner, and outside.

Light from the searchlights penetrated even the woven fabric of the cap, but the searchlights were everywhere and Matt couldn't orient on them. He was sure he was being turned randomly to confuse him and panic again threatened to overwhelm him.

Stop and think, he told himself. *Your true form may be a bunny, but you're a thinking person as well.* Rabbits, he knew, spend much of their lives underground, living in narrow tunnels and twisting passageways—all in complete darkness. There, they rely on other senses, scent, touch, their natural sense of direction, to navigate. He could do the same.

After what seemed like hours but his watch confirmed was only five minutes, Larry shoved him through a doorway and pulled the stocking cap from his head.

Three overstuffed sofas and a couple of leather recliners sat in front of a huge plasma T.V. What looked like the remains of Hoffbrewer's spread filled the tables.

A large stain on the ceiling gave evidence of why the building had been abandoned, but apparently the group had made repairs—nobody was going to let a T.V. like that get rained on.

Inside, at least twenty guys and maybe four girls gathered around him. Some smiled, others looked merely curious. A few wore openly antagonistic sneers.

"Welcome to the Hans—if you can cut it." Marcus said. "The Hans rule the school."

"I thought Hoffbrewer—"

Marcus snapped his claws like a pair of scissors. "Hoffbrewer is a nothing. The guards control the exterior—they're beyond our reach although a few of them take bribes to smuggle stuff in. The teachers follow our orders, not Hoffbrewer's. We get the best stuff—as you can see. Stick with us, do what you're told, and you'll be part of the elite. One of these days, you might even get a girl."

As a Carnecereo, Matt had always been part of the elite. Staying there sounded better than the alternative.

Still… "What about my friends?"

"Don't worry about the chicks—they're not your concern any more. As for Fatboy? He doesn't have what it takes."

"Barley is nice. He—"

"Enough."

Marcus puffed out his chest, and mounted on the stand in front of the T.V, and thrust his claws high in the air. "You all know that I've waited longer than anyone. It's my time and I claim the pretty one. Does anyone dispute me?"

"What is he talking a—"

"Shut up," Larry hissed. "You're only here because I stood up for you. Most times, they don't even consider first years. Too many of them don't survive the hazings."

"But they're talking about the girls like they're property or something."

Larry shook his head. "I told you, we don't have enough chicks." He didn't bother with the podium but he raised his voice. "If that is Marcus's claim, so be it. It isn't for me to dispute him. I claim the one with long dark hair. Will any dispute me?"

"You want her, you can have her," Marcus fired back. "Good luck, though."

A tall guy with black stripes across his face and arms stood and thunked Marcus in the chest. "The pretty one is for me."

Larry snickered. "I knew Marcus wasn't going to get Taylor. I had to time things just right so he'd think he'd get his claim and waive any right to Annie. Now he gets nothing."

Matt couldn't believe this was his own cousin. "You're talking about people here. What if Annie doesn't like you? And I don't think anybody would like Marcus. He's weird beyond belief."

"There aren't that many were-ground sloths. Besides, I already said Marcus gets nobody."

Marcus didn't look happy. "I called her first, Justin. It's fair that I get the chick."

Justin halfway transformed to tiger form. "I dispute you."

Matt would have ended up in the middle if Larry hadn't grabbed him by the collar and pulled him to the wall. "I know Carnecereos like to fight, Matt, but this one isn't yours."

He supposed his family did have that reputation. Maybe if he'd lived up to it, he would still be free. Which made him wonder what Larry had done to get sent to the school. He was pretty certain the werewolf hadn't been too much of a sissy to stay in Frisco.

A scream drew his thoughts from home to the fight.

He wasn't sure what he expected, but it wasn't the violence that followed. Marcus tried to keep Justin away, slashing his claws whenever he tried to close the distance.

Bloody gashes opened on the Justin's hide with every strike Marcus landed, but the half-tiger kept coming, ignoring wounds, distaining even to avoid Marcus's blows.

It wasn't even close to a fair fight.

"Marcus is going to kill him," he whispered to his cousin.

"You're losing your touch, Carnecero. Justin doesn't want to hurt Marcus more than he has to, that's all."

Marcus must not have recognized whatever Larry saw, either. He pressed his attacks, going for a vital strike rather than just nipping at Justin's arms. His claws moved so quickly, they were almost a blur.

Abruptly, though, the blur froze when Justin reached out a huge paw, grasped that claw—and tore it off.

Marcus collapsed, his pained squeal so penetrating, Matt couldn't help covering his ears.

"I claim the pretty one." The words, through a tiger mouth, were barely understandable.

"Guess ole Marcus won't be challenging me for the ugly one," Larry said. "And don't worry, Matt. I'm sure you wanted one of the chicks for yourself, but it's not your time. Wait a couple of years and put some muscle on that scrawny body. Any Carnecereo is bound to be a tough enough fighter to win one."

Matt let himself be blindfolded again and led away from the Hans lounge. He hadn't imagined things were so rough at the School. He certainly wasn't going to get involved in owning girls, but he didn't know what he could do about the practice. Maybe Annie and Taylor would be better off having someone powerful look after them. Still, he might not be an expert on girls but he knew they wouldn't put up with it. Not without a fight.

When it came down to it, though, one bunny couldn't change a situation controlled by trolls and predators.

* * * *

Barley grabbed his third danish, stuffing it into his mouth on top of number two—which he'd only partially swallowed. Number one sat in his tummy like a comfortable weight holding him down.

So far, school was working out well. The dining room looked like the devil, with most of the overhead fluorescent lights burned out and remnants of petrified food hanging from the institutional-green walls, but there was plenty to eat and the cafeteria server had just raised an eyebrow when Barley had loaded his plate.

He closed his eyes, savoring the pastry's sweetness and the slight tang of its lemon fill. On his iPod, he listened to a Chopin mazurka, tapping his foot along with the traditional dance tune that talented and tragic composer had used as the basis for the composition. Sure Barley was stuck in hell-school, but life still didn't get better than this.

People were moving around him, but Barley didn't care. He could stay here forever, centered on his music and his food.

"Move, cockroach. You're sitting with my girl." Someone ripped his earbuds from his head, then threw them into the dishwater.

"Hey."

The furry-armed werewolf had already turned, but he spun back when Barley complained. "You have a problem, kid?"

"You're the one with a problem." He struggled for the jerk's name. "You owe me a new set of earbuds, Larry."

"Okay, I owe you." The werewolf slapped Cameron, one of his troll-buddies, on the back. "Good luck collecting…. Or maybe you think *you're* tough enough to make me pay up."

Barley glared at the werewolf. In a fight, Larry would turn Barley into ground meat.

"Come on, Barley." Matt grabbed his arm. "He's too strong for you to take."

Barley looked around to see if any of the faculty were watching, but saw only other students. Annie looked curious, but Matt's face said he knew more than he was letting on and was trying not to let on. One table over, Taylor sat by herself. She looked at Barley with disgust, as if it was *his* fault he'd been lost in the music and hadn't seen the attack coming. It wasn't even as if the werewolf wanted his buds, he was just being a jerk.

Annie got up and fished the buds from the water. They had to be ruined from the bath already, but she spent enough time swishing and splashing them around to make sure of it. Annie certainly had a thing for water.

The werewolf tried to get between her and the table, but Annie stepped around him more quickly than Barley'd guessed she could move and handed Barley the buds. "They should be okay, Barley."

He kept an eye on Larry. "Are you kidding? They're electronics. They're ruined."

"They're not ruined." She turned to the werewolf. "No thanks to you. Don't you understand that we're in this together? Hoffbrewer wants to get us all out, but an attitude like yours is going to hold everyone back."

"I like a girl with spunk."

"If you want a girlfriend," Matt said, "maybe you should try being nice."

"Don't push it, Matt." Larry stepped closer to Annie. "As for what Hoffbrewer wants, don't be a sucker. Sure, he *says* he wants to get us out. They all talk a good line—they'll say anything to keep us from acting up." He grabbed Annie's shirt and jerked her to him, lifting her off the ground. "When you've been here for a while, you'll learn the difference between promises and delivery. The cool thing about me is, I both promise and deliver."

"That makes one of us," Annie fired back. "Because if you really are looking for a girlfriend, you're looking in the wrong spot."

"I'm in the right spot." He lowered his voice. "I just need to do a little… training."

He twisted her top so his fist pressed against her throat.

Annie clawed at his hand, but he only tightened his grip.

Barley knew he couldn't do anything. He couldn't do nothing, either. He shoved back from the table and started toward Larry. "Leave her alone."

One of Larry's buddies—from his stripes, a weretiger, grabbed him before he'd taken two steps. "Let's keep this a fair fight."

"A full-sized werewolf against a girl? Like that's real fair."

"Fair as it's going to get in the School, tubby."

* * * *

It had been so easy for Annie to take her Murdhuacha form the previous night. Now, panic made it impossible for her to think, let alone transform. She pawed at the werewolf's hand—as if that would do anything.

He tightened his grip.

Black spots danced across her vision.

Barney stood and tried to help her, but a weretiger stopped him, spoke to him, then, when Barley argued back, shoved his face into the remains of his breakfast.

She didn't think Larry meant to kill her, but she'd just as soon die as become the kind of girlfriend he was looking for. If he did kill her, would they bother punishing him? He'd already been sent to the School for Monsters and Misfits. Was there anyplace down from here?

"What a wimp." Taylor's voice sounded like it had traveled a hundred miles to get to her. Even at the distance, though, it seemed filled with Taylor's usual negative attitude.

Sometimes Taylor made her so angry.

Annie let her anger well through her body—and strength poured into her, just as it had when Taylor had told her to raise the window the previous night.

All of a sudden, she had all the time in the world. She grasped one of Larry's fingers and peeled it from her throat—then continued peeling until it snapped.

"You..." he hurled her across the room, but the action felt like slow motion so she had time to react. "You broke my finger, you little witch."

The were-tiger laughed. "You're going to have fun with that one, Larry."

Annie used the momentum of the werewolf's push to spin into a cartwheel, rolling to where the tiger still held Barley.

Stripes backed off like she'd pointed a gun at him.

"Don't mess with me or my friends." Her voice was a low croak, but it must have sounded like a growl to the werewolf and tiger.

"You just made a big mistake," Larry blustered. "You're messing with the Hans. Make an enemy of one of us, you've got trouble with *all* of us. We rule the school."

"Must have made up some new rules, then," Barley shot back.

Despite the pain he had to be in, Larry laughed. "Big talk for a punk who just got rescued by a girl."

The slam must have hurt. Barley's face fell.

"Don't listen to them." Annie's voice still sounded like the booming surf to her.

She threw a glance Taylor's way. She could never have gotten away from Larry if Taylor hadn't gotten her mad and wondered if the little witch had done it on purpose. Considering Annie didn't know how to control her powers, Barley shouldn't have to feel bad just because he didn't know how to fight against a tiger.

"We'll see you around, girlie," Larry said. "Because this isn't over. I've staked my claim. Like it or not, you're going to be mine." The werewolf would have been a little more frightening if he hadn't bumped his broken finger against a cafeteria tray and whimpered the last word. Only a little more frightening, though. Because without Taylor around to help, Annie was in trouble—and Taylor didn't even like her.

* * * *

Matt hadn't had time to tell his friends about the Hans, and he wasn't sure how he'd tell them, anyway. He hadn't known Larry would actually attack Barley and Annie. He'd sort of thought he'd send Annie flowers or ask to carry her books, which probably said more about the way Matt had been raised than he wanted known. Still, he couldn't believe his own cousin had behaved so badly—or that he'd just sat there when it happened.

What kind of person, what kind of friend, was he when the going got sticky?

Classes should have been a relief from his self-recrimination, but they were so bad, he'd just as soon close his arm in a shop vice and squeezed it.

Dozens of students crammed into every classroom. They would have spilled into the halls but uniformed guards patrolled the halls, twirling expandable batons and hiding behind dark sunglasses despite the dim interior lighting. Every single guard wore the third eye tattooed in his forehead. That had to mean something.

From the way the older students moved, Matt didn't want any attention from the guards.

The classrooms were equipped with what looked like cast-offs from public schools of the 1960s. Green chalk blackboards were shiny from wear and barely held marks. Ancient maps of the world still displayed French and English colonies in Africa. Germany and Viet Nam were still shown as divided.

Overhead, the ceilings displayed a history of the School's losing war with roof leaks—multiple layers of brown stains making it impossible to determine whether the original color had been white, green, or something else entirely.

All that would have been okay, though, if the classes had been interesting.

The teachers might know their stuff. Unfortunately, he had no way of telling. One thing Matt was sure about, they'd lost any interest in teaching what they did know to their students.

That wasn't so bad in ordinary classes. Matt could read his history and English books without someone looking over his shoulder. And outdated history books weren't really a problem. Algebra was a bit tougher to learn alone, but Matt hoped he could get together with Annie and Barley in the evenings and review the material together. Between them, they should be able to figure it out and if Taylor wanted to join in, that would be okay too.

Oddly, the problem came with the classes Hoffbrewer had promised would help them the most—the classes dealing with magic.

There were two of them—Similarity and Shape. The Shape instructor for the male students was a were-coyote named Dr. Pallendike. For obvious reasons, the female students studied shape with their own instructor—a woman.

Pallendike stood in front of his class, took roll, then announced that Marcus Grant, an annoying were-ground sloth, would take them through their changes. Each student was supposed to change into his alternate form as many times as he could during the class.

There was no way Matt would change into a rabbit in front of a dozen predators.

When he saw Barley wasn't changing either, he pulled out his algebra notebook. "Did you get what Professor Testa was saying about domain and range?"

Barley grinned. "I'll bet we can figure it out if we work together."

The two put down their heads. Barley wasn't brilliant, but he could logic his way through anything which turned out to be a good counter for Matt's more impulsive approach.

Matt looked up once in a while, but Pallendike kept staring out the window, gazing at the razor-wire fence that surrounded the School.

Around him, the other students managed an occasional change, but also wasted a lot of time whispering, passing notes, and even playing chess. Matt figured he and Barley were safe as long as they kept quiet.

Only minutes before the class was scheduled to end, though, Pallendike blinked, turned away from the window and glared directly at Matt. "So?"

He halfway transformed, letting his voice waver between the whine of an aging man and the snarl of a coyote. "Mr. Carnecero and Mr. Harris, is it? Perhaps you think you're already too much the experts to shift for us."

Matt's rabbit instincts told him to run and burrow someplace deep. There was no way he could get out of this without increasing his trouble. Unfortunately, rabbits don't have to worry about what happens when they show up in class again.

"Well—"

Barley cut him off. "Actually, I have been transforming. For me, it's not that dramatic a change, which is probably why you didn't notice."

"Oh, really?" Pallendike's obvious skepticism twisted laughter from most of the other students. "I've never heard of a true form that looks like a fat kid. But maybe—"

Matt couldn't let Barley take all the blame for this. "It's my fault," he interrupted. "I—"

"Dr. Pallendike asked me." Barley shocked Matt from interrupting back. "I'm not especially proud of my alternate form, but I guess there's not a lot of point in keeping it a secret."

He pulled off his cowboy boots—something he hadn't done even when he'd gotten into bed the previous evening.

Like most Texans, Matt often wore boots although he never rode a horse—horses tended to have negative responses to the predator scent the members of the Carnecero clan couldn't shake even when in human form. He knew taking boots off could be a struggle—you had to grab them and yank, hard.

Barley, though, slipped out of his colorful snakeskin boots as easily as if they'd been loafers.

"Oh, great," Justin the tiger shifter groaned. "One of those. Just what we need."

Barley's hooves clattered as stepped away from Pallendike. His bare ankles were hairy and he brushed back his curly hair to show two nubs growing from his head.

Matt swallowed hard, shock making him feel unsteady on his feet. Barley was a Satyr.

Pallendike looked as disgusted as the weretiger. "Are you in true form or human form now, Mr. Harris?"

"I—I'm just me. When I became a Satyr, it stuck."

"So, when you said you were practicing your transformations, you lied?"

"Well—"

"Think about this, fur-foot. I don't allow lies in my class. You may consider yourself on probation. As for you, Mr. Carnecero..."

A bell rang in the hallway signaling the end of the period.

Pallendike shook his head. "I'll finish with *you* tomorrow, Mr. Carnecero. Mr. Harris, you may stay and scrub the toilets in my suite."

"But I've got Similarity next period," Barley said. "Perhaps I can come afterwards and—"

"Perhaps you should learn to listen to your instructor," Pallendike said. "If you want to attend your classes, you should plan on participating in class activities. Now, was there something else, Mr. Carnecero, or are you planning on standing there with your mouth open when you should be heading for your next class?"

Matt just didn't get it. "But I thought you were supposed to teach us. Headmaster Hoffbrewer said—"

"Headmaster Hoffbrewer is a kind and generous man. He's also a sucker for the sad stories you monsters always come up with. He'll toughen up in time. Until then, the guards will make sure you rejects don't run wild."

If the students had to wait for Pallendike to sign off that they were low risk for re-integrating into the Fae community, Matt figured they would wait forever. Helping with Hoffbrewer's plan was going to be harder than he'd imagined.

Chapter Five

"**M**s. Ottawa couldn't pull a shape out of a *Victoria's Secret* catalog," Annie grumbled as she walked to their next class—Similarity. "Do you believe she actually poured water on me to see if I'd sprout a tail."

Taylor considered ignoring the mergirl. Annie had been pathetically grateful that morning after the incident with werewolf and had only shut up when Taylor had threatened to call Larry back if she didn't.

Still, Ms. Ottawa was an unusually bad instructor—even considering how useless the rest of them had been.

"Headmaster Hoffbrewer said they don't get enough money to pay for better instructors." Taylor rolled her eyes so Annie could see how unlikely she thought it that Hoffbrewer was telling the whole truth. "If you had any talent, any choice at all, would *you* teach here? It's got to be as much a prison for them as it is for us."

"Then why the devil don't they work to get us out of here? Do what Hoffbrewer said?"

Taylor shook her head. "Doesn't work that way, not for them. Suppose they send us home all de-monstered and supposedly safe? The Fae will just send them a new lot. Besides, what happens if they made a mistake, let someone out who went rogue? You know the Fae would hold them responsible. Letting anyone out is all risk and no reward for them. Then again, I'll bet lording it over us is the only good thing they have in their lives."

Annie gave her a strange look and Taylor realized she'd been talking to the mergirl almost as if she were a person—maybe even a friend. Of course, anyone who could move as fast as Annie had moved the previous night deserved a bit of respect. Respect but not friendship—no way was Taylor trusting anyone again.

She figured she should back off a bit, though, just in case Annie got the wrong idea. "I'm just saying—"

"Are you ladies planning on participating in this class? Or perhaps you have more important things to do?" Miss Olivetti, a withered crone who might once have had some magical powers but who certainly didn't have much left, tapped her foot.

Taylor looked around to see a classroom full of strangers looking at her. Every one of them had to be thanking their stars that Olivetti had found someone else to pick on, a new victim for her rampages.

Annie shuffled her feet and Taylor realized she was going to do something heroic, like take all the blame for herself. *Not happening.*

"Unfortunately we've missed the first couple of days of your fascinating class." Taylor spoke fast so none of her non-friends could try to jump in and rescue her. "I figured I'd just bring Annie up to speed since her people aren't big on magic."

"Really?" Olivetti's voice was cold enough to freeze mercury. "You thought she could learn more from you than she could from me?"

"Oh, no. How could anyone dream of learning more than what you have to teach? As I said, I merely wanted to help her get started so she'd be ready to listen to your brilliance." Taylor had never run into the teacher yet who didn't like being buttered up.

Olivetti stepped close enough that Taylor could see every clogged pore on her nose and the line where her makeup ended and the real skin of her neck began. *Imagine, a mage having to use makeup to alter her appearance.*

"Are you being sarcastic with me, missy?"

"Sar-what?" Being pretty had been more of a problem than an advantage for Taylor, but it did have one plus—people automatically assumed she wasn't very bright.

Olivetti's sadistic grin promised no end of trouble, but also no hint she'd seen through Taylor's ditz act.

"All right, Miss Bang. Since you feel capable of explaining Similarity to your friend, why don't you let the entire class assess your teaching style? I'll let them judge. If you do well, you can continue tomorrow. If you do poorly, well, then we'll know, won't we?"

Olivetti was supposed to be a mage. To Taylor she acted more like a weasel. She'd set things up so Taylor would either be humiliated or end up doing Olivetti's job while the other students thought she was a suck-up.

"I'd rather not take up your valuable class time with my limited understandings." Taylor didn't think it would work, but she had to try.

Olivetti laughed. "It isn't as if any of these so-called students are going anywhere. Waste a day or a year—all they have is time."

Taylor nodded. Matt and Annie might have bought into Headmaster Hoffbrewer's story about turning the school into a place where students could be reformed and then returned to the Fae. She knew better. Everyone in the school had been given a life sentence. Which brought up another issue—given the number of Fae who'd been shipped to the School over the years, where was everyone? A few of the students looked to be in their twenties, but there should have been dozens, maybe hundreds more. A life sentence couldn't last longer than a life—and the evidence seemed to hint that lives didn't last long here.

She wondered if walking into Olivetti's trap had shaved *her* expected lifetime. "I'm sure I'll make a botch of teaching." Taylor wasn't very good at giggling but she tried one for the occasion. "I don't have any experience. But if you really want me to, I'll try."

"Not only do I want you to, I'm sure the entire class is dying to hear you."

Considering what Taylor had just been thinking, the extra emphasis Olivetti put on the word *dying* made her skin crawl.

"Okay," she chirped. "Here goes, then." She grabbed a ruler from Olivetti's desk and banged it on the whiteboard.

"Everyone, be quiet. Miss Olivetti has asked that I explain the laws of similarity, at least for the benefit of those of you who need to do some catching up. Considering we're supposed to spend a year studying this, we might as well start with the basics. So, everyone knows all matter is made up of atoms, right?"

At least thirty faces stared at her from the over-crowded room.

Annie gave her a green-toothed smile and an encouraging head-nod. Couldn't the girl get it that they weren't friends, weren't going to be friends?

Other looks weren't so positive. Miss Olivetti's face turned so purple she looked like she might have a heart attack at any moment.

"Atoms in turn are made of smaller particles—ultimately fermions, consisting of quarks, leptons and bosons. Basically these are the little pieces of semi-reality that are so small we're not sure if they're matter or energy or something else.

"And when you get down to the level of quarks, there's something called entanglement."

"Come entangle with me," Cameron, one of the trolls who hung with Larry and the other Hans, shouted. "I'll show you some new tricks."

"An excellent metaphor," Taylor lied. "When people get involved, what happens to one affects the other, even if they're at a distance. When things become entangled, same thing. What happens to one happens to the other—even when there's no obvious connection anymore."

"Yawn." Marcus said.

"Similarity," Taylor continued, "is about creating entanglement that scales from the subatomic to the macro level."

"Which means squat," Larry added in a stage whisper.

She wondered who he was trying to impress—for sure it wasn't her. "Surely you remember the basic laws of magic. Similar effects, similar causes. Contagion—once connected, always connected. The basic laws of magic hold that like attracts like. Right? Now, you can define similarity as just causes similar to effect, or you can wake up and recognize that similarity runs through all of magic, maybe it's the basis of all magic."

Taylor knew she would get blank faces. She was pleased to see that a few, including Matt and Annie, seemed to get it.

"Similar to a pile of dog poop," Cameron joined the chorus of cat-calling Hans.

"Let's do an example, then." Taylor had long before figured Olivetti wasn't going to keep the Hans punks quiet. She'd have to take it to them.

She smiled and looked around, tracking down the werewolf who'd attacked Annie that morning and was harassing her now. "Larry, would you come up here?"

He crossed his arms across his chest. "I'm fine where I am."

"Really? You've been holding your hand like it's about to fall off."

"I, uh, caught it in a grinder in shop."

"Yeah, that can hurt. Almost as much as if a girl had broken it for you."

The giggles from half the class indicated not everyone liked Larry.

"Want me to fix it or do you want your bones to heal all crooked and gnarly?"

"You'd probably make it worse."

"One nice thing about similarity is, you can do either." Taylor spoke to the class. "Another nice thing is, if you change your mind, no problem. Take away pain now, put it back later." She put a bit of compulsion in her voice. "Do you want me to fix your hand or not?"

"Uh, well…"

"Come along, Larry." Miss Olivetti tittered. "We all want to see how Taylor mangles, I mean manages the magic."

Larry looked more like he was walking to his own funeral than a healing session, but he shuffled to the front of the class.

Taylor grabbed two pencils from Miss Olivetti's desk, snapping one in half and the other into thirds.

"Hey. No destruction of—"

Taylor pretended she didn't hear Miss. Olivetti. "These are the bones of your fingers, Larry. Do you see that?"

"I see some broken pencils."

"Broken just as your fingers are broke—in the same way."

"Look like busted pencils to me."

"Lucky for you I'm the mage and not you, then." *What an idiot.* "Now, pencils look a little like bones, but there are some major differences. Pencils are made of carbon, for example.

Your bones have carbon in them but they're mostly calcium. This would have worked better if I'd had finger-shaped oyster shells but Miss Olivetti didn't have any of those on her desk. So, I'll make the pencil and your bones more similar by putting a bit of your blood on them."

She flashed her razor fast, hoping nobody but Annie would see it—the mergirl seemed to see everything.

"Hey. You cut me."

"Oh, look, your ear is bleeding. What a lucky coincidence. I can use that as a source of blood. When I dribble a bit on the pencil, the pencil and your fingers become more similar. Get it—similar, similarity? It helps that it's *your* blood—my blood, for example, would be less similar."

She smeared the pencil with blood from the notch she'd put in his ear—like a feral cat that had been spayed.

She concentrated on driving the similarity home, then tipped a bit of the white glue that seems an inevitable part of every classroom on the shattered pencil ends, finally pressing them together.

The other students hovered nearby and Larry groaned when she pressed the pencils back together. Groaned, then wiggled his fingers. "Hey. They don't hurt anymore."

She tucked the repaired pencils into her bag—you never knew when power over another could be handy. "You might want to look out for those shop grinders in the future, though. They can do worse than snap a finger bone or two."

Larry glared at Annie, who gave him a green-fanged smile back. Dang, Taylor didn't want to like the girl, but she had a certain style to her.

Chapter Six

After Taylor finished showing off in Similarity, Matt stopped by Pallendike's classroom and helped Barley with the last of the floor-mopping. He wasn't jealous of Taylor, exactly. But she seemed to have it so easy. On her first day in the School, she was already the teacher's pet—and seemed to have intimidated some of the worst students—people who scared him spitless. The look on Larry's face had been precious when Taylor had scooped up the healed pencils—and tucked them away. Keeping the threat unstated had made it more intimidating rather than less.

Barley cheered Matt up right away with a game he'd invented. A sort of shuffleboard using the wet floor and their algebra books, Barley's game took Matt's mind off everything—including what he was going to do next.

They had become real experts at skimming their Algebra textbooks across the slick floor when Matt heard a noise.

"Ahem."

Matt's heart lurched at the sound and he spun around—but it was Annie, not one of the teachers.

"We're just mopping up." Barley's head bobbed in time with music only he could hear. "But I came up with a game. What you do is skim your book. You want it as close to the wall as you can get, but if you touch the wall, you lose. Wanna play?"

Annie looked from Matt to Barley, then back again, her face unsmiling.

"Are you seriously challenging *me* to a *water* game?"

Barley shook his head. "I guess not. Everyone knows girls throw like, well, girls."

She giggled. "I can't believe you're trying that reverse psychology thing on me."

"I'm not…" Barley stopped short when Annie pulled out her own Algebra book.

Yeah, Annie threw like a girl. It turned out her awkward style didn't matter—not at all.

The thin layer of water on the floor seemed to go completely frictionless as Annie's book slid across it and then, just when it seemed inevitable that the book would smack into the wall and she'd lose, the shimmer of moisture on the floor reared up into a wave and brought the book to a stop.

"Cool but I think it's touching," Barley crowed. "Disqualification."

"Not hardly." Annie took a sheet of notebook paper and slid it between her book and the wall.

It fit, but barely.

"How nice that you've found something useful to entertain yourselves with." Taylor was her normal snarky self.

Matt wanted to explain that he'd meant to do more, that he wanted to get together and work on his plan. As his algebra book dripped soapy water, he realized Taylor wouldn't buy it—although it was mostly the truth.

"Now that we're all here," he said as if he'd called the meeting, "I learned something important last night. I think I can explain what happened this morning between you and my cousin Larry. I think—"

"Larry the werewolf is your cousin?" Barley balled his fists. "No wonder you didn't do anything when he gave me a hard time."

"It isn't like that."

"It looked exactly like that to me. You sat there and Annie had to rescue me. Can you imagine how humiliating that was?"

"Why would it have been better if *he'd* helped instead of me?" Annie demanded. "Just one friend helping another."

Barley shook his head and glared at Matt. "You explain."

Matt looked between Barley and Annie. He just couldn't explain that Barley was embarrassed because Annie was a girl and because Barley sort of liked her. Better, he decided, to change the subject.

"The thing is," Matt said, "there aren't enough girls to go around at the school. So, the Hans get together and decide who gets a girl and who doesn't."

Taylor had always looked controlled, but this time her face got red. "And the girl doesn't get a choice?"

"Not that I could tell."

"So, you're saying Larry picked Annie. And he's harassing Barley because he likes Annie."

Barley put his hands over his face.

"That's exactly right."

Taylor glared at him. "Is there anything else you forgot to mention?"

There were a lot of things. "I've been thinking about Hoffbrewer's—"

"Did they just forget about me?" Taylor interrupted, "when it came to picking girls?"

"They didn't forget you. Justin the were-tiger and Marcus the were-sloth both claimed you. They ended up having a big fight. Justin won."

"Oh, really. He's the only Hans who didn't give me a hard time today."

Matt felt about two inches tall. "I didn't."

"Oh, yeah. You—the guy who knew Annie and me were in for trouble and didn't bother telling us. You've been a peach."

Matt glanced at Barley, then at Annie, hoping for a little support. Barley refused to meet his eyes, and Annie was playing with the water in Barley's mop pail. Every time she touched the water, she seemed to absorb more, leaving the remainder dirtier and soapier.

"I meant to tell you. I didn't know it would happen so fast, so I thought I'd have more time to figure out the situation."

"Well, you didn't," Taylor said.

Matt nodded. Now that he thought about it, he realized he'd listened to his rabbit side. He should have warned his friends the instant he'd seen them. "Sorry."

"Maybe Annie and I put enough scare into them so they'll leave us alone," Taylor suggested.

Barley perked up at the idea. "I sure wouldn't want someone to rip off *my* fingers."

"Larry's a werewolf, remember," Matt said. "He probably thought he'd get some sympathy from Annie if he left himself injured. That's why he didn't change and heal himself."

"Boy did that not work." Annie laughed. "Then again, your cousin may not be the brightest star in the sky."

Taylor gave him a sour expression. "Figures he's your cousin."

Matt shook his head. "Justin and Marcus almost killed each other. A broken finger isn't going to scare either. The way I figure it, we've got to work on Hoffbrewer's plan. We've got to find a way to let people out of here. It's the only way to stop this insanity."

"There's one slight problem," Annie pointed out.

"Yeah," Taylor agreed. "As in, we don't know what the headmaster plans, or even if he has a plan?"

Matt squared his shoulders. "I'm going to talk with Hoffbrewer."

Annie's eyes widened. "He's the headmaster. Aren't you afraid? I mean, before we were invited to his home. He might not like it so well if we burst in on him."

"*We* aren't going to burst anywhere," Matt said. "I am. And yes, I'm petrified. "

* * * *

Searchlights cast incandescent brightness as they swung back and forth along the perimeter of the grounds. The light from dozens of lights cast hundreds of shadows, all moving apparently at random.

Taylor blended with those shadows, cutting across the patrolled grounds separating the boys' dorm from the girls.

"You're an idiot," she muttered to herself. "This is his business, not yours."

It was excellent advice, but clearly she wasn't listening to herself.

The boys' dorm was loud with music, the blaring TV set tuned to some sort of reality fight show, and shouting males engaged in some weird guy-display.

She'd worked with Annie to make herself as close to invisible as the two could manage. Annie had spun water around her, and Taylor had charmed the drops with their similarity to a rainbow, reminding them of their ability to shift and reform light. Without Annie to hold the water in place, the rainbow cloak wouldn't last long. It might last long enough.

Matt emerged from his dorm during a commercial, just as he'd told her he planned and she let out a breath she hadn't known she was holding. If she'd miss-timed this, things could have been bad.

He glanced at the path between the dorm and Hoffbrewer's house, then froze as the heavy clump of footsteps approached.

Taylor slunk deeper into the shadows. She and Annie hadn't planned for delays.

"Carnecero." She recognized the voice as belonging to one of the students. Whatcha doing out here?"

"Uh, hi Banjo," Matt said. "Too many of the guys had second helpings on the beans at dinner and I needed a break, know what I mean? What about you? Do they have you playing trustee or something?"

Banjo waved a hand. "It's Justin's idea. We patrol and make sure nobody goes near the guards. I think it's just something to keep the Hans busy."

"Yeah. Like anyone is going to be dumb enough to approach a guard."

Taylor couldn't disagree with that. The way the guards watched everything creeped her out—and those eyeballs tattooed to their foreheads following her everywhere.

She had an uneasy feeling that third eye would catch her in her rainbow cloak as well—at least if they were looking. She'd do more research after dealing with Matt.

"Good point. When *you* get to the top of the Hans, you can change the rules."

"Like that'll happen. Still, staying away from guards seems obvious."

"Obvious or not, I'm doing my job. Be careful out here."

"Got it."

Banjo strolled off.

"Plan not working out?" Taylor said.

Matt practically jumped out of his skin. "Taylor, are you crazy? What are you doing out here?"

"Checking to see if you were going through with your plan."

Matt waved at Hoffbrewer's home—a good two hundred, searchlight-lit, yards away. "You wouldn't think it would be hard to get there. It's not close to the wall, so why should the guards patrol it? But they do—and I haven't been able to spot the pattern yet."

"This isn't like in the movies. The guards probably schedule random sweeps so nobody can just wait for one to pass and take advantage of the gap."

He shook his head. "I guess I hadn't thought of that."

He probably hadn't been a prisoner before.

"You have any ideas?"

He shrugged. "Run real fast."

"Think you can outrun a searchlight—or a bullet?" She stepped from the shadow where she'd hidden so he could see her face from where it wasn't covered by the rainbow cloak.

"Look at you—that is so cool. I read about something like that—blends into the environment. It is magic, right?"

She nodded. "Annie did most of it."

"She's amazing."

Just for an instant, Taylor wondered what it would be like to have someone thing *she* was amazing. Then she pushed the thought from her mind.

"You gone crazy?" Banjo turned back when he heard Matt's voice. "I *really* recommend against talking to yourself. If the guards decide you're insane, that's when you vanish."

"Uh, thanks."

Taylor sank deeper into the rainbow cloak and suppressed her giggles.

"No offense," Banjo said. "I think it might be too late for you, Carnecero."

"I'm going to pull it together."

"You'd better." Banjo resumed his walk.

Matt waited until Banjo was out of range this time, but clearly his brain has been scheming during the interval. "Taylor. I wonder if you could—"

She recognized that look in his eye. "No."

"But I was—"

"I'm not going to meet with Hoffbrewer alone. First, I don't have a clue what to say. Second, I'm not going to sneak into some old guy's house in the middle of the night." Just the idea made her hair stand on her arms.

Matt kicked a chunk of loose concrete. "Sorry. I know this is my job. Just for a second, though, I—"

She slipped out of the cloak and passed it to him. "Annie and I made it for *you*, idiot. We saw the searchlights and the guards last night. We knew you wouldn't be able to make it through without help. The only problem is, I didn't count on you having a long conversation with your buddy, Banjo. The disguise might not last long enough."

"You're kidding? You made this for me?" Matt slipped the cloak over his shoulders and pulled up the hood. Instantly, he was just another shifting shadow. "What about you? How are you going to get back?"

"Guys and girls are always sneaking between dorms. Haven't you learned that?"

"Uh, I guess not."

"Well, I'll be fine."

"I can't begin to thank you, Taylor. It's—"

"I did mention that time is running out, right?"

"Yeah. Thanks again." He pulled the cloak more closely around him and dashed across the open space between buildings.

"Be careful," she whispered. But she'd waited until he was out of hearing range before she said it.

* * * *

Matt stared at Hoffbrewer's door. He desperately needed to believe that Hoffbrewer had told him the truth, that the headmaster wanted to transform the school into something better, something healthy. Yet what if the Hans and the teachers were right, if Hoffbrewer was simply a naive man with good intentions?

Abruptly, the door opened and the headmaster peered out. "Ah-ha. I thought I scried something at my door. Come in, young Carnecero. Mathew, is it?"

"Matt."

"Of course."

He followed Hoffbrewer through the small house that must once have belonged to the base commander. Hoffbrewer had decorated it with prints showing mythological themes and framed photos of famous mages including the non-Fae Siegfried and Roy and possibly fae Harry Houdini.

Hoffbrewer gestured for Matt to sit at a small table on which someone had placed a glass of milk and a plate full of assorted Girl Scout cookies.

"I'm not much for baking," Hoffbrewer admitted when Matt stared at the cookies for a second too long.

"I just wondered if you always had these out."

Hoffbrewer laughed. "Of course not. I knew you'd be coming and I put them out for you. Have one. This isn't Hades. You can eat here without being cursed."

Matt wasn't so sure. A life sentence in the school seemed a lot like Hades to him. Still, he was long past any chance of rescue. He took one of the peanut butter cookies and washed it down with a swallow of milk while he considered how to approach the subject.

"If you knew I was coming," he finally said. "Perhaps you know why I'm here."

Hoffbrewer laughed again. "You want to know what we can do to change this nonsense. You want to know how to get your friends out. I hardly need to be a seer for that."

"Well, yes. That's exactly what I want."

Hoffbrewer's eyes twinkled. "And your friends are willing to help?"

Matt took a deep breath. This was his chance. "Headmaster Hoffbrewer. I think everyone in the school would be willing to help if they only knew what to do and thought it had a chance. Give them a real plan, real hope, and they'll pull together."

Hoffbrewer shook his head. "It's easy to complain. But change can be scary."

"Give them a chance." Matt thought about all the times his father had lectured him on getting better grades, on finding summer jobs, on pack leadership. Everyone thought his father was smart and a great businessman. He wished he could explain what he wanted in words his father would use. "Suppose there's a program where students can officially given a certificate that announces they're cured of anti-Fae tendencies."

Matt recognized Hoffbrewer's upturned lips as the typical *I'm going to ignore this kid*, smile adults give.

He worked harder at channeling his father. "Make the qualifications specific, measurable and clear. If you give people goals, with paths to achieving them, they won't waste their energies fighting among themselves, they'll get out of here."

"Now you sound like your father, Matt."

"You know my dad?"

Hoffbrewer nodded "He is a major leader among the Fae."

"Well? What do you think?"

"I think your plan has two small flaws."

"Really?" It had seemed obvious to Matt. "What flaws?"

"First, I have no idea how to certify someone as harmless to the community. What measurable steps would we require? How could we be certain we were measuring the right thing?"

Matt nodded. "I'm sure there are psychologists who could help us with that."

"Perhaps." Hoffbrewer didn't look convinced. "That doesn't address the second flaw." He held up a hand. "Assuming I could certify someone as harmless, I still couldn't set them free."

Matt battled down anger. "Of course you could. Why would you want to hold—"

"I didn't say I *wouldn't*. I said I *couldn't*. The guards wouldn't let them out no matter how many certifications or qualifications I gave them."

"But they have to follow your instructions, don't they. You're the headmaster. They work for—"

"They work directly for the Fae communities of Texas, which gives them all that money for exactly one thing— keeping the misfits *inside* the confines of the School. Forever. It isn't me you need to convince, you see. If I had my way, we'd tear down the razor-wire fence tomorrow. I want students, not inmates."

Goosebumps raised on Matt's arms when he thought about the guards with their third eye tattoo, their grim faces, the way they never took their hands off of their clubs—except when their hands were on their guns.

"But if you don't control—"

For just an instant, Hoffbrewer looked about as unlike Santa Claus as possible, then he pulled back his jovial aspect as if it were a true-form. "Exactly. If I don't control the guards, what am I but another prisoner?"

Matt had come with visions of some master plan. But if Hoffbrewer was ineffective…

"Do you know how Diesel engines work?" To Matt, Hoffbrewer's question came completely from left field.

"Uh, no."

The headmaster nodded. "We need to add engineering to our program here." He pulled an empty two liter Coke bottle from his recycling bin, then fetched a bottle of rubbing alcohol from his medicine cabinet and poured in a cap full.

He shook the Coke bottle, then smiled at Matt. "A small amount of vaporized fuel is injected into a cylinder and put under pressure."

He squeezed the Coke bottle lightly, but it reacted as if he'd caught it in a vice, scrunching up more tightly than Matt had imagined possible.

"Don't touch it," Hoffbrewer warned. "It's hot. Unlike a standard gasoline engine, a Diesel engine has no spark plug, no electronic ignition."

"That's very interesting, but—"

"The heat from compression does all the work."

The instant he said the word 'work,' the Coke bottle exploded with a huge bang and a flash of blue flames that seemed to reach through the entire kitchen before quickly vanishing.

No ordinary human could have squeezed the bottle hard enough to set off that explosion. Yet Matt hadn't seen Hoffbrewer do any of the things Taylor had said a Mage had to do. Which meant Hoffbrewer was far more powerful than he'd imagined. It was lucky, Matt thought, that Hoffbrewer was on his side.

"What did—"

"That's what we have here, Matt." Hoffbrewer wiped up the shattered remains of Coke bottle. "All the bad elements of Fae pushed together. Sooner or later, there's going to be an explosion."

"But if you have no power—"

Hoffbrewer nodded. "I've proposed ideas of certification similar to what you suggested to the Fae council. When I learned that *you* were coming, I called your father and begged him to reconsider, to imagine that he could have you back by his side if he supported me. To my shock, he refused to listen, even when I told him it could lead to your release."

Matt snapped his mouth shut and swallowed down the sudden lump in his throat. He'd imagined his parents really believed the line they'd given him about making it through the school, being able to find a life. Now, he knew the truth—they didn't want him, had no use for a boy whose only talent was to transform to a pathetic rabbit.

"I'm sorry." Hoffbrewer patted Matt on the hand, then opened another box of cookies and slid them in front of Matt. "That wasn't very sensitive."

Matt swallowed again. "So," Matt said cautiously, afraid a huge sob might sneak out if he wasn't careful. "There's really nothing we can do."

"I didn't say that." Hoffbrewer gave him a sly look.

"What, then?"

"If there's a hole in the piston, the diesel engine won't work. We help students escape. That takes the pressure off."

Matt thought about some of the guys he'd met since coming to the school. He certainly wouldn't counting on them to behave well if they got.

"But not just any student," Hoffbrewer said, as if Matt had spoken out loud. "That's something I'd like your help with, Matt. We need to find the right ones."

"I can see that."

"And Matt?"

"Huh?"

"We need people who can be trusted rather than people who seem nice or harmless. The guards are always watching and they'll be happy to murder anyone who attempts an escape. And too many of your fellow students are taking their pay."

Matt nodded. Maybe it was the idea of students turning on each other for whatever rewards the guards chose to give them but he felt uncomfortably like he'd walked into a trap he couldn't escape.

Then he thought of the way Hoffbrewer had squeezed that bottle. With the headmaster to help, maybe escape was possible.

Chapter Seven

Sleeping was the worst.

As long as Taylor stayed awake, she was in control. But she couldn't maintain her wards while asleep. All she could do was keep her makeshift knife close, and wait.

She didn't bother hoping against attack. Her whole life proved that *hoping* didn't work, that an attack would come. Despite her jerk of a stepfather, in a way, she'd been relieved when her mother had remarried. Instead of the unnumbered men her mother had dragged home nightly from the strip clubs where she spent her evenings, her stepfather had been just one threat. The strip peekers had been unpredictable.

She'd halfway expected the attack that first night. Matt's story of the fight among the Hans explained the delay. And it identified the likely assailant.

He came just after she'd fallen into a troubled sleep.

Justin would have done better if he'd used his tiger stealth. The weight of the magic weighed on the room like a load of cement, yanking her to wakefulness.

"Sleep," it whispered, tugging on her eyelids. "Let nothing disturb you."

She grasped the knife, her lips pulled back in a grin. She'd barely managed a flesh wound on her stepfather. Justin the were-tiger was in for so much more.

He poured into the room. In full tiger form, he was beautiful—and close to ten feet long, not even counting the tail. His scent was of lush forests and snow-packed mountains.

She tightened her grip on the bar of soap with its embedded razor blade and worried. Armed or not, she couldn't win a fight against a tiger, especially a tiger with magical defenses. His basketball-sized paws could knock aside any attack she made. His six-inch claws could kill her in an instant. With his size, even striking from the top bunk gave her no advantage.

He glided closer, then slowly transformed into near-human form, retaining hints of his tiger markings on his face and in his hair. He grabbed a towel from the doorknob and wrapped it around his waist just before it was too late.

Taylor had brushed off Annie's offer of a t-shirt to sleep in, and worn her normal clothes to bed. She'd abandoned sheets and blankets years before—after the night one of the strip club perverts had showed her how well they could hold a girl still and helpless, better than any rope. Now, without any covering and with the nearly naked male in the room with her, she felt as exposed as if she'd been the one undressed.

"You're not sleeping." Justin's voice was conversational. "The little spell is for your roommate."

Apparently, Annie's fight with Larry had created a bit of apprehension among the predator community. That wouldn't help Taylor, but she was happy for Annie, at least. A sleep spell probably meant she would survive this night.

"I don't know where you learned your pickup technique," Taylor tried, "but sneaking into a woman's bedroom is definitely not any way to win her over."

Justin chuckled. "I do fine."

"Right. You do so well you have to claim your girlfriends in a fight, then sneak up on them while they're sleeping."

"Your friend Matt has a big mouth."

"I don't have friends."

"Which is why you're so easy to find alone." Justin shook his head. "You're always surrounded by your buddies."

"And you're so afraid of Matt and Barley?"

The human-tiger laughed. "You got me there—I'm not afraid of *them*. But I *am* afraid."

Despite herself, he'd piqued her curiosity. "Oh? Of what?"

"Of lots of things. Of the guards. Of being stuck here for the rest of my life. Of some idiot deciding he wants to rule the school and starting a bloodbath. If you want the full list, I'll give you a printout. The type is small, though."

This conversation was definitely not going the way Taylor thought it would. "Why did you stop Barley from helping Annie?"

"She wasn't in danger but he was."

"Larry was choking her."

"Larry is not the brightest star in the sky, but he wouldn't kill her. Killing girls brings down the guards, and Larry doesn't want that. Also, he'd never have another chance at a female. He meant to scare her, intimidate her, that's all."

"That's *all*?" Apparently Justin had no idea how horrible intimidation felt.

"I also knew *you'd* keep it from escalating any further."

"Me?"

"You, magic-girl." He gestured toward the window. "You radiate power like one of the guards' searchlights. You weren't about to let anyone hurt your friend."

"I already said I don't have friends."

He reached a pawlike hand toward her, stopping just out of striking distance. "Is that what you tell yourself, little mage?"

"It's the truth."

"How does lying to yourself help?"

"Look, tiger-boy. If you want to chat me up, call me and ask me for a date. Otherwise, give me a break. In either case, spare me the psychoanalysis. My mother sent me to enough shrinks when I was young—something about paranoia. As if."

"You can feel my magic," Justin went on as if she hadn't said anything. "Most shifters are too caught up in their true-forms to worry about similarity but I've always wanted to cover my options. Still, I'm not as good as you. I need someone with your talent to help me get out of here."

"If you want out, why not go along with Hoffbrewer's plan?"

Justin shook his head. "You don't know what you're talking about."

"Hoffbrewer wants to set up a certification, so we can prove we're not a danger to society..." She trailed off at Justin's disgusted look.

"If he told you that, he was lying. There's only one way out of this place—and that's in a coffin. Unless you help me create another one."

"If that's a motivational speech, you need practice."

Taylor would have sworn Justin hadn't moved, but abruptly, her pillow was a mess of loose feathers and her bar of soap had vanished from her hand.

"I normally don't need to talk to motivate."

If he'd used magic to move like that, she would have felt it, could have countered. But this was pure tiger.

He tossed her makeshift knife from palm to palm, not watching it but not slicing himself with the blade, either. "See what I mean?"

"I see that you're a bully."

"Last year, I helped Aeneas disguise himself as a guard. We'd gotten hair, a scrap of uniform, saliva, the whole similarity grab-bag, so Aeneas practically *was* the guard."

"I don't know anyone named Aeneas."

Justin stared at her for a moment. "Think about what you just said. He didn't escape and he isn't here anymore."

"How do you know he didn't make it out, then?"

"I felt the magic. I couldn't tell what they did, but the surge of magic was so strong it knocked me on my butt—and when I'm in tiger form, nothing should be able to shift my balance. The way I figure it, I need major magical help if I'm getting out. And I am getting out. I've been here a long time, Taylor." His voice dropped two octaves. "A very long time."

His last words faded and she felt herself peculiarly moved. How would she feel if she remained trapped here, year after year, watching new guards, new instructors, new students arrive but with no hope of escape?

"What about me?"

He shrugged. "This isn't your time. But don't worry. I've claimed you. That'll give you protection even after I'm gone."

"You're so full of it, Justin."

He reached into a bag she hadn't even noticed he'd brought with him. "I've got even more this time. A couple of weeks ago, I lifted one of their wallets. They weren't even sure he'd lost it inside, but believe me, they cracked down on the School something fierce. It's got an ID card with an embedded chip, so that'll help with the similarity. But there's got to be something more. They have a way of—"

"The third eye."

He stopped, then stared at her. "Huh?"

"Did you think the guards just wore the eye as a tattoo? I'd only heard rumors about it before coming here, but I did some research this evening. The third eye is a major working. Casting it on every guard here has got to consume a substantial percentage of the Fae energy in Texas. But it's effective. Ordinary eyesight lets people see what light reflects. The third eye lets them see reality. That's how they caught your buddy, Aeneas. He was similar, but not real."

"Want to know something funny, Taylor? I'm what you pretend to be. I really don't have friends, just people I use and people I make deals with. Aeneas was one of those. Now, you're another. It's your choice. We can do a deal, or I can just use you."

Despite herself, Taylor shuddered. Justin's words had been harmless enough, but something in his tone conveyed a threat far worse than anything her stepfather had ever dreamed of.

"I'm always looking for the win-win," she admitted.

"Good. I'm a patient man. I'll give you thirty hours to come up with an answer to the third eye problem. If you can't, well, I guess I've got myself a new girlfriend."

* * * *

On his fifth day at the school, Barley had a revelation.

Back home in Richardson, everyone in the Fae community condemned him for becoming a Satyr, forcing him to struggle to keep himself from manifesting his Satyr abilities. That he'd been unable to do so was reflected in his presence here in the School.

Now, though, as he sat with his friends, the thought occurred to him that the worst had already happened. He had no reason to continue to hide his true form because everyone knew what he was. He had no reason not to experiment with what it meant to be a Satyr because he'd already been given the punishment.

The old saying, *Don't do the crime if you can't do the time,* could be reversed. He was stuck doing the time—why shouldn't he go ahead with the crime?

As he ate his third sandwich, the one Annie had nabbed for him, he considered what he might do. Maybe he could…

"You look like you're a million miles away."

Matt's voice jerked Barley back to the reality of stale bread, questionable peanut butter, and not enough jelly. "Huh? Sorry. I was just thinking."

"That's what gets me nervous."

"Meaning what?"

Matt put both hands in front of him. "Hey, don't get sensitive. You just looked like a cat who'd spotted a quadriplegic mouse."

Barley sighed. He liked Matt, but his friend always wanted to analyze things, plan things out. Like when he'd gone to Hoffbrewer's house—he'd made sure to clue the others in first, as if hoping they'd talk him out of his idea.

Barley wasn't like that. Now that he'd decided to experiment with his Satyr side, he didn't need conversation—he needed an opportunity.

He couldn't explain that to Matt. Then again, it was easy to change the subject with Matt. "Have you ever wondered why some of us are Fae and others mundane?"

"You're thinking the guards, aren't you?"

"Huh." All he'd been thinking about was who he could play Satyr tricks on. "Uh, yeah. That's what I meant."

Matt lowered his voice to a whisper. "I think you're right. I don't believe the guards are Fae."

Now, that was ridiculous. Those third eye tattoos had to be Fae. And there was no way a bunch of ordinaries could hold the Fae captive. "Of course they are. Look at their tattoos. They—"

Matt leaned closer. "I meant, I don't think they were born Fae. I think they are *made* Fae when they come to work here. Otherwise, someone would know them. We've got students here from just about every part of the state, and with connections throughout the country. But nobody has ever heard of any of these guys. Nobody knows their families. So, if they're Fae, where do they come from? And if they aren't born Fae, how come nobody's ever mentioned people can convert?"

Those were good questions. Sometimes, Barley realized, changing the subject caused more problems than it solved. Still, he'd gotten Matt off his case.

Barley dumped his tray in the trash bin, then smacked his forehead as if he'd messed up. "I just trashed my silverware. You guys go ahead while I fish it out."

Matt looked down into the disgusting mess in the bin. "Better you than me."

Exactly.

Once Matt and the girls had gone, Barley gingerly reached into the garbage and pulled out his carefully napkin-wrapped silverware. He walked it over to the kitchen attendant who collected the silverware and checked his name off on a list.

"Don't play jokes with your trash, kid," the attendant said. "The guards are watching."

What was everyone's problem with the guards? Sure, their third eyes were weird, the searchlights at night made sleep tough, and their dogs howled at all hours. Still, they didn't do anything. As far as Barley was concerned, they seemed harmless.

Thanks to the conversation with the kitchen attendant, he was the last one out of the dining hall. And good ol' Larry, a jerk even if he was Matt's cousin, was showing off in front of a crowd that included Taylor and Annie.

Worse, the girls were laughing at his antics. That wasn't right. Barley was the Satyr, they should be laughing at Barley's stunts.

Although Larry had apologized for trashing Barley's buds, he'd accused Barley of hiding behind Taylor's skirts. Barley also suspected Larry had put the wad of gum on Barley's chair in English.

Rather than compete with Larry, Barley decided to make him look silly. Heck, silly was practically Larry's true-form.

Barley hummed to himself as he hurried down the hall. He could move faster when he had music, and it somehow made those around him get out of his way. This time, though, he didn't use his magic to walk faster. He let it gather around him like a cloud.

Larry finished a joke, then tried a cartwheel.

If he'd settled for one turn of the wheel, he would have made it. The second spin, though, gave Barley a chance to hit him with that gathered power.

Larry's arms buckled and he landed splat on his head.

Barley had inhaled deeply in preparation for a good laugh, but he let out the breath in a gasp, instead, when Larry stayed down. He hadn't intended to hurt anyone, just cause a little embarrassment.

Instead of giggling at him, Taylor and Annie were all over Larry, asking him if he was all right.

When Larry finally stood, Barley thought he looked fine, that he'd stayed down as long as he did to get their sympathy. What a jerk. He tried another hum, then caught it short when a too-large hand grasped his shoulder.

"Very funny, Harris."

The music and the magic melted away like a drop of water on a hot iron. Gus, the guard who'd picked them up at the bus station, didn't look like he had even heard of a smile, let alone thought something was funny. Then again, maybe he did— maybe he thought student suffering was amusing.

"Would have been funnier if he'd landed harder," the guard continued. "Don't you think?"

"That, uh, doesn't sound so funny."

"Doesn't it?" Gus tightened his fingers on Barley's shoulder. "We haven't had a Satyr here for decades. But I've read the records. You can affect people with your music, right? Make them drunk. That's what you did to the punk, right? Gave him an instant buzz with no need to drink at all."

"I, ah," Barley was tempted to brag, but he caught himself in time. "I'm sure I don't know what you're talking about."

Gus jerked Barley around, hard, his fingers digging deeper into Barley's shoulders. "Don't lie to me, putz. You think I can't see your magic? You think you can keep secrets from us?"

"Uh, no, sir."

"Here's the thing, jerk-face. You're supposed to be the life of the party, right? That means you'll be invited everywhere. I think we can work together."

"I don't know what you mean."

Gus shook his head slowly, his bald spot gleaming and his third eye glittering. "There are a lot of real creeps in this school, kids who are here because they represent a real danger to society. Put them all together and they make more trouble. We try to keep an eye on them, but we don't get invited to their parties. A satyr will. You watch them, tell us what they're planning, and we'll make sure you're safe."

"Oh. You want me to be an informant."

"Don't say that word like it's a curse. You'll be doing yourself a favor, and you'll be cutting down on the problems we have. So, think about it, kid." Gus dug his nails deeper into Barley's shoulder. "It's as good an offer as you're going to get. If you don't take it, I'm putting you down as a troublemaker. And troublemakers get extra attention."

"I don't want—"

"And try a joke like that on a guard and maybe I won't laugh so hard."

"Oh." Barley knew he was repeating himself but his brain had stopped working.

Gus shrugged. "Trust me on this. There are a lot of kids here who've already made the right choice."

Barley nodded. This time, he'd really blown it. He'd have to tell Matt, which meant explaining what an idiot he'd been working his magic where a guard could see him.

One thing for sure, his Satyr magic had gotten him into trouble—he'd learned his lesson: no more magic.

* * * *

"What have you got for me?"

Taylor cringed when Justin threw his arm around her shoulder, just the way her stepfather used to do as he pretended he was being paternal but really feeling up her chest.

"I beg your pardon?"

"That's 'I beg your pardon, sweetie,'" Justin reminded her.

"In your dreams. You may think you won me in your fight, but I never agreed to that silly machismo display."

Justin shook his head. "You don't get it. I'm protecting you, here. When I get out, the guards will go nuts. They'll know we spent time together. If you're not my girlfriend, they'll look for other reasons."

Taylor didn't like it, but he made sense. "I can be your sulky-pissed-off-because-she-got-stuck-with-you   girlfriend, though, can't I? How would that be?"

"Not exactly ego-gratifying, but I guess I can live with it. Anyway, you said you learned something. What is it?"

She drew his head close enough to kiss. Not that she was interested. "Matt put together a listing of the guard shifts and stations," she whispered into his ear. "Also their training schedule, for when they bring new guards into the rotation. I made a copy and hid it in the library in a Latin copy of Ovid's *Metamorphoses*."

"Ovid should be safe."

"*Anything* in that library should be safe. I've never met such a bunch of unmotivated students, which is practically funny considering that's exactly what all of my teachers called me back when I was in the real world."

"Okay." Justin ran his hands down her sides in a gesture that probably looked incredibly intimate and even sexy from the distance the guards were watching from, but actually barely made contact. "That's part one of the esc... uh, the plan—knowing when they'll be changing guards, when there's bound to be some confusion."

She wondered for a moment why he didn't even let himself say the word *escape*, then realized that the guards would be magically attuned to that word. Anyone using a list of dangerous words within a hundred feet of a guard, even under her breath, could count on being swarmed and questioned at length. If the guards didn't like what they heard, that person would vanish—apparently forever.

"I've been working on the other part." She handed Justin the leather armband she'd constructed through similarity. The strap looked like something Justin might wear—and something his girl might give him. In fact, she'd woven in the fabric strip and the button he'd given her from the guard uniform, and the tiny RFID chip she'd removed from the guard ID.

He hefted the bracelet. "This is it?"

"What were you expecting, a genie in a bottle?"

He grinned. "You know, I always wanted one of those. Rub her and there she is, willing to do every bidding. Put the cork in and she's gone—and quiet."

Taylor shuddered. "It sounds good to you because you're a creep."

"Oh, sweetheart. You say the most endearing things. Anyway, how does it work?"

"You know about the magic of true name, right?"

He shrugged. "Call something by its true name, it has to obey. Supposedly that's one of the reasons why the *Bible* says not to take God's name in vain, right?"

"Something like that. I've been researching the third eye. Nobody talks about it much and what I did find was contradictory, but—"

"So, we really don't have a clue?"

She dangled the bracelet. "Nope. But my theory is that the third eye works on true name. It sees what's really there because it can pierce the veil with which similarity covers things. Just because it's similar doesn't make it the same, get it?"

"But if two things share their true name, they really are the same?"

She smiled. "Exactly."

Justin scratched his head and studied the armband. "I thought the whole point of a true name is that it's unique and can't be changed."

"That's an oversimplification. Things change, so their names change. Turn it around—change its name and you change the object. It takes a lot of effort and—"

He grabbed the armband. "So, I just put it on and I'm a guard? In reality rather than just in disguise."

"Sort of."

"But if I'm truly a guard, I won't be me. I won't even know I've got to escape."

Taylor patted him on the head. "Guess you did listen in some of your classes after all. That's where the trick comes in. If I changed your true name permanently, you wouldn't be you. So, what I did was let you be a guard for about half an hour—just enough time to get outside the school. Then the spell ends and you become you again. Don't invoke the spell on until shift change, when you'd be supposed to leave if you really were a guard."

He glared at the band as if it had turned into a poisonous snake. "And if I don't make it out in half an hour?"

"Then they'll catch you and kill you and I had nothing to do with it. When you're ready to escape, pull it up your arm as high as you can. It's idiot proof. I designed it—"

"With me in mind. You are such a sweetheart."

He bent and kissed her, but he moved too quickly, surprised her. She'd already pushed him away, had her little razor blade out from its hiding place beneath her blouse, before she realized he was just acting.

Around her, too many people noticed. A couple of guards headed her way.

"Sorry," she whispered. Then she turned and fled. She needed to find some place to dump her knife before the guards searched her. She really needed that knife. And definitely not just to keep Justin from getting frisky.

Chapter Eight

After the first morning, Annie noticed that most people backed off—both from her and from Taylor.

She went to class, studied with Barley and Matt, and spent as much time as she could in the pool.

Unlike ordinary humans, unlike even ordinary mermaids, Annie needed a steady source of water to stay hydrated.

On the way to class on Saturday, a loud horn blast caught her attention.

"You remember I said I had a bad feeling last night?" Taylor whispered.

"Yeah."

"This is what it was about."

They marched the students out in the hot sun and made them stand there while the faculty searched their dorms.

After an hour, though, Annie felt a little faint. A murdhuacha is not designed for the Texas sun. To distract herself, she tried to figure out what was going on.

Although she didn't know all of the students by name, she was good at faces. She mentally counted off the different groups—and came up one short.

"Do you see Justin anywhere?" she asked Taylor.

"Taylor Bang." They hadn't seen the headmaster since they'd arrived, but he stood before them now, his face a stone mask.

"Yes, headmaster."

"Step forward, please."

Taylor looked like she'd rather face a pool of piranha, but she followed instructions.

"Taylor. I understand you have threatened people with a razor blade."

She shook her head. "Why would I do that?"

"That's what I'm interested in finding out."

Annie didn't have premonitions. As far as she was concerned, magic was too much bother. But she didn't need magic to figure out what was going on. Taylor had been set up.

"Excuse me, Headmaster Hoffbrewer," Annie interrupted. "Did something happen to Ernie?"

He whirled on her. "What makes you think that?"

"He's the only student who isn't out here suffering in the sun. What else—"

"It could be a lot of things, Annie. But you guessed it was something bad happening to him. Or was it a guess?"

"I don't know what you mean." Actually, she knew exactly what he meant. He meant she should have kept her mouth shut. Instead, she hadn't helped Taylor, she'd just gotten herself into trouble as well.

"Tell me where your roommate keeps her razor blade, then."

She shrugged. "Probably in the shower. That's where I keep mine." Not that she needed to shave. Her legs didn't grow hair, they grew tiny scales.

"All right." Hoffbrewer turned to the assembled students. "There will be no classes today. You're all confined to your dorms. Television privileges are withdrawn. The student store is closed until further notice."

Annie grabbed Taylor's arm and turned to go.

"Not you two."

"But—"

"I know you've only been students here for a week, Ms. Fish and Ms. Bang. But surely even that is long enough to learn that there's no such thing as a coincidence. You arrive flashing around your razor blades and five days later, a student is murdered with said blade. What are the odds that you aren't involved?"

"One hundred percent," Annie said. "I don't know what time Justin was murdered, but I'm sure we can tell you where we were."

"Headmaster Hoffbrewer?" The other students had vanished as quickly as a puddle of water on a flat iron. Matt, though, stuck around despite Barley tugging on his sleeve.

"Are you trying to confess, Matt?"

"Confess what? I don't even know what this is about. I wanted to talk to you about your plan to find a way for students to return to the Fae community rather than rot here indefinitely. I was thinking—"

"At this moment, letting a group of murderous students loose on the innocent Fae community is not high on my list."

"But—"

"Enough. When I arrived here, they told me my plans were idealistic, naive. They said you were depraved and twisted— that you wouldn't have been sent here otherwise. I didn't believe them. Maybe I should have."

"Don't give up on your ideals," Matt urged. "Whatever happened, I suspect it also happens in the outside world."

"You raise a good point, young Carnesaro. And in the outside community, there are severe consequences for committing murder. I intend that there be such consequences here as well."

Matt dredged up what he hoped would be a convincing laugh. "Surely you don't suspect Annie or Taylor."

"That's where the evidence leads. Now, unless you want to join your friends in a cell, I suggest you head back to your dorm."

"I still want to talk about—"

"What *you* want isn't high on my list. Just in case I haven't made myself clear, get lost."

"But—"

Hoffbrewer turned to Barley. "Get your friend out of here. Now."

Without waiting to see that Barley followed orders, the headmaster whirled back to the two girls. "I want that razor blade. And I want a confession, not more lies about how you were with each other the whole time—unless you're prepared to admit you were together in committing the crime."

* * * *

"We've got to get them out."

Barley looked at Matt and shrugged. Classes had been canceled and they'd just learned dinner was canceled as well.

Matt looked determined—and deathly afraid. Which seemed typical of Barley's mysterious friend. He trembled at even a hint of danger, yet everything he did ended up getting himself, and those around him, into trouble.

"First," Barley said, "you were the one who said we can't escape. Second, there's no way through the guards and barbed wire even if we could get the girls out of their cell. And third, how do you propose doing that?"

Matt paced their dorm room. Despite the gathering dusk, he'd refused to let Barley turn on the lights. "That was before Hoffbrewer threatened to execute them. It's ridiculous."

"What's ridiculous?"

"That anyone would suspect Taylor and Annie of killing someone. They're girls."

Barley shook his head. "So what if they're girls? From what I've picked up, Ernie was sick, liked to hurt people. No girl would let him touch her if she could help it, which meant he'd try to find someone he thought was helpless. Neither Annie nor Taylor would put up with that—and they're both capable of defending themselves."

"They would have come to us."

This time, Barley couldn't help laughing. "Us? For what? Weren't you listening when Taylor told us what losers we were? As for Annie, she's polite and nice about it, but face the facts—we *are* losers. Either one of them can handle trouble better than both of us put together."

"We're not losers. We're just not—"

"Not dangerous?" Barley felt his face getting red. "Not criminals? Not escape artists? Not bodyguards? You're right—we're none of those things. We're a couple of kids in trouble."

"Not as much trouble as Annie and especially Taylor are in."

Matt had a point, but not much of one. If they got caught trying to help Taylor and Annie escape, Hoffbrewer would take that as a confession of guilt—and assume all four of them were involved. As it was, Barley suspected Hoffbrewer would have to let Annie go—she'd never been seen with a razorblade and she'd shown plenty of capability to take care of herself without the need for bladed weapons. Now, if Ernie had been sliced up by razor-sharp teeth.

"From the start," Barley said, "we offered to let Taylor be one of us. She as good as spit on us in return. So, why on earth should we put ourselves in danger to help her? You don't seriously think she'd risk a broken fingernail if it were us in trouble, do you?"

Matt set his jaw. "She's innocent. It's everyone's job to help those falsely accused—whether you like them or not."

Barley flopped on his mattress—their room contained two mattresses but only one chair and no bedframes. "Tell you what—you let me know when you come up with a plan. I'll let—"

Matt took the single chair. "You want a plan, I've got one. My plan is that we help them escape, then together figure out a way to get through the fence and to freedom. Once we're outside, we should be able to—"

"To get tracked down and sent back here. Besides, I said a plan, not some idealistic hope."

Matt scratched his head. "Tell me about satyrs, Barley."

Barley shook his head. "Everyone knows we're useless. What else do you need to know?"

"People say you're drunk all the time but you never seem drunk. What's that about?"

"You think drinking might help us feel better about being losers?" Barley didn't follow the logic but staying sober hadn't done much for him. Maybe—

"Do you actually make alcohol? Can you make it for other people?"

"How the heck should I know? It's not like anyone offered to train me in satyr 101. The only things I know about magic is that guys look dorky changing form all the time, especially when they're naked. Oh, I also know that Taylor knows more magic than most of the teachers here. Does that help?"

Matt pulled a tablet from his pack and turned it on. "Let's find out, then. I can't believe any Fae talent is useless."

"What about you, then? Maybe you could turn into an elephant and pull the bars out of their cell wall."

"Unfortunately, my skill isn't one I'd care to demonstrate." Matt snatched Barley's phone and brought up the Fae Wiki.

I won't fall for this, Barley promised himself.

Two minutes later, though, he was looking over Matt's shoulder.

"I was right." Matt turned and gave Barley a high five. "You can make alcohol."

"Oh, joy. I'll run to the IRS and sign up for a liquor license, shall I?"

"If you could get the guards drunk, we could sneak in, grab the keys, unlock the cell, and have the girls out in no time."

This was his plan? "Are you sure you're not the one who's been drinking? First, no guard, not even an idiot, would take a drink from the two guys known to be friends with the prisoners? Second, they wouldn't be stupid enough to keep the keys on them. And third," he paused for a moment. He'd been sure he had a third objection, a complete killer, but now he couldn't remember it. "Well, two reasons are plenty."

"The satyr is especially dangerous" Matt read, "because their flute music and dance create alcohol directly in the victim's bloodstream." He grinned. "We just need to find you a flute and we're good to go."

"I don't know anything about playing the flute?" He'd never agreed to this, so, why was it happening to him?

"I'm sure it'll come naturally." Matt stood, grabbed Barley by the arm, and yanked. "Come on."

"Where?"

"The music room. Where else would we find a flute?"

Chapter Nine

He'd been wrong about one thing, Matt decided. Whatever musical talent Barley had, it didn't roll over to the recorder. Barley's playing was all shrill squeaks, discordant moans, and steady grumbling.

"This isn't working," Barley complained.

"You're supposed to be having fun. Party animal, remember."

"I did party." Barley's face turned blotchy red and his voice cracked. "What do you think was the final straw that got me sent here?

Matt didn't know how to respond to that. He'd assumed Barley had been sent to the School because he didn't fit in, because he was a satyr and nobody had anything good to say about them. He should have realized there was more to the story. "Try dancing while you play," he suggested. "In those old Greek urns, they're always dancing."

"Dance? I can hardly walk."

"That's because of those silly boots. They aren't fooling anyone any more, you know. You might as well take them off and learn to accept what you are."

"Oh, sure. Just like you have, right? You're so accepting of what you are, you haven't even told your best friends."

Matt felt like a hypocrite. What Barley didn't realize, though, was that Matt would become a walking target the instant his secret came out. He'd been sent to the School to get away from predators and so far, his secret had held. "If it could possibly help Annie and Taylor, I'd broadcast my problem to the world. Until then, it's better for all of us that I keep it a secret."

"Says you."

"That's right. Now, forget about boot-scooting. Strip down to your hooves and—"

"Maybe I should strip completely naked. Don't they do that in those Greek pots?"

Matt shook his head and lied. "You must have looked at the X-rated ones. As I only turned thirteen a week ago, I never got to see those."

Barley grumbled but he finally kicked off his boots, picked up his recorder and blew.

The change wasn't sudden, but it was dramatic. After a couple of minutes of dancing, Barley sounded better than good.

Matt tried to keep the beat on a bongo drum they'd found in the music room, but Barley shuddered and made him stop. "Don't you have any rhythm at all?"

"I guess not." Matt was a bit miffed, but Barley was following his suggestions so he figured he should cut his friend some slack.

"This is as good as it's going to get," Barley admitted a few minutes later. Time to distract some guards."

* * * *

"What are we going to do?" Annie held onto the bars of what had clearly once been the army base's stockade.

Taylor wondered how many students had been sent into this room over the years since the army had moved out and the Fae took it over. Dozens of names were carved into the wall, but she couldn't tell whether those names were students or soldiers.

"Why are you obsessing about those names?" Annie demanded. "What can it possibly matter whether they were soldiers or students—they aren't here anymore."

"That's why it matters," Taylor explained. "Think about this. Students come into the school, but they don't come out, right? So, where do they go? A set of prison cells at a school might hold part of the explanation, especially since I don't recognize a single name."

Annie's swallow was loud enough to echo. "You mean—"

"Maybe Barney was right about them turning us into dog food."

"That's ridiculous."

Annie didn't sound any more convinced than Taylor felt. What she sounded, though, was weak. "You dehydrating on me, Annie?"

"Maybe a little. I need—"

"I know you need a lot of water, Annie. I watch you." She didn't really think Hoffbrewer would intentionally let Annie die of dehydration, but she it didn't always take bad intentions to lead to bad results—simple carelessness could be plenty.

She'd already beaten on the bars trying to get the guards' attention—and been ignored.

"I'm going to try to break us out of here," she said.

"Where would we go?" Annie's voice sounded weaker with every minute that passed.

Taylor had considered running when her stepfather had announced he'd enrolled her in the School. She'd considered running again when the trolls had attacked in Austin. In both cases, she'd decided she had no place to go, no way to support herself, would be exchanging a lingering death for a quick but painful one. Now, though, she wondered if she'd made a mistake. If she'd taken off in Austin, at least Annie wouldn't be in trouble now.

"We'll worry about that after we get you to water."

They'd searched her clothes and taken all of her equipment, but Taylor had found a worn hard-plastic spoon stuck into the muck at the base of the wall.

Someone had tried to dig their way out of the cell with that spoon—and gotten nowhere. Annie wasn't going to repeat that failed attempt, but she saw a way to kill two birds with one stone.

"I read that the moon is filled with water," she said. "The only problem is, it's locked in rocks. It would take too much energy to free that water to be useful to astronauts."

"No offense, Taylor, but that isn't really what I need to hear."

Taylor ran the spoon along the mortar that held together the bricks that formed the prison. A combination of tiny bits of concrete and even smaller flakes of plastic formed behind the spoon and she caught it in her hand.

"My dad wasn't Fae," Taylor said as she collected that precious bit of dust. "He worked for the city repairing the roads."

"That sounds hard."

"Yeah it was." It was also a job most of her friends had laughed at—making fun of Taylor's plebian background. Annie, though, didn't seem anxious to condemn her for her parents—although marriage between Fae and mundane humans was rare. "Anyway, he took me to his jobsites a few times. I was interested in the way concrete dried." She scraped another round of dust. "If you think about it, things generally dry from the outside in. But concrete is hard and impervious. So, what happens to the water that's locked inside the middle of the concrete?" She kept scraping as she talked, gathering more and more dust.

"Good question. But it's gone all right. Cement is like a hard dry rock. And all this talk about water is making me feel sick."

"I asked my dad where the water went. He said it didn't go anywhere." Scrape, scrape, scrape.

"If it—"

"It's locked in the concrete. There's a chemical reaction between the calcium silicates and the water. That reaction, not drying out, actually creates the cement."

She looked at the small mound of mortar dust and plastic chips, then at what was left of the spoon. Friction had worn the already distressed plastic to the stub of a handle.

It would have to be enough.

"The laws of magic," Taylor spoke as much to herself as to Annie, "say that time is a convenience but that all things are really as they ever were. If the cement holding these bricks in place was ever wet mud with no more strength than Jell-o, it still is—if a wizard can convince it to return to that form."

"Oh. Be careful."

That was good advice. All she needed was to collapse the walls and bring the roof down on their heads. Even if the damage didn't kill them, the noise would bring the guards running and then they'd never escape.

Taylor focused on the layer of concrete holding the bars in place, spat into her pile of dust and thought about wet concrete.

Dry concrete was *similar* to wet concrete. The fine dust in her hand was *similar* to the cement used to create wet mortar—and because it came from the wall, was, in fact, part of the wall, it stayed entangled with the cement that remained. The addition of her spit made the similarity to wet cement more complete.

The trick, of course was convincing the wall that the larger should transform to the smaller rather than following the normal pattern. Especially as drying cement released energy—and undrying it required that energy to be added back. The only place that energy could come from was inside Taylor and she wasn't sure she had enough.

Still, Annie was weakening with every moment and Taylor didn't notice getting any stronger herself. If she didn't do it now, the timing would only get worse.

Barley's idol, Harry Potter, would probably just wave his magic wand, say a couple of words of schoolboy Latin, and the walls would open up into a nice door for him. Taylor didn't want to say there weren't mages who could manage that kind of trick, but she needed more than just a novel to convince her. Similarity didn't violate the laws of entropy. If you wanted change, you needed to add energy.

She focused her will on the mud in her palm.

The walls were old. For decades, maybe a century, they'd stood still, resisting the efforts of rain and heat to wash them away or blast them out of existence, standing firm against countless prisoners' attempts at escape. Walls didn't have feelings, exactly. These walls, though, had something—the closest word Taylor could find was "pride." The walls were proud of their work, proud they had restrained countless drunk airmen, and then uncounted monsters and misfits. They didn't want to yield to her, didn't want to fail, didn't want to give up on what they existed to do.

She put more of her energy into her magic, reminded those walls of their long-ago childhood when they had been fluid, spontaneous, capable of becoming anything at all.

Sullenly, begrudgingly, they gave way before her force of will.

Too slowly. Her own energy drained away and Taylor realized she would die before she could create an opening big enough for them to wiggle through, but she intended to keep trying until she collapsed.

"Help... me... pull out the... bricks." Every word felt as if torn from her.

Annie grasped one of the loosened bricks—and the instant her finger brushed against the wet cement, it hardened again.

Rats. Taylor had forgotten about Annie's affinity for water. She'd sucked the moisture from the newly wet concrete.

"Don't do that." Her voice was barely a harsh whisper.

"But it's not the same anymore." Mortar flaked away as Annie picked at it with her fingernails. "It's more like powder now."

Taylor lurched over and looked.

Sure enough, Annie's dehydrating touch removed the water Taylor had freed from the chemical bonds inside the concrete. What remained was not rock-solid concrete, but soft flaky cement, ready to bag and take to a construction area.

What remained was perfect for the similarity working Taylor wanted to do.

She joined Annie in flaking out the loose chunks of dry cement, then again tried to find enough moisture in her mouth to wet it.

Nothing.

"Maybe I can do something." Annie made a fist over the mound of cement and squeezed.

A thin trickle of water appeared from inside her fist and dribbled down.

"Okay." Taylor's mouth was so dry, her voice was a whisper. Still, she had something she could work with. This wasn't just similar in appearance to the primal mud that had formed the basis of the concrete, it *was* that mud.

Still, the walls resisted—at the risk of anthromorphizing them though, Taylor didn't think their hearts were in it the way they had been.

She struggled to the wall and thrust her weight against it—then croaked to Annie to do the same.

Annie seemed to draw strength almost as quickly as it drained out of Taylor. She was, Taylor knew, sucking up moisture as the concrete gave it up, ensuring that it couldn't change its mind, couldn't revert to its original state.

One brick came loose. Then another. Taylor scrabbled for an opening. This was going to work. Incredibly, they were getting—

"What the devil?"

Her hopes crashed. No one had responded when she'd called, desperate to get water for Annie. She'd let herself believe they'd trust the walls, rely on the cell that had held so many for so long. The Fae, even more than normal humans, have an almost religious reliance on patterns. The pattern of decades of success should have created a trust that went beyond simple confidence.

"Looks like we decided to party with these little girls just in time. You think you're going somewhere?"

Taylor wished she'd found a way to hold onto her razor blade.

* * * *

Barley loved music.

He'd sung before he could talk. He'd been the only boy in Miss Turner's Ballet School—until the guys in first grade had made fun of him. Then he'd dropped out, of course. A boy couldn't afford to be considered weird… the other boys would gang up on him, make his life miserable. He wondered, for a moment, if girls were the same, but they couldn't be. Girls, in Barney's opinion, were nice.

Considering that he needed music as much as Annie needed water, dancing and playing the recorder should have been a joy. Instead, he felt slimy, as if he had sat down for a meal only to realize he was dining from the toilet.

"Come on." Matt's voice was just a hint of breath in his ear. "Time to start."

"I just can't—" He cut off his whispered response when an adult voice spoke.

"Looks like we decided to party with these little girls just in time. You think you're going somewhere?"

He almost didn't recognize Taylor's voice when she responded. He was used to her sounding confident—obnoxious sometimes but always confident. Instead, he heard a cringe in her tone although he was too far away to make out the words.

Matt quivered beside him and Barley desperately wanted to head back to their dorm room, to hide his head, to pretend he hadn't heard anything.

But he had heard. Taylor wasn't a friend, exactly, but Annie certainly was and Taylor was, well, a girl.

He shuffled into his dance and brought the flute to his lips.

For a moment, the recorder bleated like a bagpipe deflating. But within two steps, he had the rhythm and the music took over.

He wasn't much closer to the adults, but with his music settled around him, his senses were more acute and he felt as if he could discern every secret.

It was a heady feeling—one he'd learned not to trust in the couple of months between his birthday and when his clan had given up on him and relegated him to the School. He didn't just create alcohol, he shared in the drunken revelry. His sudden sense of invincibility was just a feeling, with no basis in fact.

He danced forward, his recorder blaring like a trumpet, moaning like a saxophone, hitting impossible notes like a classical guitar.

"Bring the chicks." It was the first guard speaking. "Sounds like there's a party. We can check it out."

"I don't know. Two little girls and two of us. Are you sure you want to share?"

"They share the booze, we'll share the girls. Fair is fair."

"Guess you're—huh?"

Barley's dance had brought him within sight of the two. He thought he recognized them from one of the guard towers where they'd sat around smoking during their breaks. They weren't faculty, didn't associate with the students—or their teachers. To Barley, their souls glowed with pure evil—

although he wasn't certain whether he really saw anything at all or was simply reaction to their disgusting words.

"It's a party." He took the flute from his lips but it kept playing, keeping time with his dance, even though nobody blew on it.

"Feel the joy. Feel the intoxication soaking through your skin. You have to dance."

"I'm not much of a dancer," the second guard said. He seemed to be trying to keep his feet from tapping but couldn't.

"Go crazy, go wild." The words sprang from Barley's lips without conscious volition. They just seemed the thing to say.

"A party," the first guard protested, "is for drinking and girls, not dancing."

"Leave the girls." Barley was beside them now. If they drew their guns, they could shoot him down and the alcoholic haze would quickly fade from their brains. "Love each other. The girls are too little, too tired. They wouldn't be any fun."

The first guard snarled at him. "Like he would."

Okay, that idea hadn't worked. But nobody had shot yet, and nobody had hurt the girls.

He couldn't hold the guards indefinitely. Already, the strain on his concentration was growing. Each step needed to be perfect to keep the magic flowing, but each move in the dance got more complicated and each second he spent pumping alcohol into the two guards fed intoxication back into him. He thought, then sang. "Matt whisks the girls to safety while Barley stays and dances."

"But—"

"Barley will be fine, so long as the girls are safe." He had no idea how he could be fine, but it would be better for one of them to be caught than all.

"Sorry, no martyrs." Somehow, Taylor's voice had regained its normal strength and standard snarky attitude. "I've got your guns, gentlemen. I can either shoot you or you can stop dancing and lay on the ground with your hands behind your backs. Considering what you wanted to do to us, I'd rather shoot."

Barley finally missed a step—and tumbled to the ground. The recorder smacked into his teeth, driving one sideways and sending blood dribbled from his mouth.

The two guards shook their heads as if they'd been sleeping, then stared at Taylor. "How'd you get our weapons?"

"Be more worried about what I do with them, perverts."

"If you shoot, guards will come running from everywhere."

Taylor shrugged. "What do I have to lose? At least you perverts would be dead and no other girls would have to worry about you pawing them."

"I think she has a point." The second guard flattened himself on the ground. "Besides, they don't have anyplace to go. They can't get past the perimeter guards."

Annie pulled shoelaces from their boots and tied their hands behind their backs, then tied their feet to their hands.

They were completely immobilized when she finally looked up. "So, guys. What's your plan for getting us out of here."

Chapter Ten

Matt felt worthless.

Barley had distracted the guards, made them slow and drunk, confused them with his song. Taylor had reacted to the distraction and stolen the guards' weapons. Annie had tied up the guards, giving the four students a chance to get away. And Matt had stood there like a, well, like a frightened rabbit, doing nothing.

If he could manage a plan, at least, he could tell himself he was pulling his weight. But his plan was as big a nothing as what he'd done.

"These perverts are right about the other guards," he said. "I haven't figured how we'll get past them."

"Well." Annie smiled at him. "At least we're out of the cell. And after what Taylor did to it, that cell is going to need some major rebuilding before it holds another prisoner."

"They have more cells." Barley broke the bad news. "We found at least six cells with prisoners already in them and a couple of empties."

"For sure we can't go back to our dorms. That's the first place they'll check. And with the searchlights, we can't get out of the campus." The Hans hideout flashed into his mind. "I've got it. We could hole up in one of the old barracks."

Taylor's look could have fried eggs. "Second place they'll look. They've got to have had runaways before and the abandoned barracks are obvious."

"Maybe we could hide in an unused cell," Annie suggested. "You know, the old purloined letter trick."

Matt considered. It wasn't a bad idea. Nobody would think they'd be dumb enough to break out of one cell only to climb into another.

If there hadn't been other prisoners in many of the other cells, Annie's idea would have been great. With so many others locked inside the various cells, there would always be too many guards on watch. No matter how long they hid, eventually they'd have to get out. And when they tried, they'd be found. If the current batch of guards was indicative, that was not something he wanted to experience.

He looked at Annie. "Just how good at managing water are you?"

She flushed bright red. "I guess I'm all right."

"I'm not asking out of curiosity. I have an idea. And I know what you are."

"You can't."

He wondered if he should tell her what he was to build trust between them, but couldn't make himself say the words out loud. A bunny? That was just too humiliating, too small. He might have been able to tell Barley, but Barley was a guy. Humiliating himself in front of a girl would be so much worse.

"You're a murdhuacha, like Jenny Greenteeth. A sort of proto-mermaid out of Celtic legend that lives in swampy waters, grabs men as they walk—"

"You don't have to tell me what that is."

Matt gestured at the looming shadows of the rusty water tower. It stood on steel legs that held it high above the rest of the school—and above most of the rest of San Antonio. Because it was dozens of yards from the razor-wire fence surrounding the school, though, the searchlights never played over it. "If we were able to go in there, if you could keep us from drowning in our sleep, maybe—"

Annie considered. "I think I could do that."

"I can help." Matt hadn't forgotten that Taylor was there—her skirt was so short he found himself distracted every time he let his gaze slip her way. He hadn't, though, thought that she would volunteer for anything. Taylor wasn't the volunteering sort of person.

Then again, maybe the guards had scared some sense into her.

He looked at the sky—he hadn't been able to replace his cellphone since the trolls had destroyed it in Austin. Maybe some people could tell what time it was from the stars but Matt wasn't one of them. All he knew was that it had been dark for a long time.

"We'd better get to it, then," he said. "If we get caught in the open during daylight, we're dead."

* * * *

The iron steps creaked under Taylor's weight and rust crumbled off on her fingertips, but she swallowed hard and kept climbing.

She'd insisted on going up last, of course. No way was she going to let one of the guys come behind her and look up her skirt. But that meant she had to worry about Barley falling and smashing through her.

His cloven hooves clattered and slipped on every step. At least three times in the first twenty feet of climbing, they'd skidded completely off the ladder-steps and he'd dangled above her, those sharp hooves cutting through the air like samurai swords.

"Find your footing first, then raise your hands a level one by one." She spoke softly although he was making enough noise climbing that if anyone was listening they'd be caught.

"What do you think I'm doing?"

She thought he was making a mess of himself. Considering he was going to fall and splat at the bottom of the tower, maybe she should have let him go last. He might look up her skirt, but if he fell he'd never tell anyone about it.

Since her life was at stake, Taylor decided she'd better not let him fall.

Hooves and steel were both hard, both minerals. She needed a third similarity.

A trickle of moisture on her nose gave her an idea. "You sweating, Barley."

"What if I am? This isn't easy for me."

"Can you wipe a bit of sweat on your hooves and a bit more on each railing."

"I'm not sweating that much."

"Then try to sweat more. I'm willing to help you but I can't do it without at least some cooperation."

A splash from above told her that Annie had reached the top and found some way to get access to the water inside—

which had been a primary concern. As far as she knew, most water towers weren't designed to double as swimming pools.

Barley muttered something that sounded vulgar but Taylor pretended not to hear. His hooves clattered against the side of the tower and, for a moment, Taylor thought she'd made things worse.

He held on, though. "Okay. I've got sweat on my feet and on the steps. That should be sexy for you."

She hadn't thought about putting her own hands where he'd sweat but she could deal with this.

She whispered the words to a makeshift spell. "Hard as rock, similar minerals, same sweat. Hoof and ladder will adhere."

"Hey, I'm stuck."

"Keep greasing the rails with your sweat as you climb," she said. "Your hooves will stick but not so much you can't tug them off."

From his muttering, Barley didn't have much confidence in her magic, but he didn't have any alternatives.

Three steps up the ladder he stopped. "You know, that helps."

"Well, yeah."

"I mean, thanks."

"No problem, Barley. Just keep climbing, please."

A second splash told her that Matt had joined Annie inside the water tower.

She looked to the east and thought she saw a hint of gray on the horizon. It would be morning soon. If they didn't move more quickly, they'd be spotted.

Unfortunately, Barley was quick only when he was dancing.

She wondered if he could dance up the vertical walls of the tower and decided he probably could—but that his lack of belief in his powers would destroy him. His family and clan had done a number on him before they'd sent him to the School, persuading him that Satyrs were worthless. The funny thing was, they probably hadn't meant to be mean about it—unlike her own family who had to work at coming up with an acceptable excuse to get her sent to the school.

"Keep climbing, Barley. If they spot any of us here, they'll guess where the rest went."

"I'm... trying. Used up...lot of energy earlier."

She knew he couldn't see her but she nodded anyway. She and Annie had been caught fair and square and, unfortunately, their guards were the kind who found teenage girls attractive. If it hadn't been for Barley and Matt, she didn't want to think about what would have happened. They knew her kind of magic and wore charms against it. Because his magic was different, something intrinsic to his Satyr shape rather than the ordinary magic of similarity, and because he hadn't been their prisoner, they hadn't fully prepared. She hadn't want to owe anyone, but it seemed she was stuck with it.

"Do the best you can, Barley. You won't fall."

She didn't put any working into her words but he seemed to move a little more easily.

A couple of minutes later, he splashed into the tower and it was only her.

Scampering up what remained of the ladder wasn't difficult. Although she'd been exhausted earlier, Barley's dance had given her an energy recharge. She paused, though, when she reached the top of the tower and looked into the pit.

She'd assumed there would be dry spots, maybe galleries inside where workers could stand while they scrubbed the walls. Instead, there was only water and painted steel. She'd promised she could help once they'd gotten inside but she realized she'd been mistaken. Water, with its constant movement, its lack of shape, its invasive nature was the antitheses of magic.

If she jumped in, she would have no more power than the weakest human. If she jumped in, she wouldn't even be able to climb out. The slick painted walls and the twenty feet of space between the water line and the top of the tower meant there was no way out."

"Hurry up," Matt called. "Your silhouette is dark against the sky so dawn can't be more than seconds away."

She opened her mouth to promise she'd cast a glamour, let herself hide in plain sight. But the idea was ridiculous. The School faculty had mages—and the guards had their charms and counters. They'd expect a hiding spell. Even if they couldn't see her, they would detect the energy draw the working entailed.

Taylor could think of lots of times when she'd trusted others and wished she hadn't. She couldn't think of *any* times when she'd failed to trust others and wished she had. Trusting three kids wasn't easy.

She climbed inside the portal at the top of the water tower and hung.

Her arms screamed at being asked to carry all of her weight and her sweat combined with the moisture welling up from the water below to make her grip slick.

"What are you waiting for?" Barley demanded. "Drop in."

"She's trying to shut the trap door behind her," Matt said.

"Isn't it dark enough in here as it is?"

"Not if you don't want to get caught. The hatch was closed when we got here. Annie and I opened it. Taylor must have—"

"You don't have to talk about me like I'm not here," Taylor said. "I think I can swing it into place."

It took more than just swinging, but the heavy weight slammed down just as she lost her grip and plunged into the water.

From a distance, the water tower hadn't looked especially large. Up close, it was huge.

It seemed like she fell forever—and when she hit the water, she wished she was still falling. She'd fallen far enough that the water felt almost solid when she hit it—and because of the motion from her swinging, her back smashed into the water first, knocking her wind out.

She descended into the water, hitting the tower's bottom hard enough that it hurt.

She'd thought the water would be warm—this was Texas, after all, and the sun beat down on the tower all day. Whether from evaporation, because it was constantly being pumped up from deep aquifers, or because of magic, this water was bitterly cold and leached out her power like a vacuum cleaner sucking up garbage.

She told her muscles to move, to swim for the surface, then realized she didn't even know which way was up. The impact, combined with the darkness, left her disoriented.

The tug on her arm seemed to come from below. Someone was pulling her deeper.

She struggled, but she had no strength left.

She stared—and saw only darkness. Could one of the others have taken offense at something she'd said and decided to drown her? If so, they'd committed the perfect crime because no one could see, no one would know.

She twisted around so her legs would hit the bottom first, hoping to push off when she was shoved into the bottom. Abruptly, though, her legs were splashing. She'd gotten so completely turned around, she'd thought down was up.

She let whoever had her turn her around, then tried to suck air into her lungs.

"Can't breathe." That was what she meant to say, anyway. It came out more "ka, ka."

She must have had the wind knocked out of her. Annie's voice seemed to be coming from a long way away. "Keep her head above the water and she'll recover."

"Shouldn't we try artificial respiration?" It figured Barley would want to try that—any excuse for another guy to stick his tongue down her throat.

Barley was a long way off as well, which meant it had been Matt who'd sought her out in the middle of the tower, dragged her to the surface despite her struggles and, she realized grimly, more than one fingernail gouge when she thought he'd been trying to murder her.

"I'm not sure that's a good idea." Matt's breath caressed her ear as he spoke. Yep, he'd been the one who had rescued her.

She should have been relieved he wouldn't insist on some sort of reward for saving her life. She'd suffered from that enough. Perhaps she'd been wrong about Matt—perhaps he wasn't interested in her at all. Which was a useful reminder that she was not part of this group, just someone who'd gotten caught up in the same mess.

Except *she* hadn't gotten caught up in the mess. She'd caused it. She'd been the one who'd waved around her knife like a trophy. And the others had gotten caught up in her problems because she hadn't been careful enough to separate herself from them.

"I'm all right." This time the words were close enough to English that they could be understood.

"Good." Matt kept a hand on her shoulder but backed off a bit. She realized he hadn't groped her when he'd rescued her—another first.

"You do know how to swim, don't you?" he continued. "Can you tread water?"

"The answer is sort of and yes. I'm not that good a swimmer but I can keep my head above water." For a while, anyway. Already, though, she felt tired.

Heading for the water tower had seemed like a good idea—someplace the guards would never think to look. But she couldn't stay down here indefinitely. And there was no way for her to escape.

She'd been trapped in the prison cell, but at least she'd had power, had ideas. Now, with the water draining her powers and its chill sucking her energy, she was really in trouble.

Worse, there didn't seem to be a way out.

Chapter Eleven

Barley knew he should be scared. They were, after all, on the run from evil guards—practically dementors—stuck in a dark water tower, and Taylor had almost drowned.

Instead, he felt like celebrating. Maybe it was the power called up when he'd performed the Satyr dance on the guards who'd tried to hurt Taylor and Annie, maybe it was the adrenaline rush from their escape, maybe it was the sense of friendship he got from working together with the others, being treated as an equal, as someone valued rather than an inconvenience at best and a monster at worst. He didn't really even care if Taylor had killed Justin and gotten them all in trouble in the first place. He'd had it coming the way he'd gone after her.

He paddled over to Annie. "So. What's next?"

"How did you know I was here?"

"Huh? You are, aren't you?"

Annie looked a bit dangerous. Her hair had gone wild, flowing around the entire pool like creeping vines and her teeth seemed to come to sharp points. Her arms trembled as if they carried a heavy weight although she didn't have anything in them at all.

Matt swum over, using a side stroke with Taylor tucked into his shoulder so her head stayed above water. "You know, Annie, I really could have used your help there. You're supposed to be the one who knows water but Taylor almost drowned."

"Sorry."

"That's it? You're sorry? I thought we were all together on this."

"Cut her some slack." Barley avoided conflict where he could, and hated it most when his friends fought each other. But he couldn't just sit by and watch Annie get hurt. He didn't know why she hadn't done anything for Taylor but he knew she had good reasons for anything she did.

"I'm not going to hurt her," Matt fired back. "I just want to know what's going on. We came here because we needed a hiding place and because Annie said she could keep us safe. So, if—"

"I was wrong." Annie's voice came fast, high-pitched—so much Barley could barely make out the words. She sounded almost like a dolphin to him.

"You can't control the water?"

"She's doing the best she can," Barley insisted.

"Don't defend me, Barley. I don't deserve it. I knew Taylor was drowning and I didn't do anything about it."

"But..." He couldn't think of anything else to say.

"She's a murdhuacha." Taylor spoke for the first time. "It's in her nature to reach out and pull things down into the depths. She can't stop that any more than you can stop listening to music."

Being the son of mages, Barley had been forced to listen to the legends of Fae since before he'd been able to speak. He couldn't remember anything about a murdhuacha, but Fae legends held more monsters than he could count. It turned out that Annie, the girl he'd thought most normal of any of the four, was one of those monsters. He really should back away, find a corner of the round tower where she couldn't find him.

"She hasn't drowned us." Barley was probably more surprised than anyone when he recognized the voice as his own. "Can't you see that she's fighting to keep herself under control? That's why she's shivering—it isn't the cold water. That's why she didn't go to Taylor—because she was afraid she'd be more hurt than help."

"How long am I going to be able to keep control?" Annie demanded. "How long before I let the water have its way. It doesn't have to support you, you know. It can go all soft and weightless so you sink into it no matter how hard you try to swim. It can suck you down like a giant toilet, hold you like a clamp, suffocate you—while I sit back and enjoy it. I didn't mean to, but I've led you into a trap."

* * * *

Annie fought the need to consume, the overwhelming desire to be one with the water, to help it do its job.

She should have known it would hit her like this. She'd discovered her murdhuacha aspect when she'd been swimming with her pod in the abandoned water park they'd taken over and made their home.

"Come on, Annie." Matt still held Taylor over his hip, but he paddled close enough to get into her face—although, unlike her, he had to be effectively blind. "Pull yourself together and help us out."

"I...can't. I'm not strong enough."

"That's complete bull. I've seen you. You're probably the strongest of any of us."

"Taylor lent me that strength with her magic."

"Oh really? Well, now's the time to pay her back, then."

He was so unfair. Couldn't he understand that she was doing everything she could? It would be easy to teach him a lesson, to let the ever-lengthening strands of her hair entangle him, pull him down, to let the water close over his mouth and keep him from—"

She couldn't believe she was thinking like that, contemplating exactly the kind of thing she'd been sent to the school to prevent.

"The water is like an overdose to her." Taylor's voice was little more than a frog's croak—but it reminded Annie all too painfully of what she'd done. Despite her often harsh words, Taylor had always come through for her. In return, Annie had left her to drown.

She forced herself to think rather than react. Could Taylor be right? Could the overwhelming pool of dark water be working on her system like a drug? When she'd been with her pod, her symptoms had appeared when she'd been in the water, but that hadn't meant much—merfolk spend their lives in the water.

"It doesn't matter." Barley panted the words. She'd thought he would float better than the others but it sounded like he was already running low on energy. "It isn't like we can go anywhere to get away from all the water. We're stuck here. I know you did the best you could, Annie."

"If it's a water overdose, maybe we can do something about it." Matt sounded desperate. "Can you transform it to alcohol, Barley?"

"If I could, we'd die even faster. Alcohol is a poison, remember?"

Annie suspected someone had said something important, something valuable, but it was so hard to think straight when the water flowed through her body, when her body flowed through the water. When both body and water became one. Maybe she would think better when the others were silent. It would be so easy to pull them down.

* * * *

Barley wouldn't last much longer.

He had to kick his cloven hooves twice for every kick the more human types had to manage, but even that barely kept his head above the water level.

He wanted to scream, to demand that the others hold him up, save him. But if he did, they'd simply tire more quickly themselves.

"Too dark," Taylor moaned.

"We're in the water tower," Matt explained.

"Make light."

As if they could. Barley had never been the world's best student but he sure remembered the time his science teacher had lit oxygen and hydrogen to make water. Water was what happened after the burn—it didn't burn itself.

It sounded to Barley like Taylor was trying to snap her fingers—and failing because they, like everything else, was wet. On the fourth try, though, she succeeded.

The tiny stub of a candle glowed to light, floating in the water a few feet from him.

He took one look at Annie and had to resist the urge to blow it out.

Annie was a monster.

Her hair, normally a bit longer than shoulder-length, had grown to fill the entire water tower. Long hanks of it caught around his ankles, threatening to pull him down and helping explain why he was working so hard merely to keep his head above the surface. Her teeth glowed green—which was bad enough. But they'd elongated into inch-long fangs that appeared razor-sharp.

She, unlike the others, didn't have to swim. She appeared to be sitting on a chair whose seat was a couple of inches beneath the surface of the water.

Her eyes, normally sea-gray, were a vivid and dangerous green and she drooled as she looked at him.

"How can you sit like that?" he demanded.

Annie shook her head as if waking from a dream. "What?"

"The water is supporting you, isn't it?"

"So?"

"Maybe it could support more of you. Maybe you could stand on it."

She smiled, showing more teeth. "Why would I want to do that?"

"You don't want to hurt us, Annie. We're your friends. We're going to get out of this together. But Taylor is right, you've overdosed on the water and it's changed your personality."

"Maybe this is my personality."

"That's the water talking." A strand of Annie's hair circled his ankle and he kicked it away just in time to keep from being dragged under. He didn't want to tell her his secret—knew she probably wouldn't have anything to do with him once he did, but he didn't see any choice. "I snuck a beer from my father's refrigerator the day after I transformed. The alcohol hit me, made me act like someone who was me, but without me actually thinking things through, if that makes sense. Those crazy things I sometimes imagine but would never do, all of a sudden I was doing. It's the same with you. If you can get out of the water, you can come back. The real you, I mean."

"Will it work?" Barley wasn't hurt that Annie asked Taylor rather than him. What did he know about magic?

Taylor shrugged. "Maybe."

"Worth a try." Matt grinned at him. "Good thinking, Barley."

That, Barley knew, was because he hadn't admitted what he'd done, that he was a worse monster than Annie could dream of being.

"I don't know how—"

"Don't give us that, Annie." Taylor seemed to have recovered from her near-drowning and was back to her normal witchy self. "You're the queen of water, remember? Think about it—water can be liquid, solid, or gas. Just tell it what to be."

"But ice is cold."

"For ordinary people it's cold. For you, it's what you want it to be. There's enough energy here in the water that you can move around the heat and cold."

Barley had no idea what Taylor was talking about. But Annie seemed to get the message. The tentacles that had been tugging on his ankles for what seemed like forever withdrew at least a little.

"I'm making an ice raft," Annie announced. "Don't try to get on it yet because I'm still practicing, but if you need to, you can lean your weight on it."

Barley didn't wait for a second invitation. The second a block of ice about a foot on a side formed out of the water, he paddled over and rested against it.

To his surprise, it was warm to the touch—warmer, even, than the water it had come from. The block sank beneath him as he put his weight on it, but its buoyancy meant he didn't have to kick to stay afloat. He could catch his breath.

"Great," Taylor said. "Make more, Annie. We'll put them together into a float that can keep all of us, especially you, dry."

Barley watched with interest as Taylor encouraged Annie through her occasional failures and setbacks. Sure Taylor was looking out for her own interests—she wasn't any more interested in being drowned by a crazed sea monster than anyone else. Still, he would have bet against her being able to summon that much patience even if she'd needed to to save her life.

Finally, Annie announced it was done and Barley let go of the warm ice block that had saved him and joined the others on Annie's makeshift raft.

Taylor's candle flickered out just as Annie flopped onto the raft like a seal sliding onto a concrete slab to catch her bite of fish and darkness descended on the tower.

"We're safe," Matt said.

"Only," Barley replied, "if you consider it safe to be stuck on an ice raft twenty feet below the lid to a water tower while guards hunt for us outside and knowing that someone framed one of us for murder."

Barley halfway hoped someone would laugh, point out that all of those other problems had been taken care of, and maybe call in Spiderman for assistance. Naturally, nobody did.

* * * *

Taylor paid her debts.

She owed Annie, Matt and Barley. The frame had been for her, not for the others. If they'd been smart, they would have let her take the heat. A part of her said that she hadn't asked, that they'd been idiots to butt in. That didn't alter the debt, though. Without help from all of them, she'd still be stuck in her cell—unless the guards had taken her out to play their sick games.

Almost, she'd rather that—better in trouble on her own than in debt to the others. That choice, though, wasn't available. Annie had stuck up for her and gotten sent to the prison cells with her. The guys had come for her when they could have walked away. Now, she had to figure out a way to pay them back.

The water had destroyed all of their phones but Barley had a watch with an alarm function.

She tried to remember what time the sun set, then told him to set the beeper to wake them up half an hour before that. After that, she curled up on the pleasingly warm and surprisingly comfortable blocks of ice Annie had built the raft out of and caught some sleep. Being held prisoner, thinking they were caught, almost drowning, and confronting a monster who really wanted to tug her under the surface had taken a lot out of her.

"Do you really think she has a plan, or is Taylor just jerking us around?" She'd slept through the whispers going on around her, but when Barley spoke her name, she snapped awake.

"Of course she has a plan." Taylor wondered if Matt was a confident as he sounded—or if maybe he needed to convince himself.

Well, he was right… she did have a plan—she just wasn't sure it would work.

"Here's how I see it." She didn't bother telling them they'd awakened her. Let them think she could hear everything. "If we escape, the entire Fae community will be on the lookout for us. They'll have good descriptions and if they latched onto our trail, there aren't many things we could do to mess that up. And believe me, there are some good trackers in the Fae community. Of course, if we stay here, we'll either starve or we'll get caught."

"You don't have a plan at all." Barley's voice was a moan. "We already knew the bad news."

The others couldn't see her—well, maybe Annie could—but Taylor shook her head anyway. "That's if it's just us. What if we weren't the only ones to escape? What if everyone got loose? As long as Barley stays away from alcohol and keeps his boots on, and as long as Annie doesn't get too waterlogged, we're about the most normal-looking of the monsters here. Even if we can't live with the Fae any more, we can probably blend in with ordinary humans."

She knew the others would object. Matt was a Carnecerro. He'd probably never even met a normal—other than the bus driver. And Annie's people stayed clear of normal humans as well. She wasn't sure about Barley—but he didn't strike her as the most worldly guy she'd met, either. She also knew that their objections didn't change anything.

Unless they got out, the guards would find them. And if they got out without creating the biggest diversion in the history of the Fae community, they'd be back in a cell before the night was over.

The argument took the full half hour she'd allotted, plus another hour besides. Finally, though, they agreed they had no choice.

Taylor felt certain that they would have kept both shifts of guards on duty since the escape had been discovered. Which meant the guards had to be tired. That might help.

Or maybe it wouldn't. Tired guards might miss something but they were also more likely to shoot than ask questions. Still, Taylor figured it gave them a small edge—and they'd need every advantage they could get.

"There's one small problem," Matt announced when the arguing had died down and everyone agreed that Taylor's plan was their only hope.

"There are probably a lot of problems, starting with how we get out of this water tank."

"Starting before that," Matt said. "Somewhere out there, among the people we're trying to help escape, is the murderer who framed you. First, if we help him escape, we'll be letting a killer free. And second, if he hates you enough to frame you for murder, he probably hates you enough to tell the guards about it when we try to help him escape."

Taylor shrugged. "Maybe when he realizes we're helping him get away, he'll back off."

She couldn't see it, but she could feel Matt's grimace. "And maybe he won't."

* * * *

An hour after sundown, Matt nodded to Annie. "Time for more blocks."

He heard a splash, then felt the dripping weight of a cube of warm ice in his hands.

He stacked the block on top of the raft, then took another from Annie and placed it on top of the first. With luck, Annie could carve steps into the makeshift ladder.

When he tried to set the fourth block, though, the entire structure collapsed. From his shouts, Matt judged Barney more scared than hurt, but those big hunks of ice, a foot to a side, weighed enough to do some damage if they hit anyone square.

"Any chance of getting some light in here?" he asked Annie.

"I can see in the dark."

"Which makes one of us."

"Sorry. I can't—"

"If I hadn't burned out my candle, I could do something," Taylor said. "Without fuel, though, any sparks I set will go out before they could do any good."

Barney stopped his muttering. "What sort of fuel do you need."

"Something that burns. Oil or propane. You want to fart for me? I could probably use that—if it didn't suffocate all of us."

"Actually, I wondered if alcohol could do the job."

Taylor paused. "Where would you get it?"

Barley laughed. "I'm a satyr, you know."

"You could be Merlin the great but you still can't make something from nothing."

"You know what alcohol is, right? Hydrogen, oxygen and carbon. Water is hydrogen and oxygen. After us breathing for however long, there's plenty of carbon in the air."

This time, Taylor's pause was longer—and more thoughtful. "With your satyr abilities providing the energy... you know, it might work."

Matt could hardly believe the two of them were working together, bouncing ideas off one another, coming up with solutions.

"Not too much alcohol, though," Taylor said. "Annie's probably safe in the water, and alcohol can't hurt you, but its fumes would kill Matt and me."

"We need a small container—like a cup," Matt said. "And something for a wick."

A tearing noise from Taylor's direction suggested the wick had been taken care of.

"Can you make a small cup out of water, Annie?" he asked. "Something that could stand up to fire."

"No problem."

Less than a minute later, the blue glow of burning alcohol lit the inside of the water tower.

Matt had expected rusty metal and mucky water. But Annie had transformed their steel cage into a fairy palace. Frost hung down from the curved walls of the tower like Spanish moss in a subtropical forest. Annie's raft had a pointed prow like something an ancient Pharaoh might have used to navigate the Nile.

Then there were the girls.

Annie had been scary before, when she'd barely held onto her control. Now, she looked beautiful—flushed with energy from the water. His mother would have said Taylor looked trashy. The wet plastered her white uniform blouse to her body and she'd ripped a strip from her skirt, shortening it even more than before. To him, it didn't look trashy, it looked good. He had to force himself to look away from her legs. He did it, though. He needed to be thinking about their escape, not about Taylor's legs.

"Okay." He took a deep breath, then repeated himself. "Okay. Here's the plan. We use Annie's blocks of ice to build ourselves a pillar up to the top of the top of the water tower. Annie can cut some footholes into it and we'll use them to climb out of here. Once we're out, we'll split up. Annie and Taylor, I need you to work together. We need a couple of things. First, either the searchlights need to go out, one way or another. Second, the fences need to be cut. And third—"

"How are they supposed to do that?" Barley demanded. "And what am I going to be doing while they're working miracles?"

"They're supposed to work together. Annie is the queen of water and Taylor is the best mage I've ever seen. I'd think they could rust holes through the fence in no time. I don't know about the searchlights, but if you guys put your heads together, I know you'll be able to think of something. As for you, Barley, you're going to do the pied piper thing. Once Taylor and Annie have breached the fences, you're going to lead everyone out."

"What about you?" Taylor asked. "Or are you our general, giving us orders but not actually doing anything yourself?"

"I'm going to talk with Hoffbrewer. If he's serious about helping us get out, he'll have some thoughts about who might be too dangerous to let escape. Once I've done that, I'll come help whichever of you needs anything."

"Hoffbrewer?" Taylor didn't just sound skeptical, she sounded downright negative. He's the administration and am I the only one who remembers what he did to Annie and me? A mass escape has to be the last thing he wants."

Matt had been thinking about that ever since Pallendike had told him that Hoffbrewer's plans could never amount to much. By now, Hoffbrewer had to be realizing the same thing. Matt didn't know whether Hoffbrewer would agree to the escape or not, but he knew they had a much better chance of success if he did. And even if he didn't, the guards didn't trust him—they'd take anything he said with a grain of salt. Maybe that would confuse their response. Explaining all of that, though, would take hours—hours that would be better used managing the escape.

"Let's try again with those water blocks," he told Annie. "With this light, we should be able to wrestle them into place."

Chapter Twelve

Taylor reached the top of the impromptu stairs Annie and Matt and built and pushed against the seal at the top of the tower.

It rattled in place, but didn't move more than an eighth of an inch.

"Girls," Barley muttered from beneath her. "Push harder."

"It's locked."

"Why would they lock it? You're probably just too weak."

"It's definitely locked." Taylor wouldn't call it a phobia, but her stepfather had locked her up often enough that it made her nervous. Once he'd forgotten about her for a week and she might have starved if she hadn't managed some similarity magic. She'd learned the feel of locked doors and she had that feel now.

"Water rusts steel, right," Matt said. "With Annie's water talent, maybe we could cut our way out."

"Anyone notice there's water and metal here and it hasn't rusted yet?" Barley demanded.

"Anyone notice someone else has become Mr. Negative?" Taylor fired back.

"Give me your belt," she told Matt. Barley was closer, but she didn't want to put up with his reaction to that kind of request.

As she'd known he would, Matt simply pulled off his belt and handed it over.

She examined the metal belt buckle. Sure enough, the back was flatter and hadn't been smoothed like the front. She went to work scraping a circle around the locked hatch.

"My psychic powers say you'll cut through in about three years, if you've got a couple of hundred belt buckles," Barley said.

"We understand that you're scared, Barley," Annie said. "But you're not helping."

Taylor had said almost the same thing two minutes before, but Barley responded instantly to Annie's correction. "Sorry."

"No problem. Hold the lantern a bit closer so I can see what she's done."

The light flared up and Annie widened the water blocks so she could stand beside Taylor.

"The paint is tougher than I'd hoped. You think I've got enough?"

"Definitely." Annie traced a finger along the faint scratches Taylor had made in the top of the tank.

Her finger turned brown with rust, but it wasn't from picking rust up—because rust spread like frost behind her finger.

The scratches started it. Without Annie's efforts, the unprotected steel would eventually have rusted, gradually weakening the metal until it gave way. What would have taken years in the ordinary course of chemistry took seconds with Annie, queen of the water, working her magic.

Less than three minutes after Taylor started scraping, the hatch groaned, then collapsed, falling straight down.

Taylor recognized the danger less than a second before the heavy hatch fell.

It was too late to call out a warning and nobody could go anywhere, anyway.

The rusty steel gave way on the right side first, and the hatch sagged straight toward Matt.

Taylor didn't think. She shoved her feet into two of the footholds Annie had built into her ice block and launched herself.

If she missed, the hatch would fall and crush Matt. She didn't miss, though. She grasped the metal, ignoring sharp edges that cut into her hands and arms, and willed her strength to shove those hundreds of pounds of rotting steel away from her… friend.

Her hands caught in the metal ring that sealed the hatch closed, giving her a better grasp, and she fell.

Catching it, holding it aloft was beyond her strength. Instead, she held her footing as long as she could, using her body like a lever to redirect the downward pressure outward, away from Matt.

It almost worked. The heavy metal plate missed his head entirely, seemed barely to brush against his shoulder before she shoved it away. Then it plunged straight downward, pulling her with it.

For the second time, she plunged toward the depths of the drowning water. Except this time, instead of liquid water, the water-block raft waited beneath her.

* * * *

Barley had blown it.

If he hadn't been sarcastic and negative, Taylor would have been more clear about her plan, Matt would have insisted that the others be careful and cooperate, and Annie would have let the rust work more slowly.

As it was, he barely had time to give Taylor an extra push as she fell past him, sending her over the water rather than landing on the hard water blocks. Unfortunately, her hands had gotten tangled in the wheel of the hatch and something snapped when she landed.

It was his fault and no apologies would make it better.

"I'll help Taylor out." Matt's voice was a harsh wheeze and blood stained his shirt a crimson red in the blue glow of the alcohol lamp. "You and Annie get started with your jobs."

"You're going ahead with your plan after this happened?"

"Wrong. *We're* going ahead with *our* plan. We're in this together, Barley. And stop blaming yourself. Every one of us had a chance to do better. All of us did the best we could."

Right. The only problem was, Taylor's best, Annie's best, even Matt's best were pretty good.

"Come on." Annie tugged on Barley's arm. "We've got to get going."

He followed her up the makeshift ladder and out the top of the water tower.

Nothing had changed from when they'd gone in except he was a lot hungrier.

Searchlights still split the night. Machine guns still poked their noses out of the guard towers. The dingy ex-army base still rotted in Texas's late summer heat—sunset having done nothing to cool things down.

"This is—" he caught himself. Sure it was hopeless, but they didn't have any better plan. He didn't know why Matt thought anyone would listen to him, would follow him if he told them about the escape, but he'd agreed to do the job and complaining wasn't going to change that.

"I'll help you down," Annie promised when one of his hooves slipped across the water tower's slick paint. If he fell of the tower, his part in any plans would be finished.

"I'm—" he slipped again, grabbing a ladder rung to keep himself from falling. "I appreciate it."

"Let me go first. I'll make sure your hoo... feet are securely planted."

"Thanks." He knew he should be helping her, not the other way around, but he couldn't and arguing about it would slow both of them down.

To his surprise, it worked. Annie made sure his hooves were centered and helped hold them in place when he moved his hands. They found a rhythm, working together to climb down the ladder that arched over the side of the tower and then straight down to the crumbling asphalt yard beneath them.

"You think Taylor and Matt will be okay?" he asked when they'd passed the halfway point and it seemed he might be going to survive. Matt looked pretty bad and Taylor..."

"We can't do anything for them, Barley," she answered. "We just have to hope."

Hoping hadn't bought him much lately. Once again, though, he couldn't think of any alternatives. "Guess I can do that."

"When we get to the bottom, you should go to the boys' dorm first," she said. "Guys tend to be willing to try anything, just because it's new. If the guys get excited about the escape, the girls will probably go along, but if you ask them first, they'll assess the risks and potential rewards and they'll never go for it. Plus, they'll persuade the guys not to try it, either."

He'd been planning on starting with the guys, but only because he'd assumed they would lead. Hearing Annie's take on the difference between boys and girls was something of an eye-opener.

Then, before he was ready, they reached the ground.

Annie grabbed his arm. "Behind the leg. Quickly."

A new searchlight swung up, its beam warming from red to blue, pointing directly at the base of the tower. If Annie hadn't seen it, or if he'd been even an instant slower in responding, it would have caught him in the open.

Unlike the other searchlights, which cut patterns through the darkness, this one remained focused, searching the base of the tower.

"The guard must have seen something," he moaned.

"I suspect you're right."

"They're not stupid. They'll send out a patrol to follow up. If we stay hidden, they'll find us. If we move, the searchlight will catch us. I think we're finished."

* * * *

Taylor had managed to knock the hatch away… almost. Just a momentary brush with its sharp edge had cut deeply into Matt's flesh. With only one of his hands working properly, it would take him more than a minute to climb down the makeshift ladder. Which was way too long—Taylor hadn't surfaced after her fall.

Instead of climbing down, he dove.

The water hit his shoulder like a baseball bat and water swirled red around him as he descended.

The deep water attenuated the light from the small alcohol lamp to the point he could see only vague shapes, but only one of those shapes could possibly be Taylor.

He kicked over, only to find one her arms wedged into the hatch closing mechanism.

"Help." She mouthed the word, but even that, he could tell, took a lot out of her.

His lungs were already burning but Taylor's had to be worse. If he went to the surface for air, he suspected it would be too late to make it back down.

It was going to hurt her, but he didn't have time for niceties. He grasped her arm, planted his feet on the hatch, and lifted off with all of his strength.

For a moment that had to be both painful and scary for both of them, nothing happened. Finally, though, her arm slipped—and both were rising to the surface.

He held onto her with is good arm and put his injured arm above him. He didn't want to bash his head into Annie's water raft.

It seemed like forever before he broke the surface.

Taylor struggled from his grip, then dragged herself up on the raft. One of her legs dangled behind her, bending at a spot where no normal person has a joint.

"Aren't we just the matched pair?" she said. You're one-armed and I'm one-legged.

"It'll take time, but we can get up the ladder." Matt had been thinking about this. You can rest your weight on your good leg, then drag yourself up, step by step. It'll be easier for me. I'll just need to make sure I'm properly balanced before I let go."

"There's only two problems with your reasoning."

"Really?"

"First, you're bleeding hard and heavy work would make you bleed worse."

"I'll make—"

"And second, look around."

Thanks to the hole Taylor and Annie had cut in the top of the tower, the searchlights outside provided a bit of illumination inside—which was lucky considering that their alcohol lamp was guttering. Between the failing lamp and the intermittent light from outside, though, Matt could see what Taylor meant. The ladder Annie had built out of solid blocks of water sagged like overcooked spaghetti. As he watched, a huge hunk of water detached itself and plopped back into the reservoir. The raft that had proved their refuge had shrunk as well and was barely big enough for the two of them.

"Any ideas?" he asked.

"You're not going to like it."

"Try me." Drowning in a water tower would be a bad way to die. Letting down all of his friends while he did it made the possibility even worse.

Another bit of raft broke off and disintegrated back into the water that made it up. Without Annie here to enforce her will on it, the water was reverting to its natural liquid form.

"You're going to have to convert to your true form. It's the only way we can get you healed."

Matt recoiled. It would have been bad enough to convert in front of a bunch of predators. For the most part, though, they didn't like him anyway. The instant Taylor learned his true form was that of a brown bunny, she'd lose respect for him, stop taking his suggestions seriously, and would laugh at him as well.

He'd really rather die than humiliate himself in front of Taylor.

"You're not just letting yourself down," Taylor said. "First, there isn't enough room on the raft for both of us anymore. And second, Annie and Barley are counting on you to do your part of the plan."

He hated it that she was right.

Gathering up his strength, he transformed into what the Fae called his true form—what he called the true mistake.

He stared up at Taylor, who greeted him with exactly the grin he'd feared.

* * * *

A rabbit?

The way he'd gone on about it, Taylor had expected something truly awful—something like a rampaging elephant. Instead, he was a cute little bunny.

His clothes drooped into the water as the raft continued to shrink, and she pulled them toward her. Nobody knew the value of clothes more than Taylor did. After all, she'd been wearing the same stupid uniform her pervert stepfather had bought her for more than a week now.

The bunny version of Matt shook himself, clearly preparing to return to human form.

"Don't do that," she said.

She looked around. The raft had almost melted and only the bottom rung of the ladder remained in solid form. Unless she managed something quickly, they'd both end up back in the water. But if Matt transformed, they'd end up wet that much faster.

She examined the bundle of clothing Matt had left behind when he'd changed. They were soaking wet, like everything, but they might do.

"Here's the plan," she said. "I'm going to make a rope out of our clothes and you're going to grab it in your teeth. Then I'm going to stand on what's left of Annie's raft and throw you out. Once you get out, you transform back to human and tie off the rope. Think you can handle that?"

She didn't really expect him to answer in English but the rabbit was trembling so hard, she couldn't even tell if he was nodding or shaking his head.

"If you can't do it, I'm still throwing you." She hoped he'd get mad and hold on tighter but if he didn't, she was telling the truth. "I'm going to have enough problems here without having to take care of someone else."

Her blouse didn't amount to anything, but she stripped off the kilt-like skirt, rolled it into a tube, lengthwise, and tied it to one of Matt's pants legs. She shoved the other leg at his mouth and he took a bite.

"You're lucky it's me down here with you and not Annie," she said. "I don't throw like a girl."

His bunny eyes glared at her and she realized she hadn't made any sense at all. If Annie had stayed down, the raft never would have collapsed and he could have just climbed out.

Rather than apologize, she grabbed the small rabbit and hefted his weight.

For one glorious summer when her mother had dated a man who, for a change, actually preferred grown-up women to girls, he'd invited Taylor to join a softball league. She'd started in outfield where they put the incompetent people, but she'd worked hard and eventually she'd earned a spot at shortstop. Throwing a softball across the infield was definitely not the same as heaving a ten pound rabbit equipped with another ten pounds of wet clothing.

The raft bobbed under her feet and she realized she'd run out of time. She hefted the rabbit again. "No practice. This had better work the first time."

She reared back and threw—just as the last bit of raft gave and she splashed into the water.

Chapter Thirteen

Two searchlights remained fixed, pointing right at the spot where Annie cowered with Barley. Although she knew their escape would be over in the next few minutes, she noted that the other lights kept sweeping over the remainder of the school and playing through the fence. The guards seemed aware of the possibility of a diversion.

She wondered if the older students already knew that, or if she had discovered something that future escapes could build on.

A winking light came from one of the buildings Annie had thought deserted. Three guards, one leading a huge dog, headed straight toward them.

"I'll stay here," Barley said. "You retreat back a bit. I should be able to make them drunk, which could give you the chance you need to get away."

"We'll stick together."

"But you have a chance—"

"I said we'll stick together."

His machismo made him mutter something but Annie noticed he didn't argue with her. He had to know how impractical his plan was. The other guards would have warned them about the Satyr by now. Getting them drunk was hopeless.

Then again, so was fighting.

She closed her eyes and called up her murdhuacha form. Not that it mattered—the guards would be ready for magical as well as physical attacks. Still, she felt stronger, more dangerous, more in control.

"Psst, Annie."

The stage whisper broke her concentration just when she felt her body respond.

She glared at Barley, but he shrugged his shoulders. "It wasn't me."

"I need a ball of water—about a foot in radius. Make it extra-wet and extra-cold if you can. Use some of that bonus energy left from making warm ice to chill it down."

This time, she recognized Taylor's voice.

Taylor's plan was probably as doomed as standing and fighting, but Annie didn't know that for sure, and she did know she could no more expect to win if she fought than had the Texicans at the Alamo.

She reached inside herself.

She'd soaked up a lot of water—so much that it had made her dangerous to her friends. Building the raft had soaked up some of that, but it hadn't completely stopped her water intake. So, it was easy to find enough water to make the sphere Taylor wanted. She did her best to make it extreme water—something that held more of that special essence that defined water—wet, cold, ultimate liquid.

"Toss it up here," Taylor whispered when Annie had done what she could.

The flashlights were still a ways away, but the searchlights highlighted where she'd have to stand to throw it.

"Let me. You throw like a—" Barley grabbed the ball of water—which promptly burst.

She pulled it back together before it could splash to the ground and lose the special attributes she'd given it. A temporary coating of the warm ice she'd worked with in the water tower made it safe for Barley to handle, so she handed it back. Nobody knew better than she how incapable she was of throwing something that large.

"Wish me luck." Without waiting for her answer, Barley dashed out from behind cover. He threw it upward on the run, then rolled just as two shots rang out.

She couldn't see where he'd fallen but she couldn't just leave him there, possibly hurt.

"Hang on." Taylor's voice remained calm, which was a lot more than Annie felt. "I've never tried this with searchlights, but it works great with old-fashioned lightbulbs. Here goes."

The ball split into ten rays of pure water, each ray heading inexorably toward one of the lights.

The guards had to sense the magical energy Taylor called up, and a dozen or more bullets pinged off the water tower. Barley could only guess whether any of those bullets had gone through Taylor first.

As each line of water hit its searchlight, the lights flared— and exploded.

Darkness plunged over the campus.

More gunshots followed, louder than Annie would have thought, with smashing pings and the splashing sound of water coming from newly-cut holes in the water tower. Within a few seconds, Barley heard orders to cease firing.

"I'd intended to take out the searchlights later, when we were ready to rush the gates." Taylor sounded increasingly close as she clattered down the iron ladder. "I don't have a clue what we do now."

"We'd better do something. The flashlight had retreated when the searchlights had come under attack and the guards started shooting randomly, but Annie had no sooner thought about them than they flicked back to life and started edging closer—slowly and carefully, perhaps, but plenty fast enough to find them if she and her friends didn't find someplace new to hide.

"Grab hands, keep your mouths shut, and follow me." For a miracle, Matt seemed to be back to normal. Whatever injuries he'd suffered must not have been as serious as Annie had thought.

Annie was the end of the line, holding onto Barley who clasped Taylor's hand. Matt took the lead and Annie could hear him sniff, using his true form's sense of smell to give him a sense of direction in the darkness.

Other than Matt's soft snorts, none of the others made a sound.

But the guards used more than sight and sound to hunt. In the darkness, they'd rely on their third eyes to pick up any sense of magic.

Annie's murdhuacha true-form had saved them and she'd relied on it more, over the past hours, than any time in her life. Now, if she couldn't control it, it would kill them all. She pushed it deep within her, willing herself to be fully normal, to be a black hole in the world of magic.

Matt gave one more sniff, then opened a door and shoved each of them in.

At least twenty students glared. None looked happy to see them.

Annie couldn't help notice that Matt was completely naked.

Larry, the werewolf who though he had some claim on her, who she'd pissed off when she'd defended Barley and rejected his advances, was the first to break the silence. "What the hell are you thinking, Carnecero?"

* * * *

Matt stared back at his cousin and the guys who'd invited him to join their band. While he didn't like the way they treated girls, and while the Marcus and Justin's fight had sickened him, still, they'd reached out to him—and he'd repaid them by exposing all of them to danger.

"Would you rather keep your clubhouse or get out of this dump entirely?"

Larry laughed. "That's sort of like asking if we'd rather have chocolate cake or a visit from Santa Claus. St. Nick might be a better deal, except he's a myth. So is escape from this dump."

"If you weren't all sitting in here feeling sorry for yourself, you might have noticed that the searchlights have all gone out." He gestured toward the two girls. "That's thanks to Annie and Taylor."

"Electricity still works." Marcus had re-attached his severed claw. If hc hadn't seen what happened, Matt wouldn't have guessed it was even injured.

"I didn't say we cut the power. Taylor blew up the vacuum enclosures on all the north-side searchlights."

"If the power is still on," the were-sloth said slowly, as if speaking to the village idiot, "then the fence is still electrified. We try to escape and we'll do their work for them."

"Interesting that you say that." Matt had tried to keep all of the Hans attention on himself which should have been easy enough considering he was naked. But Taylor, with her still-wet schoolgirl top, was far more distracting. Especially as she elbowed her way past him.

Matt didn't think the silence that greeted her words had anything to do with what she'd said. Her skirt had ripped and showed her legs up to her butt. Her school uniform blouse was still wet from its soaking and might as well have been transparent.

The were-sloth practically drooled. "I claim—"

"Oh, shut up, Marcus," Larry said. "Nobody is claiming anyone tonight."

The sloth shook his head. That's where you're wrong, puppy. Just because you didn't have the nerve to suffer through a little pain to get your girl doesn't mean I won't. Nobody is escaping. Nobody ever escapes. But chicks matter. I want this one. With Justin gone, my claim has seniority."

"Really." Taylor looked she'd been struck by lightning. "Pretty convenient having Justin gone, then, isn't it?"

"I don't know what you're trying to say."

But Matt did. Someone had killed Justin. The evidence had appeared to indicate Taylor, but it had been worse than circumstantial. Everyone who'd been in Similarity knew about Taylor's razorblade. Anyone who could sneak in a high-definition video system could have planted that evidence. He burst into speech. "You were the one—"

"Let me handle this," Taylor interrupted.

"Nobody is handling anything," Marcus said. "I've staked my claim. Taylor is mine, to do with as I please." He snapped his claw. "Unless someone disputes me."

"Now Marcus—"

Marcus laughed. "Oh, no, Larry. Not you—not that you'd dare challenge me. You've got your girl, remember. You thought you were so smart putting in your claim for the ugly one, didn't you? You waited until I had made my claim, then suckered me into agreeing not to dispute you. You think I didn't figure what you were doing. Well, you were partly right. I didn't at the time. I've had a lot of time to think it over since then."

Matt looked to Larry, but his cousin shrugged. "Those are the rules."

Taylor stuck her chin out. "I'll—"

"Shut her up, Carnecero, or I'll do it for you. Girls get no voice in this. Hans rules—a girl can only speak once she's given permission by her Hans. I'm her Hans and I don't give her permission."

"You don't—"

Every Hans in the room put their hands to their ears the second Taylor opened her mouth.

"Let me do the talking," Matt said.

"Good luck."

The Hans gradually removed their hands from their ears when they saw Matt had persuaded her to stay silent.

Which meant it was up to him.

"You're acting crazy." Matt looked from one Hans to the next, all around that crowded clubhouse. "This is your chance to get out of here. They made a mistake with the searchlights—didn't count on the combination of the powers of a murdhuacha with those of a mage. But it's a one-time deal. They'll figure out what we did and tighten security. So, why are you wasting your time with a girl who doesn't even want you—when you could escape and find girls out there who actually want to spend time with you?"

He wasn't sure why any girl would want to spend time with someone like Marcus, but his experience said, even a creep can find a girlfriend. Sometimes it seemed to him that creeps had easier times finding girlfriends than normal guys.

Larry shook his head. "Doesn't work that way, cuz. Marcus has staked a claim to the girl. Until that's settled, our rules say no other business gets conducted. Once he takes off with the chick, I'm with you, though. Justin always said there was a way out and know what, I'm tired of this life. I'd just as soon get shot trying to escape as waste the next twenty years trying to work my way up to teacher."

Matt hadn't put that together, but when he thought about it, it made sense. No wonder the teachers had no enthusiasm for their subjects—they were serving the same life sentences as were their pupils.

"Looks like there's no argument about the chick," Larry announced. "So, Marcus, your claim is—"

"Just a second." At the moment, Matt was happy he hadn't eaten in over twenty-four hours because if he had, he would have lost it. "*I* contest it."

"No way," Larry said. "You've got spunk, kid, but Marcus has fifty pounds on you. And don't let the sloth thing fool you—he moves plenty fast when he fights."

Matt wondered how fast he'd moved when he'd killed Justin. Of course, Justin probably hadn't been expecting anything.

"I'll take him myself," Taylor said—as twenty Hans pressed their fingers back over their ears.

"You try," Marcus sneered, "you'll have to fight *all* the Hans. We've got rules."

Matt had to wonder how many of the Hans would still be home with their families if they'd only learned to follow the rules earlier. Still, he thought it was a good sign for when they escaped—if they escaped. Unless the escaping students figured out how to follow rules, they'd be back inside all too quickly.

Matt held up a hand. "I'm a member of the Hans, right? I say you've got no right to Taylor—that any right you might have had as a privilege of seniority, you lost by murdering a brother member of the Hans. How does it feel, Marcus, to know that you won your girl through murdering someone who thought he could trust you?"

Marcus looked at Larry. "Nothing personal. You know I've got to kill your cousin now that he talks that kind of trash at me. Everyone knows I'm as loyal a Hans as any in the organization. As opposed to the high-and-mighty Carnecero. You think it's a coincidence that things turned to elephant poop the day he walked into the School?"

"Matt, old man," Larry said. "If you have any proof, now would be a good time to share it."

"He can't prove something that isn't so," Marcus gloated.

Matt knew he had to talk fast. If he could persuade the others, he wouldn't have to fight.

"It's the only thing that make sense. Someone killed Justin, and it wasn't Taylor. It couldn't have been the guards, because they wouldn't have bothered accusing Taylor if they'd done it—why would they care if we knew? And we all saw Justin fight—he wouldn't have let anyone close enough to slice him if they weren't someone he trusted—someone like Marcus.

"Just arm-waving doesn't prove anything," Marcus sneered.

"I'm not waving my—"

"You say it wasn't the chick but I call bull. She's the one with the razor blade. We all saw it in Olivetti's class when she used it to slice Larry."

"Why would she hurt him? She was helping him esca—"

"She's a girl, right? Their logic works different from ours." Marcus rubbed his chin as if deep in thought. "But you're right—Taylor isn't the most obvious perp. After all, I sort of doubt any chick could get Justin. He wasn't the brightest, but he knew better than to trust a chick. He'd trust a Hans, though—especially a Hans who doesn't look too tough."

"You're the only Hans with a motive." Matt couldn't believe Marcus had made it so easy for him.

"Oh, no." Marcus chuckled like Matt had walked into a trap. "There is one other Hans. Someone who's been panting after the chick since before she even arrived at the School. *You're* the one with the motive, Carnecero." He looked at the other members. "I've been a member for five years. During that time, I've worked with most of you. You know you can trust me, know that I've got your back no matter how hard things get. But what do you know about Carnecero? Sure, Larry knows his family, but Larry has been inside for three years. He can't know what this Carnecero got sent up for—he doesn't even know this Carnecero's true form. Carnecero there is your killer."

Taylor chose that moment to bolt from the clubhouse. At least she tried. Marcus threw out one long arm and clotheslined her.

She landed in a heap and Matt dropped by her side, feeling for her pulse, making sure the big sloth's strike hadn't crushed her throat.

"I think that proves it," Cameron said. "Carnecero is your killer—probably working together with the chick."

The Hans gathered around Matt.

* * * *

"Are you all right?" Annie's voice sounded like it came from across the galaxy.

Taylor struggled to consciousness. "Huh?" Her voice was a creaking mess—which wasn't a surprise considering how her throat felt. Overhead, crudely painted corrugated galvanized steel said they were still in the Hans Quonset hut but the walls were so close, they had to be in a closet.

"Don't try to talk. Marcus almost crushed your windpipe."

Taylor tried nodding, but her neck hurt so badly, that didn't work any better.

Talking hurt, but Taylor needed to know what was going on. "What are they going to do to us?"

"Marcus wanted to kill Matt and Barley and toss their bodies out where the guards will find them, but Larry said Matt is a Hans. Which means he had a right to challenge Marcus. They're going to fight over both the accusations and over you."

Taylor thought about the smallish rabbit she'd held in her hands, then about the huge sloth. The fight figured to last about one second longer than it took Justin to catch Matt. If Matt insisted on running, that might take a while—except the entire Hans would go into hunt mode and chase him down.

"Maybe Matt's true form is—"

"Don't put any hope in that," Taylor warned.

"Oh. Well, maybe—"

A door opened, and light flooded from into the storage area where they'd been stowed while the Hans decided what to do next.

With the bright light behind him, it took her a second to recognize Larry. She wished she still had her pencils. Maybe she could threaten him to—

"Don't even think about it," Larry said.

"What?"

"You need to learn to control your tells. Whenever you're getting ready to do magic, you look up and to the left. So, I'm warning you, if you use magic to affect the fight, Matt automatically loses. No giving him extra strength like you did fish-girl. No blackmailing me into fighting in his place—not that I stand a chance against Marcus. This is their fight—and none of us are allowed to change that."

Maybe, but what they didn't know wouldn't hurt, right. So, if she could get Barley to—"

"And don't think about your pet Satyr. If Marcus feels Barley working magic on him, or if any of us see dancing or music, Matt loses and we've got a dead Satyr body to deal with."

There had to be something Taylor could do, but Larry seemed to have thought of everything at least as fast as she did—and he wasn't even their enemy.

She considered what he'd tried to do to Annie. Larry might not be their enemy, but he wasn't their friend, either."

"Tie them, gag them, and bring them out." Marcus's voice broke on the last word.

"No need for that," Annie promised. "We'll be—"

"Sorry." Larry seemed to mean it, but he still pulled a bundle of cowboy-patterned cotton scarves from his back pocket and proceeded to tie the two girls' hands behind their backs.

"I'm leaving the gags a bit loose," he explained. "I don't want to choke you, 'specially after your blow to the throat. But don't even think about trying to spit them out. Lot of the guys don't have much use for Marcus but if you lose your gag, the whole Hans would be obligated to take action against Matt."

Gagging a mage was good strategy. A key part of similarity is naming the similar things. The pencils representing Larry's bones had only been pencils until she'd named them as finger bones. Without her voice, her powers were cut by more than half. On the other hand, gagging a murdhuacha was about as useful as trying to hold a pair of scissors shut by sliding a sheet of paper between the blades.

Annie's dagger-shaped teeth could cut that cotton scarf to shreds in less than a second. But while Annie could be a fearsome fighter—assuming she could get over her fear, she wouldn't stand a chance against a dozen Hans predators.

Larry was as good as his word, leaving the gag loose enough that she could swallow and so it didn't cut into her lips.

Then he helped each of them to their feet. His hands lingered a second too long on Annie, but she shrugged them off. Even if Taylor didn't think Annie had a thing for Barley, Larry had blown any chances he had by calling her the 'ugly one.' Even if he was putting on an act for the Hans, the slam was something no girl could forgive.

Not that Annie was ugly. She had great hair and a slim figure. She just didn't do anything to make herself look better—and those sharp green teeth distracted from her other attributes.

"Let's go watch the fight," Larry said. "But don't worry. Girls are too valuable here to be wasted. Marcus isn't going to punish you for hanging with Matt. After all, he didn't even have a claim on you until tonight.

Taylor wasn't reassured. Marcus Grant was a murderer, a cheat and a wanna-be rapist. She'd had plenty of experience with cheats wasn't looking for magic moments with a murderer, and wouldn't mind if every rapist in the world was lined up and castrated.

If only Matt could win the fight. Unfortunately, Taylor knew his true form. Matt didn't have a chance.

Chapter Fourteen

Matt didn't have a chance.

Larry had found him some clothes but now he stripped off the shirt, ripped off the sleeves and tied the fabric around his hands to protect his fists. Then wrapped what was left of the shirt around his left arm. It wasn't much armor against Marcus's claws, but he didn't see any medieval suits of armor lying around and that was pretty much what he needed.

Everything he did, even breathing, was a fight against his rabbit instincts. His true form made two, inconsistent, demands on him. It demanded he turn his tail and hop away to find an underground warren. At the same time it insisted that he freeze, cower on the floor, and hope that the big, dangerous predator would think he was dead and leave him for more active prey. Every muscle in his legs shook and he had to lean against the wall to keep from toppling over.

Human logic said rabbit strategy—whether running or playing dead—would never work. But he'd seen a diagram of the human brain once and discovered that the part dealing with logic only made up about two percent of the whole thing. Beneath that, in every human, especially a shapeshifter, the more instinctual parts ruled.

What logic he could muster might tell him that the instincts were wrong but he hadn't come up with anything better. Which meant he was helpless, useless and generally doomed. Marcus had lost when he'd fought Justin in his were-tiger form, but he'd given the tiger a good fight. Matt wouldn't have a chance even if his true form had been something useful.

Larry delayed things as long as he could, making sure Matt got clothes, taking his time getting the girls from where they'd been stowed while the Hans discussed their, and his, fate. Now, though, Matt had run out of time. The remaining Hans had lowered barriers over the big-screen TV, pushed chairs

into a makeshift arena shape, and had begun a soft chant…
"fight, fight, fight."

Larry led Annie and Taylor, both gagged and with their hands tied behind their backs, back into the main room. He handed the two over to one of the Cameron, the troll, and headed straight for Matt.

He threw his arm around Matt's shoulders. "You're fighting someone who's bigger, stronger, and more experienced. You'll have to rely on speed. Use jabs and kicks to keep him away. If he closes with you, he'll crush you."

Matt nodded. He didn't think he could follow Larry's advice, but he it certainly made sense.

"In general," Larry continued, "matches end with submission or with a contestant's seconds throwing in the towel."

"And *you're* my second?"

Larry looked away. "I said in general. I think Marcus will try to kill you whether you submit or not."

If that was supposed to reassure Matt, it fell a long way short.

"How come you're his second and not me?" Barley demanded.

"Because," Larry explained, "you're not a Hans for one. And because I don't trust you to keep my cousin safe for another."

Matt tried to reconcile the jerk who'd attacked Annie with the man who stood up for his family—and failed. Surely there was something inherently good inside Larry, at least when it came to family and loyalty. But there was something equally broken where it came to women. If he could learn why Larry had been sent to the School, maybe he'd understand. As it was, his cousin was a mystery—and an erratic force who might favor him one moment, then turn on him the next.

"What you saw between Marcus and Justin was an exception," Larry continued. "This fight will be run like a mixed martial arts bout—with four minute rounds. Except there's no set number of rounds. You'll keep fighting until there's a decision. Anyone who strikes after the bell is a foul, but if Marcus gets you after a bell and you're not guarded, disqualifying him won't do any good."

Matt nodded again. Larry's words should have been making him more nervous. Instead, they took his mind off of what was about to happen.

"I can make everyone drunk," Barley volunteered."

Larry shook his head. "Matt made the challenge—he's got to handle the fight without help. I told the girls this, but you need to understand, too. If anyone tries magic, it's over for Matt. If you use your Satyr skills, the Hans will turn on both you and Matt.

Matt had been running complicated plans through his head since he'd realized Marcus had to be Justin's murderer. All of those plans, though, had involved combining Annie's water magic, Taylor's similarity wizardry, and Barley's Satyr skills. He didn't have a single plan that relied on just himself.

And now, he was supposed to fight?

* * * *

Like Matt, Marcus had stripped off his shirt. Matt didn't think the sloth had done it for protection. He was trying to impress the girls with his muscles.

He didn't know whether Taylor and Annie cared much about muscles one way or the other. He sure found them intimidating.

He looked around the room. The TV, table, and ping-pong set had been shoved into the storage room where Taylor and Annie had been held while the Hans discussed their decision. On the south wall, near the door, they'd set up a couple of dozen folding chairs which now held almost all the Hans. Matt's designated corner was to the northwest, while Marcus's was to the northeast. The rest of the room was bare wood floors and corrugated walls.

A stink of sweat and testosterone surrounded him—it came, he thought, from all of the males in the room, not just from himself.

Cameron the troll got out of one of the chairs near the south wall and walked to the center of the open floor. He announced the terms of the fight while Sargon, a were-gorilla

Matt hadn't really spent any time with, and an Asian-looking kid whose name he hadn't caught, patted Marcus on the back and generally encouraged him.

Matt could have used a little encouragement himself. Larry did his best, reminding Matt that he was a Carnecero, a member of the most feared predator pack in north Texas. Larry didn't know he was talking to the Carnecero clan's prey-animal failure.

Finally, Cameron stepped back toward his chair and picked up a chime. "Matt Carnecero challenges Marcus Grant over the girl Taylor Bang. Winner keeps the female. Loser is assumed to be the killer of member Justin. In the event both fighters are unable to continue, Marcus, as senior Hans, retains his claim to the girl and both will have proven their innocence of involvement in Justin's murder. Four minute rounds with ninety seconds between rounds. Corners are responsible for making sure their fighters are prepared to continue. Any questions?"

Not waiting for an answer, he rang the chime.

Matt swallowed hard. He hadn't been in a fight since Johny Trick had stolen his Marlon Byrd-autographed baseball in kindergarten. Now he was supposed to beat a monster. It just wasn't fair.

As he had against Justin, Marcus bore in, slashing with his repaired claw and reaching for Matt.

Larry had been right, Matt realized. If Marcus grabbed him, he'd be gutted before Larry had a chance to throw in the towel.

"No surrender," he told Larry.

"You got it, cuz."

Marcus was a lot bigger. Bigger has its advantages, but it had one drawback. Carrying around all that muscle and bone took energy. Maybe Matt could keep him moving, wear him down, run him until he was ragged and too tired to fight effectively.

For the first two minutes of the fight, Matt's plan actually worked—sort of. Marcus stalked forward, sweeping his claw in big slashing movements, then Matt would feint in one direction, and, when Marcus committed, dash away in the opposite.

He actually managed to land a punch on the back of Marcus's head the third time he tried that trick, but the strike turned out to be a mistake. Marcus's skull was a lot harder than Matt's hand. Despite the padding, he feared he'd broken something.

He'd have to be more careful. Which was easy to say but much harder to do when an oversized monster bore down on him.

"Now," Marcus said, his voice calm and not at all fatigued sounding, we'll see if you can do anything but run like a frightened squirrel.

Instead of chasing, Marcus moved steadily. Instead of slashing in front of him, he held his arms out to his sides, increasing his catch area as he herded Matt toward one corner of the makeshift ring where they fought.

Matt feinted to his right, but Marcus didn't buy it.

He feinted to his left, but Marcus bore straight in.

He pretended to feint to the left again, this time following through with a somersault and roll—and Marcus caught the back of his leg with his claw.

The claw ripped through the skin of his calf, and it took an effort of will to regain his feet. He might be willing to continue the fight, but his leg was ready to quit.

Marcus stalked after him again as Matt angled away, trying to stay out of Marcus's reach while keeping out of the corners.

Matt was doing everything he could and he was losing fast. It was starting to look like he wouldn't even make it to the end of the first round.

Marcus lunged, mostly missing but scraping Matt's forehead a bit as the younger man reeled backward.

The big sloth laughed and held up his claw displaying the blood dripping from it. "Ever since Larry got here, I've had to listen to stories of how tough the Carnecero are. Guess ol' Larry was trying to make himself seem tougher than he really is. My little sister could beat *this* Carnecero and that's without having to spit out her pacifier."

Enough Hans laughed to make the insult sting, but Matt kept backing up.

He'd decided the round clock must have broken when it finally rang, signaling the end to the round.

He glanced over at Larry, who immediately raised his fists into a guard position.

Matt heeded the warning just as Marcus threw a late blow.

"None of that." Cameron got between the fighters. "We'll have a good clean fight here, gentlemen. Do you hear me?"

"Sure." Matt wasn't the cheater, but Cameron was talking to him.

"All right. Gentlemen return to your corners. Second round starts in ninety seconds.

Barley toweled blood and sweat off of Matt's body while Larry yelled at him.

"What the hell was that about? You're letting him slice you to pieces and the only thing you tried was to break your hand against his thick skull. Didn't you hear a word I said? I told you—"

"I was trying to wear him down, keep him moving, turn his size into a drawback rather than an advantage," Matt explained.

"Well try something else. You'll be out of blood before he's out of energy." Larry nodded, agreeing with himself. "A long time before."

Larry was right. Matt's plan made sense, but it wasn't working. For sure, Matt would grow tired more quickly than Marcus if he kept losing blood from the cuts he'd already sustained, let alone from the injuries he was bound to suffer if he continued.

He glanced at Taylor who stared back at him with an expression he couldn't read.

Well, it didn't matter what she thought, anyway. Even if Taylor wasn't involved, he had to confront Marcus.

"The longer you take," Barley reminded Matt just before the chime rang again, "the more likely the guards will get their lights repaired. We've got to escape tonight."

Matt knew that, but somehow the necessity to stay alive had driven it from his mind. "I'll do better."

"Remember what I told you," Larry said. "Don't let him grab you. Keep attacking his arm. His claw looks fine, but considering Justin ripped it off a couple days ago, it probably isn't a hundred percent. See if you can give it a good tug, make him feel like you're ripping it off the way Justin did. And remember, there's no rule that says you can't turn into your true form. Justin didn't, because he didn't have to. Looks to me like you have to."

That, Matt knew, was the problem."

* * * *

It hurt Barley to watch his friend get mutilated.

The first round had been bad, but at least Matt had been moving then, getting out of range of most of Marcus's attacks.

In the second round, he tried to follow Larry's advice.

Unfortunately, Marcus's claw seemed perfectly attached and Matt's efforts to yank on it only resulted in putting him in range for Marcus's punches and kicks.

Near the end of the round, Marcus grabbed Matt and took him down. Only the big troll's ringing the bell and physically dragging the sloth off of Matt had saved the smaller boy.

Again, Barley was stuck wiping blood and sweat off of Matt while Larry gave him advice.

"You can't beat him on the ground," Larry said. "That's obvious. He's got good grappling skills and you don't. Keep him outside with straight kicks and jabs. If he gets through those and reaches for you, use knees and elbows to do damage and drive him back. A lot of grapplers will walk into a knee because they're not used to getting one in the chin—and that's the end of the fight."

Matt nodded but Barley wondered how much was getting through.

Barley wasn't a fighter, but he didn't need to be to know that Larry's advice wouldn't be enough.

"A couple of things," he said, opening his mouth for the first time since the fight began. "You've got to dance, not stand flat-footed. I'm going to project some music to you, but you've got to listen to it."

"They find out you're doing that," Larry said, "they'll disqualify him."

"I'm not hurting anyone."

"Just don't let them know."

"Yeah, sure. Second, every Satyr knows that when you're in the throes of Dionysus, you're stronger, you'll feel less pain. The music will help with that, too."

"That," Matt said, "would work for you, Barley. Somehow, I doubt it will do anything for me."

"What have you got to lose?"

Even if the bell hadn't rung, signaling the start of the third round, Barley didn't think Matt had an answer for him.

Marcus swaggered out from his corner, his muscles bulging, his claws snapping, and his grin confident.

Matt, in contrast, looked like he could barely move.

Barley hummed, calling on the song that had played inside of him ever since the day he'd gone Satyr.

Matt seemed to resist at first, deliberately counter-stepping to avoid the rhythm. But that was okay—counterpoint is part of music, after all, and the dance was the thing.

Then the music caught Matt and he danced.

Matt had persuaded Barley to make the guards drunk and he'd created the alcohol to fuel the lamp in the water tower. Those had both been Satyr magic, but they hadn't been the real thing—they'd been parlor tricks, not the reason the ancients had feared the Satyr.

As Barley hummed the dance he plumbed the depths of a Satyr's full power.

For countless thousands of years, billions of people all over the world had succumbed to the power of music. Fleetingly, he wondered how many had danced until they collapsed, found love at a concert or on the dance floor, or yes, fought to the beat of an unheard drum. A Satyr wasn't a helpless wimp, Barley was powerful. No wonder the rites of Dionysus had been feared in ancient times.

As Barley hummed, Matt flowed under Marcus's claw, gently pushing his arm upward, then slammed two elbows into Marcus's ribs. He continued through, spinning a kick to Marcus's liver as he cleared.

The big sloth shook himself all over and partially transformed, taking more of his animal form. The cocky look on his face faded and he looked mystified. He hadn't seen those strikes coming.

Barley kept humming and Matt kept dancing.

Barley's near-silent hum let Matt draw on the virtually infinite energy of music. The Dionysian magic would not heal his injuries, but they kept them from hurting him and reduced his blood loss.

For the first time, his original strategy of wearing Marcus down looked like it might work.

Matt actually smiled when the round ended and he ducked under Marcus's attempt at another late blow.

"Better," Marcus admitted. Then he caught Barley's eye. "In fact, too much better. Gag the Satyr. He's using his magic to help Carnecero."

"I'm just humming," Barley protested.

"Nice try." Larry nodded at him. It was the first time the older student had really acknowledged him. "That's a useful skill you've got there."

Barley wished he didn't have to use it.

Unfortunately, his wish came true in a way he hadn't hoped for. Cameron pulled a bandana from his jeans back pocket—a red one just like the one gagging Annie, and stuffed it in Barley's mouth. "It's good that you've got your friend's back," the troll whispered. "But we gotta follow the rules."

Yeah, right. Following the rules was getting Matt killed.

* * * *

Matt stumbled back into the fight.

Barley's music had given him hope, but that music had died the instant they'd gagged the Satyr. When he caught a fist to his belly and wheeled back, trying to avoid Marcus's grab, he knew it was over.

He didn't see who shoved him, but all of a sudden, he was in Marcus's arms.

The big sloth grinned as he wrapped Matt in a bear hug, his powerful arms squeezing the breath out of him. A few of the Hans cheered, but more groaned or remained silent. Either

Marcus wasn't popular, or Matt had convinced some of them with his accusations. Not that it mattered.

"This is where you say good bye." Marcus's voice was barely recognizable as human.

Marcus reared up on his hind legs, raised Matt above his head, then turned him over so his head faced straight down at the floor.

Matt had seen smash moves in professional wrestling, but he knew how carefully those were choreographed. If Marcus drove him into the hardwood floor, his skull would shatter like an egg.

"Get away," Larry screamed. "Show him you're a Carnecero."

Which was the problem. He might have been born Carnecero, but they'd rejected him when he'd shown his true form.

The floor seemed to rush at him then, as Marcus put all of his muscle into aiding the force of gravity.

With his head only inches from the ground, he relaxed and finally let his true self come out.

Marcus had to be shocked when the hundred and forty pound boy he held transformed into a much smaller five pound rabbit. He lost his hold and Matt rode with the momentum, using his powerful hind legs to bounce rather than splat.

He scurried between Marcus's legs as the big sloth wobbled, then spun, reclaimed his human form, and pounded elbows into Marcus's back.

Marcus roared, turned, reached for Matt, and missed again when Matt dropped to the ground and nimbly avoided Marcus's kick.

Matt backed up quickly, then became a rabbit again when Marcus swung his oversized claw. The hook embedded itself in the steel wall, and Matt, once again in human form, slammed punches and drove knees into the temporarily stuck sloth.

Larry had been right about the claw—it must still hurt. Marcus winced when he finally tugged it free.

Each time he transformed, Matt felt stronger as the essence of his true form healed him.

Barley wasn't humming any more but Matt reached for, and found the music again.

He gathered all of his rabbit strength and jumped level with Marcus's head, where he transformed halfway back to human form. As the surprised Marcus tried to bring his claw back into action, Matt combining his full weight with the strength a rabbit's hind legs.

And then, abruptly, the big ground sloth turned.

Hans watched with their mouths gaping, as he rambled through the ring of chairs and out the door.

He looked at Larry, mystified. "I thought the fight…"

Barley, Annie and even Taylor were pounding him on the back, screaming with laughter.

For about three seconds.

"He went to the guards," the Hans watching the door reported. "You were right—he's working with them."

Chapter Fifteen

Matt looked about as healthy as a murder victim when he shook off Barley's celebration. "I'm going to talk to Hoffbrewer. He's been planning the escape for a long time. He'll have ideas."

Barley wasn't so sure. When Matt had explained Hoffbrewer's theory, Barley couldn't help wondering whether the headmaster cared about students escaping, or if he was more interested in using students to test the guards and discover a path to his own escape. The Fae community might let a single escape go unnoticed, even cover it up so nobody else would get ideas. A mass escape was another matter.

Matt, though, wasn't listening. "Barley, coordinate logistics with Larry. Annie and Taylor, you're in charge of whatever magic we need. I'll be back as soon as I can."

With that, he headed into the night leaving Barley staring at Larry—the werewolf who'd offered him nothing but trouble and who cherished a distinctly unfriendly interest in Annie.

Larry grinned at him as the door closed behind Matt. "Your buddy has big dreams."

Barley thought back to the promises Gus, the guard, had made when he'd caught Barley working his magic on Larry. "Your buddy, Marcus, is an informant. Do you really think he won't report everyone here for attempted escape? We're the only ones who know he was beaten by a rabbit. He'll do his best to make sure none of us live to tell that story."

Larry's grin vanished as quickly as if it had been wiped with a washcloth. "Maybe. Okay, yeah. But if Justin couldn't escape, on his own, what chance do we have when we've got to drag along a bunch of first-years?"

"Justin must have shared his plans with Marcus. We'll have to make sure nobody trusts Marcus, assuming he dares leave the guardhouse. We—"

"Hadn't we better get out of here?" Annie interrupted. "It won't take the guards long to get here."

"Good point," Larry agreed. "Except they'll look in the dorms and classrooms, too. Maybe we should take everyone to wherever you were hiding."

Barley shuddered. He couldn't stand another minute in that dripping water tower.

"Not doable," Taylor said. "The guards spotted us exiting the tower. They'll look there."

"With the guards turned out in force, we won't be able to leave the clubhouse without getting spotted," Cameron said.

Barley scratched his head—there was something at the tip of his memory. Finally it came to him and he turned to Annie.

"Matt told me about some sort of invisibility cloak you two came up with. Maybe you could make one for each of us."

"It works for ordinary light." Taylor wrinkled her nose. "For their third eyes, it might as well not be there."

"From what I've noticed, they use their ordinary eyes a lot," Barley said. "Physical invisibility might not get us over the fence, but it should help with getting between here and the dorms."

Annie and Taylor conferred for a moment, then Annie went into action ordering the Hans to carry buckets of water in from the bathroom, sheets and blankets from the beds where the Hans would sleep if they didn't dare head back to their dorms during the night, and any raincoats they could dig up from old closets.

As Hans trailed in with their offerings, Annie dunked them in pails of water, did some sort of transformation, and took out smoky gray-black fabric which she handed to Taylor.

With each cloak, Taylor rubbed a little moisture from her eye and chanted something about similarity and eyes.

That gave Barley an idea. After all, drunkenness has its own blindness. "I can add a bit of confusion. Assuming that doesn't mess up what you're doing."

Taylor shrugged. "Why not." She handed him a sheet that felt heavy, cold and wet, but looked like a transparent film of plastic wrap—except he couldn't see his hands where they held it.

He shuffled his feet into a lurching dance step, sang the opening verse to ninety-nine bottles of beer on the wall, then handed the finished product to a waiting Hans.

"Girls take longer to get ready," he said. "Go to the girls' dorm first."

"Sexist," Taylor and Annie said together as the Hans headed out.

"What? Should I have sent him to the boy's dorm and not given the girls a chance?"

"Just keep working," Annie said. "We don't have much time."

He kept dancing, losing himself in the rhythm, the powerful magic of music until, abruptly, Annie didn't let go when she handed him a sheet.

"Huh? What? I thought Taylor—"

"We're the last ones left," Annie said. "And this is the last sheet."

"Oh." His heart dropped. "I understand. You've got to leave me. A satyr is too much of a risk in a serious escape att—"

"Nobody is leaving you, Barley. Come on. This one is big enough for both of us."

Barley ducked under the wet sheet.

He expected to see nothing. After all, the only way an invisibility cloak could work would be by directing light around itself, which meant no light would actually enter the fabric. Instead, the cloak seemed to form a lens, bringing everything into ultra-sharp focus.

"This is scientifically impossible," he whispered. "How did you do it?"

"Shhh. Can't you hear them coming?"

He couldn't.

Three minutes later when they huddled behind abandoned gas pumps in what had to have been the base's fueling area, he finally heard them. He still couldn't imagine how Annie had.

At least thirty guards followed Marcus at a hard run as he burst through the clubhouse door.

Moments later, the sound of shattering glass, the stink of ozone, and Marcus's anguished whine told Barley the guards were taking out their revenge on inanimate objects.

"You promised I would be the head of the Hans." Marcus's voice had taken on a tone that would have been expected, although not enjoyed, from a five-year-old.

"Shut up and tell us where they're hidden." Compared to how he sounded now, Gus must have put on a friendly act when he'd tried to persuade Barley to inform on his friends.

"If you'd come faster when I'd—"

"And walk into a trap? You don't look like the brave and self-sacrificing type, but there have been other guards and other prisoners who played that game." Gus paused for a second and Barley imagined him nodding as he agreed with himself. "No. We came as quickly as we could. You, on the other hand, could have come a lot faster. You didn't have to fight him, you know. You could have gone along and then notified us."

Marcus had to hate groveling. Apparently he hated arguing with the guards even more. "I'll do better next time."

"You'll do better this time. I want them found."

"Okay. Let me transform. I should be able to smell them better that way."

"Fine. But keep in mind that every third shell in our weapons is silver. You play games, you'll end up air conditioned."

"No games."

Annie tugged on Barley and he followed her lead away from the Hans clubhouse and toward the boys' dorm.

He couldn't help noticing that Annie smelled nice—not like rotten seaweed the way he'd always pictured a sea monster. He swallowed and hoped Annie wouldn't notice when their shoulders touched and he let that contact linger for just a second rather than jerking back.

* * * *

"So you're back." Headmaster Hoffbrewer barely opened his door and looked out at Matt, his expression about as welcoming as that of a vampire presented with a plate of garlic.

"We've got to escape." Matt let his words rush out like an oil well gusher. "The guards are after us and..."

"That wasn't our agreement." Hoffbrewer tried to close the door on Matt's bare foot, but Matt stuck his shoulder into it and held it open.

"My friends are preparing the students for a mass escape. We need—"

Hoffbrewer smiled. "There will be a time for mass escapes, but we're not there yet. First we need a demonstration, proof that the school can be escaped. Afterwards—"

"Afterwards, we're all dead. Marcus is an informant. He was the one who killed Justin to keep him from escaping. He's already told the guards about our plan. We've got to move now, before—"

"If they're warned, they'll—"

Matt had been raised to be polite to his elders and to the seniors in his pack. His rabbit instincts urged him to give up, to go along with whatever Hoffbrewer said. But it wasn't just his own life at stake, Larry, Barley, Annie, Tayor, and all the others were depending on him. "Look, Headmaster. We don't have any choice. The guards know we're trying to escape. They've got to suspect you're involved. If we wait for a more convenient moment, we'll all be executed before we can even try."

Hoffbrewer glared at him as if Matt were somehow responsible for everything that had happened. "Well. What do you want me to do?"

Matt suppressed the urge to explain, to defend himself against unfair accusations. He forced down the obvious question, which was why Hoffbrewer was asking him, a first year student, to lead the escape.

"Escape was your idea, sir. Things just got out of hand and—"

"Things got out of hand the second you arrived at the school. I should have realized that a Carnecero would be unlucky."

"Look. Either you help us," Matt said, "or you don't. Either way, I've got to get back to my friends."

Hoffbrewer blew out a big breath. "Okay, Carnecero. My instincts tell me this is going to turn into the biggest bloodbath in the bloody history of the school, but I can't do nothing while my students suffer."

Matt wished he was still naive enough to believe the man's Santa Claus act. Instead, he suspected Hoffbrewer didn't want to be the only person left in the school after a mass escape.

"You've been here longer than me, sir." Matt relied on his inner rabbit to make himself sound respectful and inoffensive. "You must know lots of tricks we can use to escape the guards."

"Maybe." Hoffbrewer grinned again, the happy elf back. Within a fraction of a second, though, that smile faded and sweat beaded on his pale face. "I'm sorry, Carnecero. But I've got to look after myself first."

Hoffbrewer stepped into a coat closet near the building's front entrance, closing the door behind him.

"What the..." Matt threw the door open and discovered nothing but closet. Hoffbrewer had vanished.

The guards didn't bother knocking. Two seconds after Matt discovered the empty closet, an ax smashed through the front door.

Matt froze for a painful instant, his rabbit instincts again betraying him, but he'd faced those instincts before—and learned to turn them to his advantage.

He shifted into his true-form and scampered to the back of Hoffbrewer's home.

The guards would surely have surrounded the entire house, but they'd be looking for a Hoffbrewer, not for a tiny rabbit. He could slip out the back door and...

When he got to the back door, though, his hopes evaporated. Dozens of boards had been nailed across what had once been the back entrance.

Matt was trapped inside—and from the sound of it, the guards were inside the house as well.

* * * *

Taylor inhaled through her mouth, trying not to let any of Larry's odor into her lungs. He was so full of fear, the stench of it threatened to overpower her common sense, make her as helpless as he seemed to be.

"Keep moving." She halfway wished for the pencils she could use to compel him, although casting magic would attract the guards.

"I... I'm trying."

"You know what the Jedi say—trying don't cut it. Come on."

Ultimately, Larry was more afraid of being left behind than of following her, so he clung to the wet invisibility blanket like it was his only security and stayed with her as she made her way to the girls' dorm.

They weren't the first to arrive, of course. The first Hans they'd sent had awakened the girls and persuaded them to pack what minimal belongings they couldn't stand to leave behind. Unfortunately, that was about it.

"Well." Phaedra, who'd been so cocky and obnoxious when she'd first shown Annie and Taylor their room wasn't so self-assured now. "How are we going to escape?"

Taylor had spent time with Justin's guard I.D. Given a couple of days, she could replicate a new set—one good enough, at least, to stand casual inspection. She couldn't, though, put something like that together in second. Nor could she hope to create enough for all of the girls—let alone all of the guys in the school. Their escape would have been much simpler if Matt hadn't blabbed, if it was just the four of them. But Matt wasn't the kind to think of himself. Whenever he found a grievance, he seemed convinced he could also find a solution.

She supposed that was admirable in a way but it was so far from how she'd grown up, she didn't know how to deal with it.

"We've taken out the lights on the west side of the base," she reported. "They've got a couple of flashlights, but otherwise they'll be blind to our escape."

"Which won't do us any good considering that the school is surrounded by razor wire." Phaedra complained. "We'd be chopped to hamburger before we got through it."

Annie and Taylor had talked about that. "Water rusts steel. I'll go ahead and put this blanket over the wire. It'll turn it to so much rust in seconds."

Coming from anyone else, she suspected her comment would have been greeted with derision. After all, the wires had been up for years and still gleamed like they were new. But word of her little exhibition in Ms. Ottawa's classroom had spread through the school. From the nods, it looked as if the girls were prepared to believe her.

"Yeah, okay," Phaedra admitted. "But the guards can see everything with their magic eyes."

That, unfortunately, was the flaw in their plan. She hoped the darkness would confuse them, that their third eyes would sense only general direction, not provide everything they needed for accurate targeting. Hoping didn't give the comfort knowing would have.

"Anyone who stays is as good as dead." Lying wouldn't help so she stuck to the truth. "Not everyone will make it. But if we give up now, none of us will escape and they'll crack down hard. I don't know about the rest of you, but half a chance feels a lot better to me than no chance at all."

Nobody disagreed with her, but she knew they would have been a lot happier if she'd just waved her hands and said she'd magic them to harmlessness. Unfortunately, that would be a lie. The guards had every protection the Fae community could provide them. Whatever magic she could throw their way would splash off them like they were made of Teflon.

"We'll hit them in waves," Larry said. "Each group will infiltrate as well as it can, then go to ground to let the next group come up. No talking and if anyone falls, leave them for the next group to help."

"What?" Taylor spun to face him. "Have you been thinking about this for a long time?"

"Uh, I read a lot of books about World War I. That's how they finally managed to go through the trenches. If you think about it, the guards in their towers are a lot like that the soldiers in their trenches."

She still wasn't sure she liked Larry, but she had to admit there was more to him than she'd suspected at first.

"Okay you guys." She picked out a group of the most athletic girls. "You're team one. You'll hit the fences first."

"What about you?" Phaedra demanded. "You going to hang at the back to make sure you get out safely once your lab rats have sprung all the traps."

"I don't know what I did to piss you off, Phaedra," Taylor fired back. "But I don't have time for your crap. I already said you're welcome to hang out in the dorm and wait for the guards to come shoot you. But for your information, I'll be going out first to make sure the fences are taken down."

"She doesn't like you because you're pretty and she isn't," one of the girls said in a stage whisper.

"Who said that?" Phaedra glared around the room.

Taylor decided her best bet was to ignore the obnoxious monitor. Whether she was an informant or not, she was slowing them down way too much. Taylor hastily called out groups two, three, and four.

She'd barely finished that when Larry popped in with one of the Hans. "Guards on the way."

"We're leaving the dorms now," she said. "Group one, your assembly area is in the parking lot with your alternate in the outdoor shower area. Group two, the dining room is your primary but if you see guards there, assemble in the handball court." She quickly gave directions for the two remaining groups, then led them outside.

Once in position, she'd make sure they synchronized their watches and then she'd attack the razor wire. She hoped Matt would show up with reinforcements before the rag-tag group tried to infiltrate. From what she could see of them as they left the dorm, this group of girls was about as subtle as an elephant with diarrhea.

* * * *

Annie led Barley toward the boys' dorm but Barley stopped her when they were still a couple of hundred feet away.

"What?" She leaned close to him to whisper and was surprised he smelled like fresh-mowed hay. It was a pleasant scent, but she couldn't understand where he'd picked it up. They'd been in a water tower and then in a stinky all-boy clubhouse without a hayfield in sight.

"I'm trying to pick up the rhythm of the place. It feels off."

"Not everything is a dance. Maybe it just—"

He pulled away from her and she grabbed him to make sure he didn't expose himself to the guards.

"Don't you think that I know that everything isn't a dance? I've only been told that a million times a day since I became a Satyr."

"I didn't mean to offend—"

"Of course you didn't *mean* to. Nobody means to offend me—they just don't care enough to avoid it."

He wasn't being fair, but she knew how he felt. She'd run into much the same reaction from her mer-folk family who just couldn't understand why she insisted on taking a monster true-form—as if she'd had any choice.

"There should be a rhythm of packing, of getting ready. Instead, it's completely chaotic."

"Maybe nobody can believe the Hans we sent ahead."

She felt rather than saw Barley's head-nod in the darkness. "That's probably it. We might as well see if we can help. Not that they're likely to listen to us if they won't listen to the older guys."

"Ah. There you are." A strong hand clamped down on Annie's shoulder.

"Huh. Oh—" She resisted the urge to scream, recognizing Hoffbrewer's voice at the last moment. "So Matt found you."

"Indeed young Carnecero did." Hoffbrewer lifted the rainbow blanket and joined them underneath. "Maintaining no-see is tough. I'm sure you don't mind sharing this with me. Now, I assume you're on your way to the boys' dorm. Let's walk together on three. One, two—"

"Just a second. Where is Matt?"

"Unfortunately the guards arrived at my home while we were planning. We were unavoidably separated. However, we were able to work out the details first. I'm sure he'll join us as soon as he's able."

That sounded reasonable but Annie felt troubled. Still, if he'd wanted to turn them in, Hoffbrewer could already have done so.

"Okay," Barley said before Annie could figure what to do next. "We may have some troubles convincing the guys that we've got to move. Anything you can do—"

"I'll do my best to be convincing. Now, are we ready? One, two, three."

They set off across the courtyard outside the boys' dorm.

A couple of times, flashlight beams clawed through the darkness and Annie wondered how long it would be before the searchlights were repaired or replaced. Surely repairing the broken ones would take a long time, but searchlights often came on wheels. And the guards must have plans to deal with at least occasional equipment failure although probably not the mass breakdown she and Taylor had created.

Barley winced every time one of those flashlight beams came near but Hoffbrewer whispered encouragement. "Almost there. A few more yards. They'll never get to us now."

Barley completely froze, though, when they reached the dorm. "The rhythm isn't just chaotic, it's counterpoint."

"That doesn't mean anything to me." Hoffbrewer's tone seemed to indicate he was being as polite as he could be in not suggesting it wouldn't mean anything to anyone.

"I think it means that the guards are already there," Annie said. "That would make sense. Matt's fight delayed us."

"Carnecero fought? I would have loved to see that."

"Well, perhaps you can before the night is over," Barley said. "And yes, now that you mention the possibility, I think it's likely there's at least one guard inside."

"Can you make them drunk?" Annie asked. "The way you made the guards who caught Taylor and me drunk."

"Won't work," Hoffbrewer said. "They questioned the two guards you surprised. While the four of you were in hiding, they upgraded the spells they use to ward off our magic. They also fired the two guards when they learned they'd attempted to molest the girls. In the old days, that was a fringe benefit, but Gus is stricter than the former guard captain."

"But without getting them drunk—"

"The four of you have done wonders," Hoffbrewer admitted. "I never would have thought to use water to take out the searchlights. Getting the girls away from the guards in the first place, hiding for two days... I never guessed any of those were possible. Now it's my turn to help out. If the two of you will step out of this magical wrapping and distract the guards by opening the door and walking into the dorm exactly as if you expect everyone to be ready for their escape, I'll follow you in and take care of the guards."

As plans went, it wasn't much. Especially because Annie just didn't trust Hoffbrewer. Which didn't make much sense considering he was working with Matt and considering he could have turned them in already. Maybe Taylor's cynical beliefs about all adult males was wearing off on her.

Unfortunately, Annie didn't have a better idea. At least she hadn't come up with one when Barley jumped out of the wet blanket and grasped the door.

"Come on. What are you waiting for? They may be torturing our friends."

She wasn't sure she had that many friends, but she wouldn't put torture past the guards. She turned to Hoffbrewer. "Without me to control the water droplets, the rainbow effect will fade quickly and this will turn back into an ordinary blanket. If you're thinking about running—"

"Running. How would that help?"

She felt like an idiot. Hoffbrewer hadn't had to track them down. Matt had trusted him and he'd acted like an ally so far. Her suspicions had to be part of being a murdhuacha—a monster who trusted nobody because nobody ever befriended a murdhuacha. "It wouldn't help," she said. "So don't do it."

"Come on," Barley insisted. "Quickly."

She let the blanket go and watched as Hoffbrewer wrapped it around himself. She could sense water, but even though the invisibility flowed from her power the man vanished from sight.

Barley threw open the door and stepped inside—and Annie followed, directly into the sights of a pair of semi-automatic pistols.

Chapter Sixteen

Barley looked at the two guards, then at Marcus who pointed at him.

"These are two of them," Marcus shouted. "The ones who murdered Justin and then took over the Hans."

The two guards looked at each other. "Gus says we can't have fun with the chicks anymore."

"Who's going to tell him?" The other jabbed Marcus with his pistol. "Are you going to tell if we have a little action with Ms. Green Teeth here?"

"I—uh, of course not."

"Because you'd probably like to have a piece of that yourself, wouldn't you?"

They were dead.

If the guards were talking this publicly about ignoring the guard captain's orders, then they weren't going to let anyone survive to give testimony against them.

Hoffbrewer had said that the guards had protection against his Satyr skills, and he didn't even have the flute he'd used when he and Matt had rescued the girls. Still, he had to do something to give Hoffbrewer a chance to act—and to keep them from seeing him with their third eyes.

He hummed a cheery tune, stepping in time with the music.

For about ten seconds, he thought it might actually work. Then the guard who'd poked Marcus laughed. "I don't mind a nice buzz, but that's enough, Satyr-boy. Sure would be handy to keep you around for a cheap drunk, but a chick is a chick, know what I mean?"

Sometimes, in Barley's experience, ignorance was safer than knowledge. "I'm confused. What are you talking—"

The guard poked Marcus again. "He talks too much. Kill him."

"Me?" Marcus's voice squeaked like a mouse being run over by a slow steam roller.

"You kill him or I kill you. Your choice, really."

"I, uh, can I borrow a gun?"

The guard laughed. "If you need a gun to—"

Before he could finish his sentence, Barley heard a hollow clunk and the guard fell forward.

"The other guard's third eye flared like a laser and he pointed his weapon at the apparently empty air. "Hands up, Hoffbrewer. Or I'll kill you like the skunk you are."

Hoffbrewer stepped into view, his hands held high. As he did, he shrugged,

The blanket dropped to the ground and went visible as the cloud of mist that Annie had created to maintain the invisibility effect shimmered into a puddle of water on the floor at the guard's feet.

"Now, little lady." The guard didn't take his eyes off of Hoffbrewer. "Suppose you tell me where your friend the killer is."

Barley had never tried poetry or beat, but rhythm meant music. He put his rhythm into his words, hitting the guard with all of the intoxication he could. Not that he thought it would work. Still, he wanted the guard thinking about him, not Annie. "If you're talking about Justin, Marcus killed him, not—"

"That's a lie," Marcus shouted. "They know I'm working with you and they're trying to destroy your confidence in me."

"Did a fine job, too," the guard quipped. Still—"

Whatever he was going to say next went unsaid as he took a small step and slipped on the water. His weapon discharged as he fell, tearing a hole in the dorm's corrugated metal roof but fortunately missing everyone.

Barley had been waiting, hoping for that moment since he'd seen the puddle of water on the ground and remembered the way Annie had made her algebra book slide without resistance.

Unfortunately, the guard didn't land on his head and he still had the gun.

Barley leaped for the guard, grasping his gun hand and trying to wrestle it away.

The guard was strong—horribly strong. He grinned at Barley as he pulled his gun hand against both of Barley's arms—and won. "Guess this means you just volunteered to be the first to die, kid. Marcus, watch Hoffbrewer. That old man may look like a jolly elf, but he's dangerous."

"Got it, boss."

Barley had given Matt strength when he'd fought with Marcus and tried a hum to see if he could help himself. The guard's third eye seemed to drain energy as quickly as he could generate it.

Abruptly, though, Annie was on the ground with them, her fingernails extending to claws, her teeth glistening to dagger points.

She jabbed those fingers toward the guard's eyes, then clamped her teeth on his gun hand.

Two seconds later, he dropped his weapon and grabbed his bleeding hand, leaving shreds behind as he ripped it from Annie's mouth. "You poisoned me."

She licked her lips. "Funny. You taste pretty good to me. Nice to be useful for something, right."

"Let's slit their throats and get out of here." Hoffbrewer grabbed the guns the two guards had dropped.

Barley was starving but he still retched at the idea. "Kill them? One's unconscious and the other's unarmed and injured. You can't just kill them, it would be murder."

"If we want to get out of here alive, we can't leave them in a position where they could hurt us."

Hoffbrewer sounded like he regretted the necessity and, just for a moment, Barley weakened at that hesitation.

"They were going to..." Annie trailed off.

The word 'revenge' popped into Barley's mind. Sure, Annie was due her revenge for the threats, the intentions, the truly evil way they stared at her as if undressing her in their minds. But that didn't make murder right. "Listen." He spoke not to Hoffbrewer alone, but to all of the students. "Suppose we kill them."

"Cool," someone shouted from behind the television. "Not like they haven't killed plenty of students."

"Not like they weren't planning on killing us no matter what we do," someone else agreed.

Barley nodded. They had a point. "If our escape fails, they will kill us. But suppose we succeed? Suppose we get out of here. We'd have to live with the knowledge we were killers."

"I think I could live with that," Hoffbrewer said slowly. "If it helped me escape."

"That's the thing," Barley fired back. "When we escape, they'll hunt for us. But after a while, if we lay low, the chase will die down. If we leave a pair of murdered guards behind, they'll never stop looking. They'll demand their revenge no matter how much it costs them. They might also give up on the school and simply execute everyone they perceive as dangerous. That would be cheaper and easier, after all, than an entire school of magical misfits."

To Barley's surprise, Hoffbrewer looked like he wanted to argue, but he backed down. "Tie them up, then. And be sure to gag them. We don't want them calling for help."

A couple of Hans leaped to handle that task. They weren't Barley noticed, any too gentle in their actions but he didn't think the guards were in any danger.

"Right," Hoffbrewer said when the guards had both been gagged. I'd planned on a lot more preparation for the escape, but this is the only opportunity we're going to get.

"The guards have spare bulbs for their searchlights, but from what Carnecero told me, Annie and Taylor smashed the entire globes, which means they won't be able to get them working for another half hour or so. I propose this. The werewolves and other fast creatures will take their true-forms and dash toward the fences. Those of us with magical abilities will come as quickly as we can behind them, using our skills to confuse the guards.

The fence itself is a problem. It's warded against magic and I don't think anyone here has the skill to take it out. So, we'll carry blankets from your beds here and toss them over the razor-wire. I'm afraid some of us will get cut, but that's the best I can offer."

Hoffbrewer's plan might not have been brilliant but it was the only plan out there. Within minutes, the lead team of true-forms dashed toward the dark section of fence.

Barley started with them but Hoffbrewer grasped him by the shoulder. "Not you."

"Why? You said yourself that the guards are warded against what little magic a Satyr can manage.

"They may be, but I'm not."

"Huh? You want me to make you drunk?"

"Don't be obtuse, goat-boy. I want you to make me fast. The rest of you are youths. You can soak up punishment and keep going. I'm not getting any younger."

Barley told himself he shouldn't hold Hoffbrewer's selfishness against the aging fat man. Still, it seemed weird, especially when the headmaster re-energized the invisibility blanket they'd used to cut across the courtyard. They were pressed for time, but it seemed some of those going in the front group could have used the invisibility more than Hoffbrewer.

"Let's go." Hoffbrewer tugged a set of wire clippers from his pocket.

"But you said—"

"I can't climb a twenty foot fence. If I had enough wire cutters for everyone, I would have passed them out."

Again, Hoffbrewer's explanation made sense. Again, Barley didn't like it.

* * * *

Matt cringed at the back of Hoffbrewer's house. With dozens of guards always on the watch, he didn't think there would be much of a burglary problem in the faculty area of the campus, but Hoffbrewer's windows were all barred and locked.

There was no escape that way. Not even for a skinny teen. Not even for a bunny if he chose to convert to his true-form.

He headed back through the house, toward the sound of guards.

"Hey. It's one of the kids."

The shout came from behind him. Some of the guards must have split up, the smarter ones getting ahead of the ones making all of the noise.

Without thought, Matt converted to rabbit form.

The instant all four of his feet were on the ground, he gave a powerful push with his hind legs—just a fraction of a moment before a crack like a breaking wall told him that at least one guard had opened fire.

Instead of fighting his instincts as he'd done since receiving his true-form, Matt let them control his movements.

His human mind would never have considered running straight toward armed guards. His true-form knew it would confuse them, that they'd be reluctant to shoot when they were far more likely to hit another guard than to connect with a fast-moving rabbit.

Rather than run straight, he altered directions, froze for a moment, reversed his course. Over millions of years, rabbits had evolved those instincts to escape from hawks and wolves. Those predators were faster than a rabbit, had more stamina. But they lacked a rabbit's mobility.

"Don't shoot him. Catch that rabbit." Gus sounded disgusted by the guards' incompetence.

"*You* try to catch him." The guard who replied was on the ground from a missed attempt to dive on top of Matt. "If you'd brought in dogs like I—"

"I don't need dogs to hunt rabbit. Now back off. I've got a drugged dart."

Matt's human thoughts froze like, well, like the rabbit he'd always worried about. His rabbit form didn't obsess about verbal threats. It concerned itself with physical danger—the risk of being hunted by a predator, eaten by an enemy. A poisoned dart was not a threat a rabbit could understand, so he didn't pause from his run.

A pop was followed by a frightened shout. Then, "well damn it, George. Don't go and stand in front of the dart."

George collapsed before he could offer any excuses. The amount of drug capable of rendering a grown man unconscious in just a few seconds would almost certainly kill a rabbit. That it would make him inedible was small consolation.

Matt dodged again, feinted, then when the guard reacted, ran straight between the legs of the man next to him.

Another puff of air was followed by a shrill curse.

"Sorry, Andrew. Don't let him get away."

Matt ran toward the small gap between the final two guards blocking the door.

No human would have seen the subtle movements as the two reached for him. No human could have stopped as quickly as he could, the small mass of his rabbit form allowing him to simply freeze in place from a full run—with none of the gradual slowing down even the strongest human must endure.

The two guards clunked heads as they completed their grabs at empty air. Then Matt gathered all of his strength and jumped.

Against even ordinary people, let alone trained guards, the move would have been suicide. Humans can judge flying objects well enough to hit hundred-mile-an-hour baseballs. But these two guards had just hammered their heads into one another.

Even with that handicap, one managed to get a hand on Matt's foreleg. Before he could tighten his grip, though, Matt bit his hand and the guard, reflexively, released his grip.

Matt flew free and continued running, but turned into the darkness and listened as the guards called off their chase—temporarily, at least.

"Psst. Matt. Up here. Where have you been? Where's Hoffbrewer?" Taylor sounded frazzled.

He looked around, seeing nothing at first. When she repeated "up here, idiot," he spotted her, along with maybe a dozen other girls, on the flat roof of a collapsing structure that probably pre-dated the Alamo.

He hopped up to a windowsill, then jumped.

Taylor snagged him out of the air and yanked him the rest of the way to the rooftop.

The girls with Taylor gripped sticks and rocks and looked plenty ready to take on a troublesome bunny. Against a guard, he didn't like their chances.

"It's just Matt," Taylor explained before Matt had a chance to transform and come up with some story to explain how a Carnecero happened to take a rabbit form.

Matt stopped transforming when he remembered he was naked. Maybe he shouldn't let it bother him, but he couldn't bring himself to let Taylor see him naked again.

"Oh, for goodness sake. Who here has a towel?"

A reluctant girl, Elizabeth, he thought her name was, finally offered him the towel she had wrapped around her head.

Taylor tossed the towel on top of Matt, which allowed him to transform back to human form while maintaining at least a hint of self-respect.

"Hoffbrewer left me to be captured when the guards arrived," Matt explained as he struggled from under the towel. "It took me a while to get away."

"Did he tell you anything first, give you any ideas at all? We're working on your escape but we could use any help he might have to offer."

Matt shook his head slowly as he tied the towel around his waist. Now that he thought about it, Hoffbrewer had been big on noble thoughts but extremely light on specifics. The only thing he knew now that he hadn't known when he'd made his dangerous way to Hoffbrewer's home was that the headmaster could not be trusted.

"*The Great Escape* is banned from the school library, but there are plenty of books about World War One. We're infiltrating, like both sides did in that war after they realized just charging machine guns was suicide."

"I don't understand." His mother had once told him that her great-grandfather had fought in World War One, but to Matt, that war might as well have pitted Napoleon against Julius Caesar.

"We're trying to get through without getting shot," Taylor explained.

"Ah. Good idea."

"Yeah. I thought so." She raised one hand and spoke in a soft whisper that nevertheless sounded as loud as a shout in his ear. "Team one ready."

She tugged her ear and listened, although Matt suspected she was hearing something far different from the sounds around him.

His suspicions turned to certainty when she stomped one foot on the ground. "Male idiots. You'd think somebody would have suggested rushing the fence is about the dumbest thing they could have tried.

Matt jogged over to the side of the rooftop closest the darkened fence and peered over the edge.

Sure enough, what looked like a hundred werewolves, werecats, and a single were-ostrich were running full speed toward the fence.

"I thought you were going to be sneaky." At least he thought that's what infiltrate meant. "And coordinate with the guys."

Taylor had joined him on the wall surrounding the flat roof. "That was the plan. I guess someone else had a better idea."

The dashing students might hope the guards wouldn't see them without their searchlights. Matt didn't think they had a chance of being right.

* * * *

Annie had to choke back her nausea when a hail of bullets cut into the werewolves and other shifters who ran toward the fence. Without their searchlights, the guards couldn't possibly see who was coming, but the nearby city of San Antonio provided a background light just enough to let them see movement. She wouldn't have thought they'd have night vision equipment that would work as well as the water droplets in the blankct shc, Barley and Hoffbrewer huddled under, but they didn't have to. None of the shapeshifters had the benefit of invisibility. Whatever they saw or not, the guards fired like they had enough bullets that accuracy wasn't an issue.

"Interesting," Hoffbrewer commented. "I suspected they had machine guns. I wonder how many bullets they hold."

"I'm betting they have enough to kill everyone in the school."

"Almost certainly. Still, many of those shots are missing."

Most of the School's misfits were true-forms, not mages. And Annie hadn't met another mage with Taylor's control over her skill. Still, enough students had some power and they sent clouds of fog toward the guard towers, erected invisible walls in front of their friends, and did healing magic on downed werewolves.

The guards' bullets didn't seem particularly bothered, though, by the invisible walls. A few clunked away, but more penetrated, leaving glowing white-hot lines through the invisible fabric. The fogs were even less effective as the guards weren't really aiming. Fog, Annie knew, was worthless against their third eyes. Why hadn't she warned them? Sure they only had a limited time window. If they weren't well away from the school by sunrise, the escape simply wouldn't happen. Still, they could have taken a few more minutes to plan.

They would have taken more time, she finally realized, if Hoffbrewer hadn't rushed them.

"Shouldn't we do something?" Barley demanded.

"Just a moment." Hoffbrewer clamped a big hand around Annie's neck. Between his smiles and his Santa Claus act, she wouldn't have guessed he'd have such strong hands. "Some of them will reach the fence. We've got to see what... ah."

Ah, indeed. The instant the surviving werewolves touched the fence, they convulsed with pain. The sound of their shrieks reached her a split second after the

Those whose true-forms had allowed them to carry blankets tossed them over the wires and tried to climb.

The blankets appeared to offer a bit of insulation from the electrical fence as well as protection from the jagged blades embedded in the wire. Still, between the bullets and the wire, more and more fell.

"Okay." Hoffbrewer sounded cheerful enough. "Time for us."

Annie planted her feet on the ground. She'd seen enough of Hoffbrewer. Wherever he went, she wanted to go the opposite direction.

"Come along, Missy."

"Not happening."

"If you don't come, I'll have to dispose of you."

"If I'm dead, this invisibility cloak you're hiding under becomes an embarrassing wet blanket."

"Really?" Hoffbrewer whirled and seized Barley. "What about him? He isn't necessary to keep the spell, is he?"

Annie's brain whirled. If she said yes, it might keep Barley alive. If she said no, maybe he'd let Barley go.

"Let him go," she said. "I'll cooperate."

"You'll cooperate anyway."

"Oh, really? Are you so sure you'll be able to tell whether I disable your invisibility?"

"Why would you do that?"

"I don't trust you, Hoffbrewer. You knew those kids were going to get themselves killed but you sent them at the fence just to see what would happen, to let them trip the traps and make it easier for you to get out. I'd just as soon get captured by the guards as be captive to you."

"If the guards catch you, they'll kill you."

"So you keep saying. Then again, we all know you're a liar."

Hoffbrewer grew very still. "All right then. We'll make a deal."

"Let us go and I'll make sure the blanket keeps you invisible all the way to the wall."

Hoffbrewer laughed. "You think I'm an idiot? You just said I wouldn't be able to tell if the invisibility worked."

"I'd keep my promise."

"How many liars have I heard that from? No, Missy. You're coming with me."

"So far, it doesn't sound like you're offering a great deal. It also doesn't sound like it's happening." Annie plopped her rear on the ground. He could drag her, but she'd slow him down—and dragging would make noise that the guards could target on. A large man standing would be a better target than a small girl on the ground.

Hoffbrewer jerked so hard on her arm she couldn't help letting out a shriek, but she didn't get up and he only moved her a few inches.

He bent over her and gave her that smile she'd gotten to know and suspect. "How about this, mer-girl. I let the Satyr go now—as a token of good faith."

"And because there's no way you can control both of us. Don't dream you're making me feel grateful."

"Like I said, I give you the Satyr now. Then, you help me get through the fence. Once we get through, You're on your own. Come back and die with the Satyr, do your own escape. It doesn't matter to me once I'm out."

"Don't do it." Barley was pale with panic and Hoffbrewre's hands on his throat had to hurt. That didn't stop him, though. "He'll never let you go once you get out."

"Why would I keep someone who wants to betray me?"

Annie pretended she believed that logic. "Come on, Barley. He's going to let you go. So, go."

When Barley didn't move, she shoved him from under the blanket. Matt and Taylor were out there somewhere. At least she hoped Matt was still alive. Considering he'd gone to see Hoffbrewer and only Hoffbrewer had showed up, she feared the worst. "Go find Taylor, Barley. She'll know what to do." If there'd ever been a time when paranoia was an advantage, this was it. And Taylor was the most paranoid person Annie had ever met.

Chapter Seventeen

No matter what Annie said, Barley didn't trust Hoffbrewer. With her power over water, Annie was a useful talent—a talent Hoffbrewer wouldn't easily let go. But Hoffbrewer added his own sharp shove to Annie's more gentle push and Barley went sprawling, his hooves once again throwing him off balance. By the time he'd regained his feet, Annie and Hoffbrewer had vanished.

He stared into the darkness, hoping that Annie would leave some glimmer, something for him to follow. Instead, he saw only dark sky, the even darker profiles of the guard towers, and the occasional muzzle flash from a guard machine gun.

Psst. Barley. Up here.

He looked around so quickly he almost lost his balance again. He needed his boots, his iPod and his music, and was suffering from their loss.

"Barley. We're on top of the old theater building."

He looked—in time to see Taylor make herself glow just for an instant.

That instant, though, was long enough for the guards to target the building where she'd hidden.

He hummed to himself while he waited for the guards to turn their attention back to the gang from the dorm. He kept expecting to hear Annie's pained scream. Each second that went by without it was both a relief and added to his sense of fear.

It took a few minutes before the guards decided they'd either hit their target or it had gone away. Only then did he take a tentative step toward the theater—and felt himself jerked back to the abandoned bathroom where he'd been hiding.

He whirled with the pull, his fists flailing—and caught Matt on the nose. "Oh, sorry."

"No problem." Matt changed to a rabbit-sized lump under his towel, then back to human. "Why charge at the wall like that? That wasn't the plan and they had to know it wouldn't work."

"It's what Hoffbrewer told them to do," Barley admitted.

Matt slapped his forehead. "That makes it my fault. I was the one who insisted we go to Hoffbrewer. I was—"

"Give it a rest, Matt. None of us had a plan and he did. So far, it hasn't worked so well but it's possible a few of us will escape. Hoffbrewer sure seemed to think he'd spotted some flaw in the defense."

Matt nodded—or that's what Barley thought he saw. San Antonio's lights gave the sky a gray glow that wasn't really enough to see anything in.

"If we're going to get out," Barley said, "we should head for the fence, too." The instant the words left his lips, though, he felt consumed with guilt. He hadn't even asked about Taylor and the last time he'd seen her, she was surrounded by tracer bullets.

"I'm here," she said before he could say anything. "Thank you for your concern."

"I, uh—"

"Some people take magic to read. You're not one of them, Barley. I suggest you give up any dreams about becoming a professional poker player.

"Barley's right, by the way," Taylor continued. "We can't follow my original plans exactly—Hoffbrewer's mad charge spoiled that option. But I kept track when they were shooting at me. The tower to my left shot thousands of rounds when the true-forms first charged, but it didn't fire a single shot at me when I signaled Barley, even though they are closer than anyone else. I submit to you that they've emptied their canisters. They've probably sent someone to get more ammunition, but that may take a bit of time."

Or maybe it won't, Barley thought. Still, they had to go with the best chance they could find.

"I think that's the way Hoffbrewer took Annie," he admitted. "But I'm not absolutely positive. I, uh, sort of got turned around.

"There is one thing," Taylor said. "Hoffbrewer doesn't belong out there. If I have a chance, I'm going to see to it that he's caught."

"He's got Annie," Barley objected. "If they catch him, they'll catch her, too."

"I'm not saying I like it, I'm saying that's the way it is. Hoffbrewer is the kind of monster the school was set up to confine. It's sad statement that he ended up in charge of the place."

Barley had a flash of insight. "I'll bet he killed the former headmaster. I'll bet that's how he became headmaster in the first place. This whole school is like the Hans—where you have to fight someone to get ahead."

"Or to get the girl," Taylor added. "As I see it, we have three goals. First, we want to rescue Annie from Hoffbrewer. Second, we want to get as many of the girls, plus any surviving guys, out of here as quickly as possible. And third, I want to make sure Hoffbrewer ends up captured. So, let's go."

"Makes sense," Matt said. "But I have the feeling we're missing something important."

* * * *

Matt watched silently as groups of five girls rushed from cover to cover, making their way to the fence line nearest the tower Taylor insisted must be out of bullets.

Each group of five had at least one mage to provide a bit of cover, to work with the faster true-forms to create a team. He suspected a few still had Annie's invisible water-cloaks although he couldn't see those.

All in all, the assault was a dramatic contrast from the mad rush of true-forms Hoffbrewer insisted on. It also seemed to work.

A few machine guns spouted off almost randomly. A few of the girls fell. Mostly, though, they slipped through the night like shadows against the blackened ground.

"Fence is electrified," Barley said. "I didn't see anyone make it through."

"I suspect Hoffbrewer has a plan."

Barley nodded. "He has wire cutters. Probably insulated. He won't use more magic than he has to because magic calls to them like one of those silent whistles calls a dog."

"Really?" Matt had to wonder how Barley knew that.

"Yeah. The one who drove us, Gus, he caught me, uh, doing a little something. That's how I figured it out."

Taylor gestured for them to move out. With Hoffbrewer's method, those going last were the safest. With Taylor's, relying as it did on stealth, those who went first had the advantage. Taylor, Barley and Matt were the last group.

"Barley says they can sense magic with their third eyes," Matt whispered to Taylor when she got near enough to hear him.

"Uh, welcome to the obvious, Matt."

He flushed. Maybe he should have guessed she'd know but he'd had to tell her, anyway. If someone got hurt because he'd assumed she'd known something she didn't, he'd never forgive himself.

"So," Taylor barely breathed the words as they dashed across an open spot in the crumbling concrete that made up the schoolyard. "Any thoughts on what we do when we get out?"

"I guess we'll have to find Hoffbrewer and make sure he gets sent back."

The three ducked behind a couple of barrels that had once served some obscure military purpose and now simply rotted in the school grounds—along with almost everything else there.

"We've got to get Annie free of him." Barley gasped for breath but what Matt could see of his expression looked determined. "He said he would let her go when they got out, but I don't believe him. He'll keep her and use her. What she can do with water could come in handy for a criminal."

"I was thinking," Taylor said, "more along the lines of how we get food and shelter. We don't have any money and I don't think any of us wants to sell what the perverts out there would be interested in buying."

"We can't worry about that yet," Barley insisted. "We've got to free Annie. She's our friend."

"I don't have friends."

Taylor still said the words, but Matt didn't think her heart was in it.

"Call her whatever you want," he said. "Barley is right. We've got to rescue her."

Something moved under Matt's feet and he almost bolted. Instead, he overcame his rabbit instincts, knelt and looked.

The wolf snarled at him.

He was a shifter—Matt didn't recognize him in wolf form, but he had to be one of the guys from Hoffbrewer's first wave.

"Are you okay, buddy?" Matt asked.

Another snarl.

Matt ran his hands over the wolf body and plucked off two darts—one from his foreleg and the other hanging from his back.

It felt as if he'd finally opened his own third eye—his whole view of the world altered as dramatically as if he'd changed channels. "They're shooting stun darts."

"Cool." Taylor grabbed one from his hands. "I can use similarity to match up a bunch of this, give the guards some of their own medic—"

"Why wouldn't they shoot real bullets?" Taylor missed what was important about it. Matt wasn't completely sure he understood himself, but he knew it was the most important thing they'd faced that night—and they'd faced a lot.

"Cause they want to stop us, not kill us." Barley's tone said he thought the answer was obvious.

Which it was, except... "It didn't make sense. Everyone knows the guards kill whenever they can. Everyone knows that anyone sent into the guard cells is gone forever. Everyone knows—"

"Everyone knows what the headmaster, the teachers, and the older students tell them," Taylor said. "And we all know that Hoffbrewer is a liar."

"So, maybe the guards aren't the enemy."

"Of course they're the enemy." Barley sounded impatient. "Friends don't act like this."

"I didn't say they were our friends. But if they don't kill when they don't have to, maybe we can negotiate with them."

Taylor bent a piece of a paper clip and whispered something. Ahead of him, the razor-wire shivered but didn't fall. "Okay, Matt. Suppose we offer to bargain. What have we got to offer?"

He couldn't blame Taylor for her suspicions. What the guards had intended for Annie and her had been purely evil. But Gus had fired them when he'd learned what they'd done. "We could offer Hoffbrewer to the guards," he suggested. "Tell them that he was behind everything."

"I hate to be the bearer of bad news," Barley said. "But we don't have Hoffbrewer and the headmaster does have Annie. I don't want her hurt."

"That and why should they believe us?" Taylor added.

They were right—in a way. But in another way, Matt knew they were incredibly wrong. If Hoffbrewer was a liar, Matt couldn't trust anything he had said. Maybe the Fae community could be persuaded to change the school, begin looking for ways to release those who'd overcome whatever problems had led them to the school in the first place. Matt himself had seen enough of his fellow students, not to mention Hoffbrewer and the other faculty, to know that simply letting all of them out posed dangers to the community—and to the students. Few of them were really prepared for a life outside, let a life on the run from Fae enforcers.

"We've got to figure something out," he said. "Because it's our only option."

"If that's our only option," Barley said, "then I think we're sunk."

Matt couldn't make himself argue. Barley was probably right.

* * * *

Hoffbrewer, Annie realized, wasn't just dragging her randomly toward the fence. He had a specific goal in mind—and a clear path he was following.

In his years at the school, he must have mapped every obstruction, every raised point, every guard tower and reinforced fencepost.

"You've been planning this a long time, haven't you?"

"I was sent to the school when I was thirteen, same as you," he said. "Like that Taylor friend of yours, I was too smart, too capable. I made those on the outside uncomfortable. And yes, I've been waiting for my chance ever since."

He'd said he'd volunteered to be headmaster, given them the idea he'd been outside. He'd lied. She also suspected he wasn't like Taylor at all. Taylor had been unfairly sent to the school because she'd fought back when her stepfather had tried to rape her. Hoffbrewer had almost certainly earned his trip to the school.

Matt would probably tell Hoffbrewer that, angering the headmaster in the process. Annie was a monster, but she wasn't crazy. She could play along with Hoffbrewer's delusions. She forced a smile. "I would have thought escape would be easy for someone of your skills."

He spit on the concrete. "The other students were slime. Every plan I made, someone betrayed. The guards had their snitches and someone always talked.

She had to bite her tongue to suggest that if he'd been a little braver, he could have made a plan that didn't rely on other people taking all the risks. Taking chances when he could make others do it for him just wasn't part of Hoffbrewer's mentality.

"So," she tried to sound chirpier than she felt. "You've been inside for a long time. What are you going to do when you get out?"

His laugh had none of the Santa Claus jolliness he'd affected earlier. "I've got a list of the people who sent me here. I only wish there was some way to make their lives hell for as long as they made mine. I'll have to settle for sending them to Hell directly."

"Ah."

She had thought he'd head for a part of the fence most distant from any guard tower. Instead, he headed directly for one tower, finally ducking under its steel legs to approach the fence.

"Good thinking," she whispered. "They'll never see us down here."

"They're so certain of their power." His voice practically crackled with contempt. "Once I handle the jerks who sent me up, they're next on my list. I'll come after every guard here. One by one, I'll show them that they're pikers when it comes to torture."

Annie would make herself sick if she tried to praise that kind of thinking. Instead, she peered at the wire.

Up close, she saw the insulators that kept the electrical charge from escaping into the ground.

Hoffbrewer handed her his wire cutters. "You'll need to cut through the bottom two strands. Don't worry, the clippers are insulated."

If he'd been so certain they were safe, he would have cut the wires himself.

She wished she were brave like Matt. He would probably throw the clippers as hard as he could outside the fence, foiling Hoffbrewer's escape without worrying about what happened to him.

As if reading her thoughts, Hoffbrewer chuckled again. "I do have a second pair of cutters. I'd rather keep you alive— you've been a big help. But if I have to go on alone, I won't be heartbroken."

He might have been bluffing but Annie didn't think so.

She reached for the fence, then stopped. A murdhuacha is a water creature and water was famous for its electrocution risk.

"What are you waiting for?"

"I'm trying to figure out how you benefit when I electrocute myself. After all, you are touching me. You'd get it, too."

Hoffbrewer jerked away from her. "Well, figure something out."

She reached a hand toward the wire, stopping a couple of inches away when she felt the first hint of pressure from the current and pulling back another inch to be safe. Then she drew on herself, pulling some of the water she'd absorbed in the tower and sending it to coat the electric wire. "Rust," she murmured.

Mist flowed from her fingers—and rebounded from the shiny wire. A spark followed the path of mist, crossing the gap and putting her down on her rear.

She shook her head, dizzied and frustrated by the electrical shock.

Hoffbrewer cursed softly. "Use the cutters."

"And trust a little bit of plastic to protect me? Not going to happen."

"If you think doing nothing will make you safer, you're badly mistaken."

She hadn't noticed while she'd been under her rainbow blanket, but now she saw a hint of gray on the eastern horizon. The sun would be rising soon. If they weren't outside the fence when it did, both she and Hoffbrewer would be killed. She wasn't anxious to die.

"You say you're a pretty good mage, right?"

Hoffbrewer gave her a disgusted look. "I'm an excellent mage."

"Suppose I create a water elemental. Can you animate it?"

"Are you insane? Why would—ah. I understand. Yes, for a moment, at any rate."

She reached for the blanket, touching it and drawing out all of the tiny drops that let it reflect and refract the light.

Even with all of that, plus what she stored in her body, it wasn't a lot. She used Barley's basic shape as a model, creating the figure hollow to conserve water, and making it about two feet tall.

"You've got a unique talent," Hoffbrewer said. "That could be useful."

Her heart pounded at his words and she involuntarily gasped for breath. She didn't want him to think of her as useful.

Either he didn't notice her reaction or he didn't care. He concentrated on the little elemental, pulling a bit of hair out by the roots and placing it on top of the figure, then breathing into its mouth.

Finally, he reached to her and reclaimed the clippers, placing them in the elemental's hand.

The little blue figure nodded, then reached for the bottom wire and snipped.

This time, the shock hit both of them. And the poor elemental steam-flashed out of existence.

Still, the bottom strand was cut. "It'll be a squeeze." Hoffbrewer breathed hard. "But I can get out."

"I guess this is where we part, then," Annie said. "You promised you'd let me leave when we escaped."

"Did I." He gave her his eye-twinkle. "Guess I lied."

* * * *

The sun hadn't risen, but Taylor could feel it lurking just below the horizon. Dark purple streaks promised what would become a beautiful south Texas sunrise.

The first wave of girls was about three quarters of the way to the fence. If they'd had another twenty minutes, even ten, they could have escaped.

"We aren't going to make it," she said. "Hoffbrewer's crazy stunt having all of the guys charge took too long, distracted us too much."

Barley grunted. "He didn't care about anyone escaping but himself."

"Maybe we don't need to escape." Matt sounded like he was musing, talking to himself more than the others. Still, considering he'd been the one urging the escape from the start, she couldn't believe him.

"You want me to turn myself in so they can torture me or do whatever else they want." Taylor's voice cracked a little and she knew she sounded hysterical, but she couldn't help it. There was no way she was going back into that cell with those guards. She'd rather get shot attempting escape. Only, unfortunately, they'd learned that those trying to escape hadn't been shot by bullets, only by drug darts.

She twirled one of those darts in her hand, letting her magical senses probe the nature of the drug. Maybe she could turn that weapon against them.

Barley had been humming to himself ever since they'd reconnected. Now, though, he started chanting.

He spoke softly, as if to himself, but she found her legs jerking in time with his movements and his words.

"Do you mind?" she demanded. "You know that won't work against the guards, but it messes with my thoughts."

"I don't care whether we escape or not, but we've got to get Annie." He turned his words into a song.

"That's it," Matt shouted, attracting a hail of drug darts.

Fortunately, they huddled behind an overturned picnic table which absorbed the darts. It wouldn't have stopped bullets, though, Taylor realized. She wondered how long it would be before the guards started shooting to kill.

"What's it?" Barley kept singing.

"We capture Hoffbrewer. Then we turn him in to the guards so they realize we're not part of his plan. And we negotiate a better deal—the kind of deal I thought Hoffbrewer wanted in the first place. Something with a program that will let people out of here once they've reformed. After all, do we really want all of these creeps loosed on the world?"

"The worst of the creeps work for the guards," Taylor reminded him.

"Hoffbrewer is probably outside the fence by now," Barley added. "He's out of our reach."

Matt peeked around the picnic table at the fence. "Call back the others. I'm going to go out myself."

"How do you expect to get out when the rest of us can't?" Taylor demanded.

"In my true form, I can run fast and dodge a lot. And I can get under the electrical fence with no problem.

"And when you get out," Taylor reminded him, "you'll be either a naked kid or a bunny. That will be so useful in tracking down and capturing a criminal like Hoffbrewer."

"It's worth a try."

Barley shook his head. "All those other true-forms were fast and could dodge, too. And the machine guns got them."

"But one creature, alone, would be—"

"Would be an easier target," Taylor interrupted. "It's getting light."

Barley shuffled a little dance. "Back on the bus, we agreed we'd all work together. You're not going out alone."

A lightbulb went off in Taylor's head. "Okay, you guys. That's it."

Barley looked startled. "Huh?"

"We need to work together, like you said, Barley. What have we got? Matt has a small and fast true-form. He's as fast as a werewolf, but he's smaller, harder to spot with normal vision, and harder to hit because he makes a smaller target. Barley's Satyr music gives him grace and speed. And my mage skills can confuse the guards' third eyes and I could also make us look like we had clothes on once we got outside."

"Except, there are three of us," Matt reminded her. "And I'm the only bunny. I can't exactly carry the rest of you on my back."

"In a way you could," she said. "Let me explain."

Chapter Eighteen

They were taking a big chance and Matt didn't like it. Although it had come in handy a few times, he'd been ashamed of his bunny-body ever since his family had barely restrained themselves from adding him to the coming of age feast. Now, it wasn't just he who'd depend on that fragile vessel—he'd be carrying Barley and Taylor inside of him, as part of him.

Which raised another point. "You're sure you won't be able to read my mind if you're inside my head?"

Taylor shook her head. "Believe me, I already know what males think."

He didn't think comparing him to her stepfather was fair but he wasn't going to argue.

"I guess I'm ready, then."

They'd signaled a retreat for the girls and for those guys who either hadn't been shot or who'd recovered from being hit by drugs. The others had returned to the guys' dorm, which was bigger than the girls' and barricaded the doors and windows. Taylor had told the students to hold out as long as possible—that they were going to try to get some leverage for negotiation, then dragged he and Barley to the art room.

Now, she created three crude figures out of clay.

Barley was easy enough to recognize. The cloven hooves and furry legs were a give-away. He wasn't sure he liked what she'd done to him but when he'd mentioned that, she just scowled at him. As for her, he didn't think she had that much of a figure. Still, the little statues were pretty good art. Taylor was talented.

She collected a bit of saliva, hair and a shaving of fingernail from each of them, touching up the clay with what he now recognized as similarity.

"How does that help," Barley demanded when she stepped back to admire her work. "Even if those were us, they're still—"

He broke off when Taylor rammed all of them together.

"Ouch." Matt felt as if his body had been seized by giant hands and was being turned inside out.

"You'll have to transform." Taylor's voice sounded harsh, almost inhuman. "But not yet. I'll say when."

Moving quickly, she changed the shape of the clay to that of a rabbit.

"Now." She groaned rather than spoke the word.

Matt changed.

* * * *

Matt felt as fuzzy as when Barley's skills had backfired before they'd gone after the guards. Every thought seemed an effort and his body didn't respond when he told it to move.

"You've got to relax." Barley's voice was inside his brain. "You're squeezing us out."

"Do you really think that kind of thing?" Taylor often sounded disapproving, but now she sounded downright disgusted.

He was lucky he was in rabbit form because he'd be blushing if still human. "I thought you—"

"Ha. Gotcha. But Barley's right. Relax. Your body knows what to do. You don't have to force it."

"I've got a question." Matt knew Barley was inside him, but he still managed to sound distant. "Let's assume all of this works. Let's assume we figure out a way to rescue Annie and capture Hoffbrewer. How are we going to get back to our own bodies?"

"No problem." Taylor's tone had more hope than confidence in it, though.

Matt quelled his inner screaming and hopped toward the partially open door. When he got there, he turned around to see Taylor and Barley apparently sleeping.

"Won't the guards see through my true form and stop the escape," he said.

"You said you were quick," Taylor reminded him.

"Oh, yeah."

"So, show us."

Barley started humming something. When he'd hummed while Matt had been fighting Marcus, the music had made his muscles less tired, his movements more fluid. The music directly in his head was the Pacific Ocean compared to a glass of water.

Although a lot of the guards surrounded the boys' dorm, some strange sense told him that there were plenty in the gun towers looking down.

"I gave you something like the guards' third eye," Taylor explained. "So you can spot anything Fae."

"Cool. Now if only I can avoid it."

"You might be able to sense their intentions a second or so before they shoot."

So that was the feeling gnawing at the back of his brain. He juked to one side just as a hail of darts smashed where he would have been if he'd stayed in a straight line.

Barley upped the speed of his hum and Matt danced to his tune, leaping, stopping suddenly, temporarily reversing his direction, but always returning toward the path his bunny nose told him Annie and Hoffbrewer had taken.

"I'm using some of what Annie taught me to make us hard to see." Taylor sounded exhausted—not a good sign since they'd just started. "It's not easy."

"Take some energy from me," Barley offered. "A Satyr can dance forever without resting."

Barley flooded energy through him. Matt just had to hope that Taylor could use some of it.

He crouched under one of the guard towers, panting as much oxygen as his rabbit lungs could hold. "Use the fear," he murmured to himself. "Don't fight it."

His wiggling nose caught the scents of Annie and Hoffbrewer more strongly here. Apparently they'd stopped and waited for a while before completing their escape. A pair of wire cutters rusted in the middle of a small puddle of water directly under a single cut strand of fencing.

"That's how they got out," Taylor said. "You can feel the magic in that water, can't you?"

"You know I can't feel magic. I'm a true-form, not a mage."

"Justin showed me you can be both. Besides, I'm part of you so you're not just a true-form anymore."

He gave a bit of control of his vision to the part of his brain that was Taylor and instantly he could recognize the fading glow left by magic.

"It was an animated water elemental," Taylor said. "Annie couldn't have done that alone. Is Hoffbrewer a mage?"

"He said he was," Barley admitted.

"Great. I'm good for a kid, but getting better takes practice. He's been an adult more than twice as long as I've been alive."

"But there's only one of him and there are three of us," Matt said. "There's probably never been a werebunny/Satyr/mage before."

"Which is almost certainly a good thing," Barley glumly surmised.

"Okay, ready, *now*," Taylor said.

Matt wasn't sure what was special about that moment, but he'd felt it too—an increase in the pressure at the back of his head that made moving more urgent than before.

He dashed through the hole in the fence. Forgetting about anything but speed, he ran pell-mell down the deserted street outside the base.

The gunshots sounded different—louder. A silver smear on the road next to him told him why. Inside the base, they'd fired drugged darts. Once the prisoner had escaped, they shot to kill.

"Can't keep them off any more," Taylor gasped.

He looked ahead. Rabbit eyes weren't especially acute but he didn't need to be a hawk to see he was too far from the built-up part of San Antonio. The area outside the fence must have been part of the base once. Every structure had been demolished, and the underbrush had been trimmed almost as close as a gold course putting green.

But the street itself had possibilities. He ducked behind a curb—and a large chip of concrete ricochet hit him in the back.

The sewer grates had extra slats welded onto them, probably to prevent even a skinny werewolf from slipping through.

They hadn't planned on a rabbit, though. It took him a couple of wiggles, but abruptly he fell into the damp muck about ten feet below the surface.

"How are we going to track Annie from down here," Barley demanded.

"We'll do better than if we'd been killed."

"Not enough better."

Matt suspected Barley was right.

* * * *

Hoffbrewer hadn't given Annie the chance to recover the water from her dead elemental.

She felt a little woozy as he crawled under the fence, then dragged her after him.

I could touch one of the higher fences. Since he's touching me, we'd probably both die. The thought was abstract. Even if she was ready to commit suicide to protect the outside world that had sent her to prison, she lacked the energy to do it.

Hoffbrewer had simply nodded, thrown her over his shoulder, and crossed the fifty feet to a well-camouflaged car.

He opened the driver's side door, tossed her across the car to the passenger seat, then got in and fired up the engine.

The car couldn't have been sitting there long because it caught instantly and Annie realized Hoffbrewer had to have contacts on the outside.

Which she should have guessed from the way he name-dropped about what leaders were doing what and how that would affect the school.

"I, uh, need some water."

He navigated down one street onto another. "You be good and I'll give you some. Later."

Her stomach twisted at the nasty way he emphasized *some*. She'd drained herself for him, after all. Then again, he'd watched her eat, knew that her teeth weren't just green, they had sharp points designed for slicing flesh. He probably though he was being smart to keep her helpless.

"That would be nice." Better to play along with him. "Can I roll down the window? It's stuffy in here."

"Would have had to pay more for a car with A.C."

"Is that a yes?"

"Sure, do it. Just keep your mouth shut."

She nodded.

She was on her own. By now, Barley would have told the others that Hoffbrewer had kidnapped her, but what could they do?

The sun had crept over the horizon just as Hoffbrewer had started the car's engine and she hadn't seen a single student follow them through the gap in the fence. Barley, Matt and Taylor weren't going to be rescuing her. Still, she combed her fingers through her hair.

Every once in a while, a hair came loose or cracked away and she licked each bit, then, when Hoffbrewer wasn't looking, let it waft out the open window.

As trails went, it was a step up from breadcrumbs. But not much of one if nobody followed.

Hoffbrewer drove without hesitation to an aging hotel only a couple of blocks from the Alamo.

"You're my daughter." He'd tossed the keys to a valet, then walked around to open Annie's door exactly as if he were a gentleman rather than a kidnapper. "We're here on vacation to see San Antonio's historical sites."

"The guards will be looking for us," she said. "It would be safer for you if you let me go."

"I wish it were that easy. But if they caught you, you'd tell them too much. It really is better that we stay together for a while. Better for you considering what I'd have to do if I couldn't keep you."

As always, his reasoning sounded so logical. Any doubts she had about his motivation, though, were answered by his next question.

"I'm intrigued by your abilities with water. Would you have to be touching someone to drain the water out of them, or could you do it from a distance?"

Annie's stomach jolted. She looked around, but Hoffbrewer didn't loosen his grip on her arm and she couldn't drain water from him—he must have used their drive time to create a protective ward for himself.

"Don't even think about trying to get away," he said, his voice low. "We can make this pleasant, or we can make it painful, but one way or the other, you're coming with me. For now, at least."

Hoffbrewer's 'for now' was likely to last as long as he could use her.

If she wanted to stay alive, she really should find a way to make herself useful, or at least make Hoffbrewer believe she could be useful.

For now, though, she didn't have the energy. Unless she could replenish her water soon, she wouldn't be useful to anyone.

Hoffbrewer finished the check-in without releasing his grip. He ignored the look the clerk gave him when he asked for a king-sized bed, collected an apple from the bowl on the counter, and dragged Annie to the elevator.

Once there, he held out the apple. "Show me how you can drain something of water. You need this, don't you?"

She reached for the apple, but he pulled it away. "Remember this, Annie. I can give you water and I can take it away. Don't even think to play games with me."

"No games," she agreed. If she ever had a chance to get away, she wouldn't play at it, she'd grab it with both hands.

"I'm glad we understand each other." Finally, he handed over the apple.

It shriveled in her hand, but the few drops of water it contained weren't nearly enough. Unfortunately, it looked as if Hoffbrewer intended to keep her starving as a part of his control. Even more unfortunately, that plan would probably work.

* * * *

The storm sewers were dark, damp and disgusting.

Taylor made gagging noises, but it didn't take her long to notice that Matt seemed able to sense direction and obstacles almost as well as if they hadn't fallen into utter darkness.

"Is it just me," Barley demanded, "or are we really spending our lives in dark, wet caves.

Matt ignored their complaints and hopped off in a direction Taylor felt certain could only lead them back toward the school.

"You got turned around when we fell," Matt assured her when she asked. He didn't explain why he couldn't have been the one who got turned around.

It turned out, though, that he was right. After what seemed like forever, he crouched under a storm drain and leaped upward. His claws scrabbled on the rough concrete, finally catching and letting him pull the rabbit body they shared into the daylight.

"We're out, but how do we find Annie?" Barley demanded.

For an eerie instant, Taylor wondered what it would be like to forget all of that, to stay in rabbit form and explore the world from a new perspective. She'd never have to worry about her stepfather, about guards with disgusting desires, or about being sent back to the school. As long as she shared Matt's head, it didn't matter what they did to her body back in the school.

Then she thought about Annie stuck in Hoffbrewer's claws desperately hoping for a rescue that wouldn't come unless she made it happen.

"Annie is smart," she reminded the others. "Even though she couldn't have known we'd get out, she wouldn't have taken any chances. She'll leave some sort of trail for us to follow. All we need to do is find it."

A car roared by and Matt ducked back inside the storm sewer, then lost his footing and slid back into the muck.

"Any suggestions on finding it," Matt wanted to know. "When I'm in my true-form, my nose is better than any human's, but I'm no bloodhound."

Taylor mentally shrugged. "If I had something of hers, I could use Contagion. As it is..."

"Take us back up, please." Barley sounded more forceful than Taylor could remember. Usually he was happy to follow along.

It took Matt two tries to scramble back out of the sewer line, the second assisted by Barley humming, with Taylor feeling like an unneeded parasite. She didn't know what they were going to do and couldn't seem to help them do it.

"This is the main road we took from the airport," Barley said. "I'm betting Hoffbrewer took it, too. We'll just head along here until we see whatever Annie left for us to find."

Matt set out, heading north away from the school.

Ten minutes later, they'd been chased by a dog and two cats, and were all discouraged.

"Maybe she didn't leave anything." Matt voiced the fear Taylor had suppressed. "Maybe she couldn't."

"You take that back." Since Barley didn't have a body right then, he couldn't be holding back tears. He sounded like he was, though.

"Sorry. I'm just trying to be realistic about—"

"What's that?" Although Matt controlled the rabbit body, its senses fed information to all of them.

Matt froze, then headed toward the thin strand of red.

"It's her hair." Barley sent an alcoholic surge through Matt's bunny body. "She's alive."

Taylor didn't mention any of the hundreds of scenarios she could imagine where finding a strand of Annie's hair didn't mean she was alive at all.

"Hop over and sniff it," she told Matt.

He took one hop and then scurried out of the way when a city bus barreled through, almost costing them a dimension. "Feel free to look both ways first," she cautioned.

"Sorry."

"If Matt kills his body, what happens to us?" Barley asked.

"I promise you don't want to know," she shot back.

With the bus out of the way and no other vehicular traffic heading their way, Matt made it to the strand of hair and sniffed. "It's her all right. I recognize the scent."

Taylor had never doubted that. "See how it's stuck to the ground, She must have wet it before she let it go. Which means she really still is alive and at least partially in control of her movement and her mind."

"What else?" Barley scoffed.

"Hoffbrewer is a mage. He'll try to take Annie over, turn her into a tool."

"Can he do that?" Matt demanded.

"Of course not," Taylor said. "It's completely against the rules. If they catch him, they'll send him to the School."

"Ah."

"Yeah, ah. They've already done their worst so there's no particular reason why he shouldn't do anything he wants. My point, though, is that he hasn't done it yet."

"So, we look for a trail of tiny hairs?" Barley sounded willing but not especially hopeful. "And we just pray he doesn't brainwash her or make her a zombie or whatever before we get there."

"Considering we've only gone a few weeks and we've already almost lost our lives about four times," Matt said, I'm not sure that's such a good idea."

"Pick up the hair and tie it around your forepaw," Taylor said. It's a part of her. Once touching, always touching—it's contagion, a fundamental law of quantum physics."

"You mean you can track her with this?" Barley asked.

"Exactly."

* * * *

Barley wondered if they'd ever eat again.

He felt guilty for thinking about food when Annie might be getting tortured, when Matt was sharing his true-form with a pair of hitchhikers, and when Taylor was casting spells on Annie's hair to remind it that it was once part of a red mop on top of Annie's head. He couldn't help it, though.

While Matt used his rabbit senses to navigate through pitch-black underground passageways, and while Taylor used magic to spell a compass that followed the trail of Annie's hair, Barley sniffed hamburgers, fried chicken, and fajita meats so tender and succulent, he kept making Matt's body drool.

Thoughts of food gave his song extra strength when Taylor announced they'd arrived and Matt found a nearby sewer grate.

"Oh, look, mama. A bunny rabbit."

They emerged directly next to a family picnic.

A little girl giggled as she pointed at Matt's true-form.

Her brother, a child of maybe three, didn't say anything. He did, though, run straight for them, his pudgy arms stretched out like a zombie's as he grabbed in their direction.

"This isn't what I had in mind," Matt muttered.

"Don't run straight away," Barley suggested. "Run toward them first."

Matt altered his plan, following Barley's advice and Barley managed to snag a hunk of cake as they ran straight through the blanket where the kids' mom had laid out the picnic.

He stuffed it into their rabbit face as they ran, ignoring Taylor's shocked screams and Matt's calm remonstration.

"I'm hungry," he explained.

"Rabbits don't eat cake." Taylor sounded almost hysterical.

"I'll bet that's only because they can't get it."

The pudgy kid kept after them, doing a lot more damage to the picnic than they had, and Barley relinquished his temporary control over their body, letting the more experienced Matt scurry through a couple of legs and into a large building.

"*This* where they're hiding Annie?" Barley asked when Matt ducked behind a statue.

"You idiot," Taylor answered. "It's the Alamo. Isn't it cool?"

Sure enough, there were the obligatory vignettes of brave Texicans holding off hordes of Mexican regulars. Accompanying them were weapons and documents supposedly dug up from the ruins.

"If Annie isn't here, why are we wasting our time?"

"Maybe," Matt said, "because someone stole a slice of cake and we had to run."

That was all the time for conversation they had, because the Alamo's security people were after a potentially dangerous rabbit and the three had to duck, scramble, and dodge to escape into the gardens behind the Alamo, then squeeze between the iron bars of a back gate.

Matt slowed. He was breathing hard, and Barley had been too intent on his cake and the one old lady who'd managed to hit them twice with what looked like an antique broom but felt like a club to do much humming.

"Looks like we got away," Matt said.

"Yeah, but—"

A canine howl cut off Barley's words. A pit bull who looked the size of an elephant was only a few feet away and heading directly toward them.

Matt whipped around, but the woman with the broom stood between them and the relative safety of the Alamo.

This, Barley thought, was completely wrong. They were supposed to be rescuing Annie, not getting eaten by somebody's pet.

Chapter Nineteen

Annie's mouth felt like the west Texas desert and her head throbbed with a headache that she couldn't get rid of.

Outside, the sun beat down on the hotel room, but Hoffbrewer refused to allow her to run the air conditioner. Instead, he stripped off his jacket and tie, unbuttoned the top couple of buttons of his shirt to expose a hairy chest, and tapped away at the hotel's TV-Internet device.

Getting rescued had never been likely. But some part of her brain had clung to the idea. Now, though, she forced herself to give it up. She was on her own and needed to think that way.

Hoffbrewer looked up just as she reached that conclusion. "You might as well give up any fantasies about escape. It isn't going to happen."

How had he done that? She'd never heard of practical mind-reading. It certainly explained, though, why Hoffbrewer had been sent to the School. Nobody wants to think that their private thoughts are being examined and judged by someone else. The Fae's leaders would have felt threatened by that ability and been worried that their negotiations would be undermined.

More particularly, it meant he would know anything Annie planned. If anyone did come to rescue her, he'd sense their thoughts before Annie even knew they were close.

"The only people coming for you are guards," he said. "If they catch you, they won't rescue you, they'll kill you." He gave her that Santa Claus smile he managed to pull out whenever he wanted. "Surely I'm better than they are."

She wasn't so sure. If she didn't get water soon, she might welcome a bullet through the head.

"It isn't that bad," he explained. "I'd give you more, but you'd just make trouble for me. Can't you understand."

She understood perfectly. Abusers always blame their victims.

"How long are we going to stay here?" she asked.

Hoffbrewer shrugged. "Until the hunt dies down a bit. You might as well get used to it."

A mer-person, whether standard or murdhuacha, didn't get used to living without water any more than a normal human would get used to living without oxygen.

"Maybe I could just take a shower." She'd do it in her clothes, though. Hoffbrewer didn't seem to be a dirty old man, but he was enough other things that she couldn't put it past him.

"That's a laugh. As if I'd be interested in your scrawny body with knobby knees and ridiculous hair." Still, he took out the key, unlocked the hotel minibar and removed a tiny bottle of water.

She looked at it longingly, unable even to summon up the moisture she'd need to drool.

"You students are so pathetic." He uncapped the bottle, tilted it back, and drank deeply, finally tossing away the empty. "Ah, so satisfying."

Abruptly, she'd had enough.

Without thinking, she dashed to the sliding door to the hotel balcony, leaped to the railing, and dove down the three stories to the swimming pool below.

The pool was shallow—a normal human making the jump would probably snap her neck. But a normal girl would never be sent to the School for Magical Misfits. She became one with the water, soaking it through every pore, breathing it into her lungs to maximize her hydration.

Her body urged her to stay under, promised the safety of water all around, but she knew that promise was a lie. A small hotel swimming pool was a trap, not a haven.

Still, she stayed under for nearly a minute before emerging to see Hoffbrewer peering at her over the balcony railing. "That," he said, "was a mistake."

She nodded.

"You know you've just put yourself in an interior courtyard. There's no way out without going through the front door, and I've already phoned and told them you're a rebellious girl trying to get back to your abuser boyfriend."

She bit down the urge to tell him what he could do with his telephone. From the blotched red that marred his face, he must have read that thought, though.

"Hey." An overly-muscular man wearing a hotel logo golf shirt that pouched out with the beginnings of a beer belly leered at her. "No diving in the pool. It's not spring break, so no wet t-shirt action, either."

Running only gets their predator-instincts active, she thought. She flowed out of the pool, heading directly for the man and flashing him with her green teeth.

He looked confused for a moment, then frightened, and bolted away.

"Get her," Hoffbrewer shouted.

But beer-belly man wasn't having any of it.

Hoffbrewer cursed, then hopped over the balcony railing.

For a fraction of a second, Annie let herself imagine the headmaster splatting on the concrete beneath him. Instead, he floated downward, as if flying were the most normal thing in the world—another mage skill she'd never heard or, or even imagined possible.

For once, though, Hoffbrewer's inoffensive exterior worked against him. Faced with the choice between letting a dangerous girl with sharp teeth catch him and bowling over a friendly guest, beer-belly chose the Santa Claus option.

Annie dashed after him into the hotel lobby, then into the revolving door that led to the outside. She'd made it. She was—

The door froze in place.

Hoffbrewer, his face nearly purple with anger, strode into the lobby as Annie struggled against the door. But glass is proof against water.

"There, now, darling daughter," Hoffbrewer said. "You know your daddy won't let you hurt yourself."

She pounded her fists against the door, but it was locked in place.

"You know I'll have to punish you for this." Hoffbrewer had on his Santa Claus persona, chuckling as he spoke. Throughout the lobby, guests and employees looked on indulgently, as he reached in and clamped down his strong fingers on her upper arm. "If you scream," he whispered far more harshly, "I may have to kill some of these others, too. Their blood would be on your hands."

* * * *

Matt froze.

The dogs, big slobbering things with sharp teeth and studded collars, probably couldn't have caught him before he managed to dash into a sewer, but he didn't even try to run.

"His family is all predators," Barley said. "It's got to be a reminder of when he found his true-form and nearly got eaten."

That must have been something they'd talked about together late at night. It explained why Matt was just waiting to die, but it didn't offer up any attractive options.

Which meant it was up to Taylor. Except dogs don't like mages, and mages dislike them back. If Annie were here, she could take on her true-form and either scare them or eat them, but Annie wasn't—

Except Annie was. Matt had managed to tie that strand of Annie's hair to his forefoot. The basic law of magic says that the part encompasses the whole. That bit of Annie should be enough.

She concentrated on the hair, on the dried moisture that had been Annie's saliva, brought the entire girl into her mind and willed.

She expected her angle to change as she grew from a six-inch bunny to a five foot something girl. Instead, nothing happened.

"They must see something," Barley said.

Sure enough, the dogs were looking up as if they saw something that wasn't there.

Taylor thought about Annie's green teeth, the way they flashed when they caught the sunlight, especially the way they came to sharp points, then projected that image at the dogs.

They weren't Fae. They would have killed a rabbit but they probably wouldn't have attacked the image of a girl. They certainly wanted nothing to do with a murdhuacha.

She laughed as they turned, tucked their tails between their legs, and dashed away howling as if they'd run into a cattle prod.

"Uh, Taylor." Matt had finally stopped making those pathetic panic noises, but this didn't sound too much better. "Everyone is looking at us. You did remember to put some clothes on Annie, didn't you?"

She was in rabbit form. There was no way in the world she could actually blush. Still, Taylor felt blood rushing to her miles-distant cheeks. Of course she hadn't dressed Annie. Tayor's spell re-linked Annie's hair to the girl, but it certainly didn't bring wardrobe choices with it.

"If you magically dress yourself," Barley warned, "you'll violate the Fae secret."

"And what?" Matt demanded. "If they catch us, they send us to the School?"

"Relax, guys." Taylor made herself sound confident. "I'm not going to put clothes on her. I don't know how."

"Relax, she tells us," Barley complained.

Momentarily she took control of Matt's body, bent down, and used his incisors to cut the strand of hair around his foreleg.

"Now get out of here," she demanded as she relinquished control.

Without Annie's hair, they wouldn't be able to use magic to track their friend. If Hoffbrewer moved her, they were in trouble. But Annie hadn't moved for a couple of hours while they'd made their way through San Antonio's sewers. Taylor just had to hope things would stay that way.

"Straight ahead," she told Matt. "She's in that brick hotel down Travis Street."

Barley hummed one of his songs and Matt put on a burst of speed.

They arrived at the hotel's front door just as Hoffbrewer reached into a revolving door and dragged Annie back to the lobby.

"Too late," Taylor groaned. "If we'd just gotten here a few minutes ago, we could have done something."

* * * *

Barley could hardly believe their bad luck. Annie had tried an escape and nearly made it—and everyone in the hotel seemed to be cheering Hoffbrewer on as he dragged the kicking Annie back toward the elevator.

From the expression on his face, only partly hidden by his jolly elf act, Barley didn't think he'd let Annie make another escape attempt. She'd just gone from potentially useful to dangerous.

"My guess," Barley said, "is that Hoffbrewer does half the killing at the school and blames the guards. What a scum."

"We need to help her." Matt sounded matter-of-fact, like he hadn't been whining like a toddler needing a diaper change just a few minutes before.

"There," Taylor moved Matt's eyes so they could all see a mail slot. "We should be able to wiggle through that."

Without more discussion, Barley began another hum and Matt launched himself at the slot.

It was a tight squeeze but Matt's bunny-body was far more flexible than any human form. After a few seconds of serious wiggle, they popped their head through—just in time to see Hoffbrewer whirl around, dragging Annie with him as he came.

"Ah, so it's young Carnecero, is it? People, this is my daughter's pet bunny. He must have escaped from his hutch upstairs."

Guests and staff nodded as if he'd said something reasonable, as if a rabbit escaping from a hutch inside a room would be likely to crawl *into* the hotel through a mail slot.

"I'll just scoop him up and take him with me," Hoffbrewer continued. "I know Annie will be much happier if he's with us."

"He can read your minds," Annie shouted.

"So, what?" Taylor said. "If we don't think, maybe we can figure out a useful plan?"

"Stop thinking so loud." Barley whispered to her rather than talking normally to both of them. "I might have the beginning of a plan."

"Here, bunny, bunny, bunny." Hoffbrewer grabbed a towel from a cleaning cart and bent to pick Matt up.

Matt hesitated, then jumped, quickly reversing his course—and ended up heading exactly where Hoffbrewer waited for him.

"So far," Taylor griped, "the beginning of a plan looks like the end of all of us."

Hoffbrewer's hands clamped down on them, then went to his throat.

"Oh, daddy." Annie made her voice a pathetic sing-song. "Can I carry him."

"Better let the girl have her pet," a beefy bald man in a navy blazer and gray slacks said. "At that age, the little animals are even more important than their boyfriends, if you know what I mean."

Hoffbrewer looked like handing the rabbit over was somewhere below eating raw crawdads on his favorites list. Until Matt's frozen worrying thawed out when he considered peeing on the headmaster's hands. Then the man handed him over to Annie so quickly she almost dropped him.

"So," Taylor whispered. "What's this big plan? And why are we whispering, anyway? Isn't the whole point that we're working together?"

"Hoffbrewer can read minds, right? But he thinks the rabbit is just Matt. He doesn't know we're here and unless we give him a reason, he won't look. So, Matt can quiver in panic, like a rabbit, and Hoffbrewer will never know what hits him."

"Like a schizophrenic rabbit is really scary."

"Confusing schizophrenia with multiple personality disorder is a common—"

"Spare me the research notes, doctor. What are we going to do?"

Annie, apparently disturbed she'd almost dropped the rabbit, clutched Matt to her as Hoffbrewer dragged her into the elevator.

"He's going to kill me when we get back to the room," Annie whispered.

"Guess that puts a time limit on your plan," Taylor pointed out.

Matt trembled like he'd been hit by a California earthquake and Barley couldn't really blame him. He'd been super-brave when he'd fought against Marcus, but his true-form changed his personality. Fortunately, neither Barley nor Taylor were really rabbits. They were semi-humans along in the rabbit's mind. Which meant he was scared, but not panicked.

"Hope it's a slow elevator," Barley muttered. He was just a Satyr. Matt was the planner, Taylor the mage, Annie the powerful and frightening one. He was the clown, the dude you brought along because you wanted a good play list. But Hoffbrewer was also a mage. If Taylor tried to use magic against him, he'd notice and shut her down before she got anywhere. Which left it up to him.

He started humming.

"You do have a plan, don't you?" Taylor sounded worried. Unfortunately, she had every reason to be.

"See if you can project this rhythm into Annie," he sing-songed his words, keeping the beat. "If she could dance even a little, that would help."

"I'll try." From Taylor's tone, the chances of success were minimal.

Which was unfortunate. Because if Annie wouldn't dance, Barley didn't think he had enough skill to do what he needed to do.

* * * *

Annie hugged the rabbit's small trembling body to her and watched for a chance. She couldn't believe Hoffbrewer had actually handed Matt over to her. If he'd held onto Matt's rabbit form, he could have used threats to Matt to compel Annie. As it was, she planned on letting Matt go the second the elevator opened. Once they were separated, Hoffbrewer would have to decide who to chase—at least one of them would get away.

"As plans go," Hoffbrewer said, "it's not bad. Except you're dealing with a mage—one who can read your mind."

He held up his hand and showed her that he'd kept a couple of strands of rabbit fur. "I can break your bunny's neck from across the room as easily as I could do it with my hands… and using magic would be ever-so-much cleaner.

Annie wanted to scream. She couldn't help her brain from working, from trying to figure a way out of her predicament. But every time she came up with an idea, Hoffbrewer yanked it out of her mind and countered it making things worse. The only time she'd come close to escaping was when she'd reacted without thought, without planning. Unfortunately, that wasn't anything she could count on happening again.

"You can count on it *not* happening again," Hoffbrewer said.

The rabbit twitched in her arms and the elevator motor seemed to take on a rhythm as it chugged its way up to the third floor. She wasn't sure if it was good news or bad that the old hotel had an old elevator. If Hoffbrewer was going to kill her, she'd almost just as soon he get it over with as keep her sick with concern.

First one of her feet, then both, then her whole body began to move in time with the beat. Like all mer-folk, Annie loved music and had spent countless hours learning the moves of synchronized swimming. Dancing on land was something she had experienced far less often. Still, by the time the elevator reached the third floor, she was swinging her hips, tossing her hair, and getting into the groove of a song that couldn't really be anything at all.

"What the devil..." Hoffbrewer shook his head. "Never mind. You have no idea." He jerked on her arm. Come on, Annie. I'm, ah, not going to hurt you. Remember, you're going to help me. Then I'm going to let you go."

She didn't need to be a mind reader to know he was lying. Which made her irrational need to dance even stranger.

* * * *

Matt felt trapped inside his true-form.

Whatever serves as a rabbit equivalent to adrenaline pumped through his arteries, froze his muscles into immobility. Yet, something not himself twitched his feet, kicking against Annie until she started moving as well.

A rabbit's ears are far more sensitive than those of any human, but Matt couldn't hear the music Annie danced to—he suspected she couldn't hear it, either. She must have flipped out. He could only conclude that the continual danger had snapped her mind, just as it threatened to snap his.

Rabbits, Matt decided as Annie danced a peculiarly lurching step while Hoffbrewer dragged her down the hall, are not built to digest cake.

What had been a nagging tummy-ache when Barley had grabbed the cake became a horrible urge.

"Oh, no." Hoffbrewer pushed away.

Too late. Barley seized control of Matt's true-form and vomited straight at Hoffbrewer.

The headmaster wiped at the mess, dropping the strands he'd pulled from Matt's fur. "What's that?" he demanded. "Barley?" For the first time, Hoffbrewer sounded concerned. "But that's—"

He pulled himself together.

"Sugar to alcohol." Matt's true-form lips and throat weren't designed for human speech. He had no idea whether Hoffbrewer could understand Taylor's words. Matt could, though. And the magic could.

Barley's song rang out.

Matt sprang from Annie's arms and danced, moving counter-clockwise around Hoffbrewer once, twice, a magical third time.

Hoffbrewer reached for him, but Matt had overcome his fear. It was easy to stay away from the big man's groping hands.

Hoffbrewer figured that out about the same time Matt did. He also realized he didn't need to catch Matt. All he needed to do was grab Annie. With her back in his power, Matt and the others would be helpless.

On the third trip around, though, Hoffbrewer's eyes crossed. He lurched toward Annie, then fell to his knees and vomited over the floor, before collapsing into his barf and snoring.

"Sometimes," Taylor's voice spoke to Matt for what seemed like the first time in ages, "similarity can get a little disgusting."

"What did you do to him?"

"Me? Hoffbrewer is ten times the mage I am. It was mostly Barley. Hoffbrewer didn't know we were here, didn't expect Barley's Satyr attack. So, we made him drunk. Alcohol comes from sugar, you know, and that cake had enough sugar in it to make the defending crew from the Alamo drunk."

"So, what do we do with him, now?"

He could feel Taylor's mental shrug. "You're the planner, right? I guess you phone the guards and tell them you've captured Hoffbrewer. Maybe cut a deal."

"Yeah."

"The thing is, you're going to need to change back to human form. And when you do, Barley and I go away."

"Go away as in return to your bodies."

"Uh, I don't... yeah, sure. That's got to be what'll happen."

Matt wished she'd said that with a little more conviction. "Annie can carry us back to the school."

"By the time we get there, Hoffbrewer will wake up and escape. And I don't think any of us want that."

"But—"

"Look, Matt. I'm no more excited about this than you are. But you need to be here, and you need to be here in human form. So, just do it."

"Hey. Don't I have anything to say here?" Barley chanted rather than spoke, his Satyr magic keeping the alcohol flowing through Hoffbrewer's body.

"Sure, Barley." Matt welcomed the interruption. Anything to delay the decision that might very well destroy two of his best friends.

"You're not a rabbit, Matt. It may be your true-form, but it's only one aspect of who you are. When it comes down to it, you're brave and you're able to make the right decision. You're learning to use your true-form rather than let it use you. So, make the decision you've got to make. I trust Taylor. If anyone can get me back to my own body, it's her."

"That doesn't make me feel much better."

"This isn't about feeling good, Matt. It's about stopping Hoffbrewer. You know he was going to kill Annie. We got here just time time."

"Okay. Are you guys ready?"

Taylor snickered. "We're ready. But you aren't."

"Oh." Fortunately fur covered his face because Matt would have blushed redder than a fire engine. He hopped down the hall to a cleaner's cart, grasped a towel with his teeth, and hid under it.

"Okay, guys." He took a breath.

How do you say goodbye when you're sending your friends into the void miles from their bodies? He decided he simply couldn't. "I'm going to change now. But I want to thank you, lots. I mean—"

"You're choking me up," Barley said.

"Okay. Here goes."

He changed—and the voices left his mind.

Chapter Twenty

The instant Hoffbrewer had let go of her, Annie had scurried away looking for a weapon. She knew she couldn't run from the headmaster—he'd proved that to her only minutes before. But she intended to defend herself and her friends, no matter how helpless the fight seemed.

She was about to smash the glass door holding the fire extinguisher when she heard the retching sound.

While the rabbit ran round him, Hoffbrewer listed to one side, leaned against the hallway wall, vomited, then collapsed.

As a mage, Hoffbrewer would probably recover more quickly than the normal human.

Using a blade of ice she extruded from her fingernail, she sliced his belt, slid it off, then used the leather straps to tie his hands behind him. She didn't know if it would help, but she didn't think it could hurt.

She heard someone clearing his throat and looked up. If the hotel manager spotted her like this, he'd probably call the police on her.

Instead, Matt looked down at her.

He was naked except for a towel around his waist, and held a washcloth in his hand. "Mages seem to use spoken words to help exploit similarity," he said. "Do you think he'd choke if I stuffed this in his mouth?"

"Stuff away. If he chokes, I won't feel too guilty." The second she said that, she realized she was lying. She didn't like Hoffbrewer, was more frightened of him than of anyone she'd ever imagined, even more than the guards who'd plotted to abuse Taylor and herself. But she didn't want to be responsible for killing him.

"I'll tell you what," she said. "I'll watch to make sure he's still breathing."

"Good idea." He picked up the plastic key card Hoffbrewer hard dropped when he'd fallen. "I need to make some calls but we should probably roll Hoffbrewer to the room first."

She looked at the fallen body. The headmaster had to weigh close to three hundred pounds. Still, if they could do it, they should get started. Sooner or later, someone was going to get off the elevator. When they did, they'd assume that Matt was the abusive boyfriend Hoffbrewer had lied about.

"How'd you do it?" she asked as they started shoving. "You're not a mage, are you?"

"That was Barley and Taylor. My part was throwing up when you danced me around too much."

"Ah." She looked around. "Where are they, then?"

"I, uh, I don't know. They were sharing my true-form, but they went away when I switched back. Hopefully they went back to their bodies."

"Oh." That didn't sound as positive as she wished it did. "So, did they escape as well? How many of the others got out. When Hoffbrewer dragged me through the fence, I thought it was too late for anyone else to make it to freedom."

"Nobody else escaped."

"You mean it's just us?" She and Matt dragged Hoffbrewer the rest of the way into the room the headmaster had rented and closed the door. "We've got to get Taylor and Barley out. The guards will kill them—and everyone else."

Matt shook his head. "Maybe. But the guards shot drugged darts when the werewolves charged the fence. The person who told us they liked to kill was Hoffbrewer, and somehow I don't think he's the most trustworthy person around."

Annie shook her head. "You don't get it. When they caught Taylor and me, they were going to..." She let her voice trail off. She couldn't bring herself to use the word in front of Matt.

"I'm not saying the guards are all nice. I'm not even saying that they're not some of the scummiest people in the world. But we don't know they arbitrarily go around killing students. I want to cut a deal with them."

A deal where one side had the power and the other had nothing wasn't likely to be fair. "What sort of deal?"

"They've got to know by now that Hoffbrewer was responsible for a lot of the problems. We turn him in in exchange for the kind of system he pretended he'd asked for— some sort of method for students to prove they're no longer a danger. So, eventually you'll be able to get out."

She shook her head. Once in a while, the naivety from Matt's rabbit true-form shined through. "They'll use their magic to track us down. They have no reason to make a deal because we don't really have anything to offer."

"There is that."

* * * *

Barley had told Matt about Gus approaching him, and shared the the contact information the guard captain had given him. Matt picked up the hotel phone and started dialing.

Just as his thumb was about to mash the last button, though, he stopped. Gus would see where the call came from and he and his guards would descend on the hotel in minutes. Annie was right about one thing—Matt had to make sure they had a reason to bargain rather than simply decide what they wanted.

He pushed the phone plunger, then listened to the dial tone.

His family had rejected him, sent him to the School when they should have known what kind of place it was. When Hoffbrewer had tried to get his father's support, his own father had rejected the idea—and his son. And..."

Except, he'd only had Hoffbrewer's word for that.

He dialed the number and listened.

"Carnecero residence." His little sister Ophelia picked up the phone before the first ring even completed.

"It's Matt. Can I talk to dad?"

"Matt, listen. I'm expecting an important call. Maybe you can just phone back later."

"And maybe I can't. I need dad right away. It's an emergency."

"And this is an emergency for me."

The clunk of the phone hitting the floor was followed by a brief whine. "Is that really you, Matt?" His brother Scott sounded breathless. "Dad just got off the phone with someone named Gus. Sounds like you're in real trouble."

"I'm in huge trouble and I need dad."

"Yeah, I get that. Just a sec."

It was only a second. "Son, are you all right?"

"The school is a disaster, dad. I—"

"It's something you've got to live with for a part of your life, Matt. Running away—"

"I'm not talking about running away. The headmaster, Hoffbrewer, was using all of us. He got a bunch of us killed just so he could escape himself."

"Hoffbrewer as in Chuck Hoffbrewer. He's the headmaster?"

"I don't know his first name. He looks like Santa Claus."

"He looked like a kid when I was in school with him, but I guess he was a little pudgy. He killed three of our fellow students and laughed when he got caught."

"He learned to hide it but kept the laughing up. And he's the headmaster."

"Okay." His father took a long breath, then exhaled it. "What do you want me to do, Matt?"

Matt felt simultaneously vindicated and discouraged. This was his dad, a leader of the north Dallas Fae community. Shouldn't he be able to turn over his problems and have his dad make them go away? On the other hand, his father trusted him, wanted his input. That had to be worth something.

"The school doesn't work the way it should, dad. There's no way out. The students are killing each other, are fighting over girls, and are manipulated by the teachers, the headmaster, and the guards. The teachers and headmaster are just students who've managed to survive. They don't care about what we're learning, and the students don't care, either because nothing matters."

"That doesn't sound good. What do you think would be better?"

"I knew Hoffbrewer was just playing with my brain, but he suggested a program where students are given goals. If they meet the goals, eventually they can get out. That would defuse a lot of the pressure."

"That makes sense."

"Also, we could use some real teachers and a real headmaster."

"That sounds reasonable, but it'll be hard to find anyone willing to take those jobs."

"Dad, you're a businessman. We've got some really capable people in the school, but they're wasting their lives. Think about it as an investment."

His father said nothing for a minute, but Matt could still hear him breathing so he couldn't have gone away. "I can see that. But that's for the long term. What do we need for right now?"

"I need you to talk to the guard captain, a guy by the name of Gus. Tell him we've got Hoffbrewer tied up and gagged. Tell him we want to come back to the school, but we don't want to get shot while we're doing it."

"Hang on. I'll get him on the other line."

Ten seconds later, his father was back, his voice no longer calm. "Matt. You've got to get out of that hotel. They're coming and it's too late for Gus to head them off."

* * * *

"We gotta get out of here." Matt looked completely panicked.

"What?" Annie felt like she'd been on the run since forever. She didn't want to stay in a hotel room with Hoffbrewer, who was wriggling and showing signs of regaining consciousness, but she also didn't want to rush off anywhere."

"The guards are coming."

"That's what we want, isn't it?"

"Yeah, but they'll be coming in shooting."

"So, we want to stay here, but we just don't want them to see us at first."

"If you're thinking about your invisibility stuff, don't forget their third eyes."

She laughed. She hadn't thought about invisibility once since escaping the School. "I was thinking, we might hide under the bed."

Matt looked at her, then nodded. "I could turn back to my true-form. I'd be smaller."

And she could take on her full murdhuacha persona. But the guards weren't going to be fooled by disguises and they'd likely see the magical forms as more threatening than if they found a couple of kids hiding under a bed.

She looked to make sure Hoffbrewer wasn't going anywhere, then slid under the bed.

It was a tight fit—no way could an adult have managed it. There was also no way the hotel maids had bothered cleaning under it in recent years.

Matt waited a couple of seconds, probably checking Hoffbrewer himself, then dove underneath. She was surprised he didn't go out of his way to stay away from her. She was so used to being the monster that being treated like just another person surprised her.

"Shouldn't be long now," he whispered. "At least I hope not. If Hoffbrewer gets loose before they open the door, we're in trouble."

The guards didn't just open the door, though. They broke it down with some magic Annie didn't know existed and didn't want to learn about, either.

* * * *

Matt hadn't thought the bed would hide them from the guards. Taylor hadn't fully explained the way their third eyes worked, but they seemed capable of peering through merely physical objects. What he hoped was that hiding would make them seem harmless.

"You mean we did all of this for nothing?" Annie whispered as dozens of guard feet filed the space around the bed. "We go back and things are just the same?"

He put a finger over her lips and nodded. If he'd been more perceptive, seen through Hoffbrewer's too-sweet exterior to the bitter reality inside, he might have come up with an escape that worked. As it was, things would probably be worse at the school instead of better.

"You under the bed," one of the guards said. "Do not try any of your magic. We'll see the flare and be forced to shoot."

"We aren't doing anything," Matt shouted.

"What about Hoffbrewer?" another demanded. "Shouldn't we let him free?"

"We'll let Gus straighten things out once we get back to the School."

"Sure." The second guard paused, as if trying to decide how to ask his next question "What about the girl? Do we get to—"

"Even forgetting Gus's rules, you're talking about a girl with razor-sharp green teeth? You sure you want to go there?"

"Ah. Right. I just meant, we want to be careful of her."

"Yeah, I'm sure that's what you meant." The first guard pulled off the bed covers, then lifted the mattress and box springs off the frame and tossed them against the wall. He stared down at the two teens for long enough that Matt wondered if he was gathering power to explode *him*.

The guard finally broke the silence. "Enough of the hide and seek, children. Let's go."

"I'd watch Hoffbrewer," Matt said. "He can read thoughts and he's got more mage power than I'd thought possible."

"We're not worried about Hoffbrewer. We're worried about how a couple of kids managed to get outside our barriers. It shouldn't have been possible."

If they weren't worried about Hoffbrewer, Matt was worried about them.

The guard tossed Annie a couple of plastic straps. "Put one of these around your boyfriend's wrists and the other around your own."

"He's not my boyfriend."

"Look, girlie." The guard got in her face. "You've been nothing but trouble to us ever since you got here. I'm looking for a reason not to hold your face under the bathtub like an unwanted kitten."

"Pete," the other guard said. "She's a murdhuacha. You hold her head under water and she'll thank you and then pull you in after her. I brought you along for muscle, not to run your mouth."

Matt wondered if they were playing the good-cop bad-comp game, or if Pete really was as ignorant as he appeared.

Hoffbrewer groaned and rolled over, straining against the leather straps that held his wrists behind his back.

"Just relax, headmaster," Pete said. "We're taking you back to the school."

Hoffbrewer tried to say something, but the washcloth made it incomprehensible.

"What is that about?" Pete pulled the washcloth from Hoffbrewer's mouth.

"They kidnapped me, made me come."

"Really? How'd they manage that? You being the adult and all."

"She's a murdhuacha. She threatened to suck all of the water from my blood. And he's a Carnecero. You know how they are."

* * * *

Taylor felt like she'd been swimming through maple syrup forever. She couldn't breathe, but somehow didn't need to breathe. She could move, but she had lost all sense of direction, had no clear concept of whether she was moving closer to her body or farther away. In fact, she had no idea whether she still had a body. Years might have passed, or decades. Her body might be a dead husk, or dust.

A glowing white ball danced beside her, the only thing she could see, if indeed she saw it. She'd followed it since the beginning, hoping it was Barley, hoping he had a better idea of where they were going than she did.

Taylor had thought she'd confronted her fears when she'd joined with the two boys inside Matt's true-form. She'd been wrong. While inside Matt's brain, she'd been able to see, she'd been able to talk. Here, she had nothing but a blind hope that the glow really was Barley and the irrational trust that he knew what he was doing when he clearly hadn't had any idea where he was heading ever before. She was the mage, not Barley. She was the one who was supposed to take charge, be responsible. But she was failing.

The glow moved closer to her, writhing in time with a tune she couldn't hear. Which made her more hopeful it really was Barley but no more confident he knew what he was doing.

He continued the dance for what might have been a few minutes—or a few years. Then, abruptly, the glow writhed, dimmed, and vanished.

Taylor was alone, and panic nearly swamped her body. Her fears urged her to run, to get away from whatever monster had claimed Barley's soul.

You wanted to be alone, she reminded herself. *You're the one who kept insisting you didn't need friends.*

But not like this.

Well, nobody said getting your wishes would make you happy.

Oddly, that internal discussion calmed her. Some amount of time must have gone by and she hadn't been consumed. Perhaps she wasn't going to be eaten—at least right that instant. Perhaps Barley hadn't been consumed by the glare that had surrounded him.

He might even have reclaimed his body. Maybe he'd been trying to communicate with her, let her know they'd arrived.

If that was the case, however, she'd let him down. She'd been able to leave her body because she'd had access to Matt's hair, to the clay shape she'd created of a simplified rabbit. She'd had her voice to control names. Then, she'd been a mage. Now, she had none of those things. She was a disembodied soul lost in the empty space between life and the hereafter—assuming there really was something on the other side and she wasn't just shunted off to some dusty closet of reality.

And feeling sorry for yourself will be so helpful.

Hey. I'm just thinking.

Think about how to get out of here.

Easy for you to say.

She giggled to herself, silently of course. Nothing was easy to say because she had no voice. Taylor didn't have the skill to read them—let alone the dance an amorphous blob had performed. Maybe she should have stayed inside of Matt, let him remain a rabbit and counted on Annie handling the drunken Hoffbrewer.

Which was absurd. The man was too dangerous and he'd had too long to learn to read Annie's intentions.

What felt like an electrical current shocked its way through Taylor's soul. Hoffbrewer had read thoughts, and he had done so without using his hands, without using his voice, simply relying on his mage skills.

She wasn't the mage Hoffbrewer was. But she was better than a lot of adults—she just hadn't realized the laws of magic allowed for that trick. Her situation was so desperate, trying seemed her only alternative.

She marshaled everything she knew about magic. Similarity: every human is similar to every other. Hadn't her biology instructor said that every human shares something like ninety-nine percent identical DNA? Each human's thoughts must be similar to the thoughts of every other human. Through the principle of contagion, a human who'd spent time as a soul, moving through the dusty closet of between, would be remain entangled with another human with the same experience. The laws of magic dictated that she should be able to read Barley's thoughts, learn from him if he had found his way out, or had been trapped in something worse than the thick syrup of between.

Taylor concentrated on listing similarities. She and Barley were both thirteen, both students at the School, both from the Dallas area in Texas. Each of them had survived their time in Matt's mind, and both had been thrown into whatever void lay between life and death.

She felt something tugging at her, but couldn't pick up any clear message. Even with everything she'd considered, it wasn't enough.

Have to dig deeper, she told herself. But what else, really, did they have in common? She was a girl and he a boy. She was a mage and he a Satyr. She relied on independence, and he was happy to go along.

At that last thought, something quivered.

Her independence had served her well. Without it, she probably wouldn't have fought back against her step-father's demands. Could her refusal to have friends, to be a friend, also be a trap? Could she be stuck between because she hadn't created a firm enough connection between herself and the real world?

The fearful part of her denied the possibility. Taylor didn't make friends—they would only tie her down.

She forced herself to relax. Although she'd insisted she wasn't one of them, Annie, Matt and Barley had treated her like a friend, had included her when they hadn't had to.

She added friendship to the list of similarities… and Barley tugged her through.

She blinked actual human eyes, sat up—and faced at least twenty guards, their guns pointed directly at her head.

"Just three more," Gus said.

Chapter Twenty-One

Matt hadn't thought the bed would hide them from the guards. Taylor hadn't fully explained the way their third eyes worked, but they seemed capable of peering through merely physical objects. What he hoped was that hiding would make them seem harmless.

"You mean we did all of this for nothing?" Annie whispered as dozens of guard feet filed the space around the bed. "We go back and things are just the same?"

Matt put a finger over her lips and nodded. If he'd been more perceptive, seen through Hoffbrewer's too-sweet exterior to the bitter reality inside, he might have come up with an escape that worked. As it was, things would probably be worse at the school instead of better.

"You under the bed," one of the guards said. "Do not try any of your magic. We'll see the flare and be forced to shoot."

"We aren't doing anything," Matt shouted.

"What about Hoffbrewer?" another guard demanded. "Shouldn't we let him free?"

"We'll let Gus straighten things out once we get back to the School."

"Sure." The second guard paused, as if trying to decide how to ask his next question "What about the girl? Do we get to—"

"Even forgetting Gus's rules, you're talking about a girl with razor-sharp green teeth? You sure you want to go there?"

"Ah. Right. I just meant, we want to be careful of her."

"Yeah, I'm sure that's what you meant." The first guard pulled off the bedcovers, then lifted the mattress and box springs off the frame and tossed them against the wall. "Enough of the hide and seek, children. Let's go."

"I'd watch Hoffbrewer," Matt said. "He can read thoughts and he's got more mage power than I'd thought possible."

"We're not worried about Hoffbrewer. We're worried about how a couple of kids managed to get outside our barriers. It shouldn't have been possible."

If they weren't worried about Hoffbrewer, Matt was worried about them.

The guard tossed Annie a couple of plastic straps. "Put one of these around your boyfriend's wrists and the other around your own."

"He's not my boyfriend."

"Look, girlie." The guard got in her face. "You've been nothing but trouble to us ever since you got here. I'm looking for a reason not to hold your face under the bathtub like an unwanted kitten."

"Pete," the other guard said. "She's a murdhuacha. You hold her head under and she'll thank you and then pull you in after her. I brought you along for muscle, not to run your mouth."

Matt wondered if they were playing the good-cop bad-comp game, or if Pete really was as ignorant as he appeared.

Hoffbrewer groaned and rolled over, straining against the leather straps that held his wrists behind his back.

"Just relax, headmaster," Pete said. "We're taking you back to the school."

Hoffbrewer tried to say something, but the washcloth made it incomprehensible.

"What is that about?" Pete pulled the washcloth from Hoffbrewer's mouth.

"They kidnapped me." Hoffbrewer glared at Matt like he was demon-spawn. "I've never felt such power."

The guard nodded. "For sure they made it through barriers that should have stopped them.

"You know I always report troublemakers to the guards," Hoffbrewer whined. "If I'd known Carnecero was so dangerous—"

"He fooled all of us."

Matt's mind whirled. He'd been sure Marcus was the traitor, the one who'd reported Justin. Maybe he had, but it sounded like Hoffbrewer was involved as well.

"He's trying to—"

Before he could get another word out, Pete grabbed him from behind and the other guard stuffed another washcloth, a clean one, in his mouth.

"Good thinking." Hoffbrewer said. "But remember, he's a true-form."

Pete grinned "Not many true-forms can get out of silver bonds.

Matt's skin didn't sizzle when they wrapped the metallic cords around his wrists. It did hurt enough that it might as well have.

The guards tied up Annie as well, despite her protests that they needed to be watching Hoffbrewer.

Hoffbrewer went along meekly, as if he hadn't been responsible for the failed escape. When they reached the tired van, though, he bent down as if to tie a shoe, then kept bending until he vanished into the sidewalk.

"What the devil."

"Oh, hell." Pete gestured at the blank spot where Hoffbrewer had been. "We knew he couldn't be trusted and he still suckered us. I thought the third eye warning was about the kids."

"Speaking of the kids, let's get them back to the school. Bad enough to lose one."

"Yeah. Not a lot of demand for guards equipped with third eyes in the outside world."

Matt shook his head. Couldn't they see that they needed to go after the headmaster right away? The longer they left him free, the more power he'd gather.

He gestured to his gag, ignoring the cutting pain from the silver cords.

"Oh, no. We've learned our lesson," Pete said. "Back to the school and then you'll talk. And believe me, you will talk."

Matt didn't resist as they dragged him into the van. But his sense of dread only grew.

* * * *

"I'm disappointed in you, Barley." Gus sat behind a battered wooden desk in an office so small it could barely contain the four chairs that hosted Barley and his friends.

"What?"

"If you'd helped me like you told me you woullld, none of this would have happened. You knew Hoffbrewer was planning something. You could have—"

"When was he supposed to tell you that," Annie demanded. "When you locked Taylor and me in your cells, or maybe he should have interrupted your pervert guards when they caught us escaping and had a reasoned discussion with them."

Gus turned in Taylor's direction, but Barley was certain the guard's third eye still stared directly at him. "Those guards have been dismissed."

"Dismissed? They should be on trial. Besides, they hadn't been dismissed at the time. And—"

"Even forgetting that," Barley interrupted, "you didn't exactly make it sound like I'd be doing anything good if I turned informant. You said I could play jokes on people, be cruel to them. Why would I want that?"

Gus slammed a fist into the wall. "Okay, Taylor is right. The guards were under my authority and they behaved badly. Dismissing them doesn't excuse their behavior or my lack of control over them. Second, I confess I misjudged you, Barley. When I saw you play your trick on Larry, I thought I recognized someone who enjoyed inflicting pain and offered you what I thought was a logical bribe. I should have looked more deeply."

"Yes you should have," Matt said. "But we're wasting time here. Hoffbrewer is the danger. Didn't you hear what Annie said? He's planning on going on a revenge rampage, killing everyone who was responsible for sending him here in the first place, then going after the guards who kept him inside."

Gus nodded. "I agree with everything you say, Matt. Except your assumption that *you* are involved. You're students here at the school, remember—prisoners, by another name. Preventing escapes, keeping the dangerous Fae inside the walls of the school, is our job. It's also our job to hunt down anyone who escapes those barriers. Don't worry about Hoffbrewer. we'll bring him home."

"Did your guards tell you how he fooled them?" Annie demanded.

"Exactly," Gus said, "like he fooled you, you mean?"

"That isn't fair. We had captured him."

"Fair or not, I'm not letting my students wander around outside, put themselves in danger, risk letting the Fae secret out. I've assigned ten guards the task of hunting Hoffbrewer down. If they can't do it, I'll assign more."

Gus made sense Unfortunately, Barley knew, he was also wrong. Ten guards wouldn't be enough to catch Hoffbrewer. And the longer they waited, the more damage Hoffbrewer could do.

"I didn't bring you here to discuss Hoffbrewer," Gus announced. "The four of you have been nothing but trouble since you arrived at the school. I've got to decide what to do about you."

"We've been trouble?" Taylor's normally low-pitched voice climbed a couple of octaves. "We've tried to mind our own business in an insane situation."

"I hardly think conspiring with Hoffbrewer to lead a mass escape, creating a charm based on equipment stolen from guards, fighting in the dining room, dueling for women in the Hans clubhouse, and blowing out four of our searchlights can be described as minding your own business."

"But we had to—"

"Don't try to shirk your responsibility, Ms. Bang."

Barley nodded. Gus was right. Although everything they'd done had made sense at the time they'd done it, they'd acted with incomplete information. They'd let Hoffbrewer give them false information about the school. Their actions had almost certainly gotten other students killed, and had directly led to Hoffbrewer's escape.

"But we captured Hoffbrewer before," Annie protested. "Matt, Barley and Taylor took a horrible chance all to save me. Matt and I could have gotten away if we'd—"

Gus laughed. "And then what? You're still children. How would you—"

"We're not children." Barley hardly recognized Matt's voice, it had grown deep and harsh, like steel grating on granite. "We have made mistakes, but they were not childish mistakes. And I ask you this. *Why* did we make these mistakes? We were new here. Shouldn't we have been told the rules? *You* brought us to Hoffbrewer, it wasn't us who sought him out. *You* called him the headmaster. *You* allowed him to set the rules, set our schedules, determine our futures. What were we supposed to think?"

"That's just it," Gus said. "You were supposed to *think*."

"You have us under your power." Matt looked at the others. "You can punish us if you wish and there's nothing we can do about it. But won't that leave things just the same—a broken system with a so-called school that's really a death-trap for the students and an opportunity for sadistic guards and for the sickest of those students to become faculty? Shouldn't we be thinking of ways to change the situation? Hoffbrewer is a monster, but I think he was right when we first arrived and he told us about the need for programs that improve students and let them get out."

Gus shook his head. "Got to give it to you, Carnecero. You've got the gift of the gab. But if you want to persuade me a mass escape attempt, one that could have cost dozens of lives if Hoffbrewer hadn't messed it up to increase his own chances of escape, is a good reason to let people out."

* * * *

Barley hummed to himself for a second, felt the music strengthen him before he spoke. "You've got to see that we can't keep going like this. Look at the four of us. Annie and I are monsters, but we didn't do anything particularly wrong. Maybe we can learn to control ourselves—or maybe we can't. Seems to me we could, if anybody had even bothered trying to teach us. And Matt? His family couldn't deal with him being a prey animal when they were all predators. So they sent him here where they thought he'd be safe. Some safety, right?

Instead, you give him a life sentence? As for Taylor, it's her stepfather who belongs in jail, not her. And—"

"That's none of your business," Taylor interrupted.

"You're my friend, so I'm making it my business."

"I don't—"

"Oh, give it up, Taylor. Of course you have friends. As for you, Gus, I can't imagine running a bunch of loser guards in a school for students nobody wants is particularly good for your reputation. Not to mention the guards who deserve to be locked up with Taylor's stepfather. Maybe you think you're one of those cowboys guarding the walls of the Alamo against hordes of barbarism, but you're really standing for something evil, same as those guys fighting for the liberty to keep slaves no matter what the Mexican government wanted."

Gus stared at Barley for a moment as if shocked he'd had so much to say. Well, Barley was surprised, too. He normally let Matt do the talking for all of them.

"The Alamo was not about slavery," Gus said. "It was a lot more complicated than that. I can see we need to get some better teachers in here.

"Maybe," Barley said, "the school is more complicated, too."

Gus glared at him again. "Maybe you're right, kid. But we sure as all gotcha ain't going to start work-release programs just after you stage a massive escape attempt."

"Not just an attempt," Matt reminded them. "Hoffbrewer is out there somewhere."

Barley shuddered. Hoffbrewer had a long list of enemies he'd look to take his revenge on, but he, Matt, Annie and Taylor had to be somewhere near the top of his list.

"I already told you," Gus said, "That we'll take care of Hoffbrewer. Y'all have given me something to think about. I'm going to make some changes in the school, bring in real teachers, make sure no guard ever abuses any of the students again, that kind of thing. As for the four of you, I'm tempted to lock you up for good but that didn't work last time I tried it. Instead, you're students again—but the guards are going to be watching you, so don't try anything."

* * * *

"Well, that was a complete waste." Taylor shouldn't have been surprised. Since when did anything change for the better? Still, it seemed like they'd been on the run, on the go, desperately trying to make a difference ever since they'd arrived at the school. After all of that, when they'd worked so hard to do something good, they were just in more trouble.

"I wouldn't say that." Matt's voice had changed during their time together. His deeper tone made her sit up and take notice. Which should have frightened her. Taylor had far too much experience with grown-up men. Somehow, though, it didn't.

"We've got friends now," Annie pointed out. "Which we didn't when we got here."

"And don't give us the line about not having friends," Barley added.

"Yeah." Taylor thought about it. "Okay."

"You know in *Through the Looking Glass*," Matt put in, "where they have to run as fast as they can just to stay in the same place."

"That's what I meant," Taylor said.

"Well, maybe it's good practice."

"Huh?"

Matt smiled. "I'll bet we're faster runners now than when we got here. Next time, we'll be smarter, too. We'll do better about trusting people who don't deserve it, we'll know more of the angles."

"Next time we do what?" Taylor demanded.

"I'm not sure yet," Matt admitted. "But I can't really believe the school isn't going to change—if we stay here."

Taylor looked at him. Matt was still a were-bunny, but their time together had toughened him. He'd learned to use the rabbit rather than let it use him. She suspected he was right—somehow or other, they were going to make some changes—changes that would last.

Books by Rob Preece

Hot in the Saddle
Hunger
In the Werewolf's Den
Kingmaker
Medium in the Middle
The Merchant Prince of Arcadia
NanoCorporate
One Handsome Devil
A Really Bad Hair Day
The School for Monsters and Misfits
Veil of the Goddess

www.ingramcontent.com/pod-product-compliance
Lightning Source LLC
Chambersburg PA
CBHW060210180626
46813CB00007B/2771